T0197109

THE BRIDE STRIPPED BARE BY HER BACHELORS, EVEN

THE BRIDE STRIPPED BARE BY HER BACHELORS, EVEN

A NOVEL BY

CHRIS F. WESTBURY

COUNTERPOINT
BERKELEY

Library of Congress Cataloging-in-Publication Data

Westbury, Chris F.
   The bride stripped bare by her bachelors, even : a novel / Chris F. Westbury.
      pages cm
   ISBN 978-1-61902-290-4 (hardback)
   1. Obsessive-compulsive disorder—Fiction. 2. Men—Conduct of life—Fiction. 3. Duchamp, Marcel, 1887–1968—Fiction. 4. Travel—Fiction. 5. Art museums—Fiction. 6. Psychological fiction. I. Title.

   PS3623.E84733B75 2014
   813'.6—dc23

   2013044916

ISBN 978-1-61902-549-3

Cover design by Michael Kellner
Interior Design by Megan Jones Design

COUNTERPOINT
2560 Ninth Street, Suite 318
Berkeley, CA 94710
www.counterpointpress.com

Printed in the United States of America

"Can one make works that are not works of 'art'?"
—MARCEL DUCHAMP

"God can only be present in the creation
in the form of absence."
—SIMONE WEIL

"I always paint fakes."
—PABLO PICASSO (ATTRIBUTED)

1

GIVEN THE ILLUMINATING GAS

Call me Isaac.

For now, anyway.

You can call my mother Julia, from now on I guess. She *was* Julia. Now she is not.

Let's say that she died of a stroke in her garden on a sunny Sunday afternoon four Junes ago while I was out at the Isabella Stewart Gardner Museum, even though it was one of the hardest museums for me get to by public transit. Maybe I was there *because* it was one of the hardest museums to get to. If I had to travel farther, it kept me out of the house longer.

It was not that I *wanted* to get out of our house. It was just that it was *good* for me to get out of the house. One of those baby steps our group therapist Jannie was always talking about.

You probably won't get Julia and Jannie confused, but just to be sure: Think of jewels when you think of my millionaire mother Jules; think of a nanny when you think of my still-in-school group therapist Jannie. I always use tricks like that.

Only my dad ever actually called my mother Jules, though.

I was the one that found Julia after her stroke. She and I were living alone together then, in a house that had been much too big even for three before my Dad died. It has *seven* bathrooms. When I starting living there alone after Julia died, I started using a different bathroom every day of the week, so that our cleaning lady Milly (whose real name is Anna Millson Tier) wouldn't feel like she was just totally wasting her time cleaning them all.

I doubt that she could really tell the difference, though. I am very fastidious.

My dad—Stanley, as he always insisted he be called, never just plain old Stan—was a man who liked to show off his money. When he was 61, he bought a brand-new bright blue Porsche. He only got to drive it for three years before he died. When he was dying he probably wished that he had bought it earlier. For him, it was extremely cool to have, and we only got half what he paid for it when we sold it. That would have annoyed Stanley. My dad hated a bad deal.

I would say that Julia looked fine, almost totally normal— even a little more beautiful than normal in an odd way; somehow younger in death than life—when I found her lying in her garden, except for her slight grimace and the fact she was lying awkwardly in the dirt, her right arm tucked half under her body, her right cheek resting on the soil.

I didn't *touch* her, of course.

When I found her collapsed like that on top of her own arm, I went in the house and called 911. I didn't go right away because I already knew she was dead and I wanted to look at her for a few minutes before I left her alone there. After I called, these two guys named Sam and Steven came in an ambulance and looked at her for a while, and then told me she was dead, and then someone else came and took her away, just like that. Our lawyer, Mr. Salandhi, took care of getting her cremated on behalf of the family (which was by then reduced to just me), so I never saw her again.

I wish that I had turned her over and washed the dirt from her cheek before they took her away. I wish that I could have had the presence of mind, the compassion, the simple reckless guts, to do that.

Julia was a fantastic mother. She looked after me for way longer than any mother should have to look after her son. I wasn't all she had hoped for in a son. She was stuck with me when I was stuck at my worst.

Everyone gets stuck sometimes. That's normal.

But I was stuck almost all the time for years.

That's not normal.

That's diagnosable.

::

You can call my best friend Greg, for now. He actually has a cooler name that I will tell you later, but Greg is his real name, and that's what almost everyone calls him.

I don't believe in God, but if I did, I would write here: *Thank God for Greg.*

This guy made my life. If it wasn't for him, I don't know what I would have ever done after my mother's cheek fell onto her garden's dirt. I am sure I would never have left Medford, Massachusetts, to buy an expensive replica of an antique chocolate grinder with legs in the style of *Louis Quinze.*

So if you read this, Greg (and you will read it, buddy, because I'll be calling on you for proofreading): Thanks, man. You *schloobing* rock.

In case you are wondering what that means (which you no doubt will be unless you *are* Greg), Greg doesn't swear. He's against it, says it promotes avoidable unhappiness by "unnecessarily stimulating the hypothalamic-pituitary-adrenocortical axis." Greg believes that we have a moral duty to avoid avoidable unhappiness. When most people would swear, he always says *schlooby* or *schloobies* (or sometimes *schlooby-pie*, don't ask why, there isn't any reason). It's annoyingly addictive once you start doing it. Try it and you'll see.

So, Greg doesn't just *rock*. He *schloobing* rocks.

When Greg and I first met, I was an undergraduate at Tufts University, majoring in psychology, to see if I could understand what was going on with me. I was having a *lot* of problems in those days. I went to a group therapy session at the hospital that we always just called "group." The same way people just say, "We went to *church.*" We went to *group.* It's like it doesn't really matter which exact church or group it was. All that matters is that we went to one.

Mr. Greg Zipf was in group with me. He did look like a crazy person. Sorry, buddy. I feel bad writing that down, but we both know it's really just true. Let's speak truth to fact.

Greg looked like an anorexic nerd in the throes of drug with-
drawal. If I write here that I mean that in the nicest way possible,
you'll probably think I'm trying to make some kind of mean joke.
I'm not. He's *Greg*. If you knew him, you'd see what I mean. The
anorexic-nerd-in-the-throes-of-drug-withdrawal look suits him.
It's just who he is.

He wore ragged, secondhand T-shirts with slogans that had
absolutely nothing to do with his life. Although he has denied it
and probably still will today if you ask him, I am pretty sure that
at that time, Greg only owned (or only *wore*, anyway) three shirts:
one promoting a chain of Puerto Rican car repair shops; one commemorating a poker tournament in Las Vegas 10 years earlier (that
he had not been to); and a blue one that had a red line drawing
of the Canadian parliament buildings in Ottawa. He always wore
old jeans, too big, that he cinched with a thin brown belt (clearly
intended for women) high up from his scrawny hips. He probably
only had a pair or two of those. I'm giving him the benefit of the
doubt in writing that: It always looked like the same pair to me.
He often wore a long gray stained rain jacket, rain or shine, summer or winter, inside or out, with its front pockets stuffed with
two or three well-used secondhand paperbacks. He smelled, not
of unwashed body odors (he is obsessive about washing his body
too, even if he does it mainly only when everyone else is asleep),
but slightly dizzyingly, sickly sweet, due to the fact that he gener-
ously applied any cologne that he found for sale for a buck at the
dollar store. His thinning, straggly brown hair was slicked slightly
too much to his scalp, styled in a poor and completely unconscious

comb-over. He had a look in his large bright brown eyes of frantic, frightened urgency, like a lamb who believes that there might be an attempt on his life at any second: maybe a little sad about how things worked out, but wide awake.

Greg was a hand-washer like me. He also had—and still has—[what some might call][1] *a symptom* that is perhaps unique in the annals of medicine: He is obsessed with spoons. He *loves* the look of spoons, especially the concave side. The outside is very good, but he much prefers the *inside* of the spoon. Of course he is right about that. The inside of a spoon invites us into a weird, unpredictable, and often beautiful world of dancing light. The outside of a spoon just pushes our attention off of itself, like it doesn't want to have anything to do with anything else. I still discuss this with Greg occasionally. The topic is quite boring now since we have already agreed about it for years. It's like two Red Sox fans getting together every few weeks to pass the time agreeing in argumentative tones that the Red Sox are definitely the best baseball team.

Greg's love of spoons was diagnosable. The reason I say that is it prevented him from performing "activities of daily living." That's what they call them in the mental health biz. Not being able to do your activities of daily living is very bad. It means that he couldn't do anything *normal*, like have a job, or a social life, or a girlfriend or anything. He spent too much time with spoons to leave room for anything that normal people did. When I first met him, he would have happily spent six or eight hours, in one

---

1. I feel compelled to note here that Greg added that parenthetical comment.

sitting, studying a spoon if he could find one. Many people in his life tried to make sure he did not. He was living with his sister at the time, not so happily. She allowed him to eat only with a fork. Greg did not find forks to be interesting. I once bought him a spork (combination spoon and fork) as a present. He told me he liked it a lot, but not as much as just a plain spoon. I told him he could use it to eat with, and he still does. He uses it as a *fork*. I also bought him a small spoon plated with real gold once, which he still keeps in his main spoon collection that he has in a large case at his place now. He likes that one a lot. It is probably his favorite. (If you read that sentence, he didn't cross it out when he proofread this, so it is true.)

The lady who was running group in those days was an officious young intern from one of the many clinical psychology programs in town, who I already told you was called Janet, or at least I said she was called Jannie like nanny. (It doesn't even matter if you forget her name completely; she is a totally minor character in this story.) We were allowed to call her Jannie instead of Dr. So-and-So because she didn't have her degree yet. She liked to wear brown corduroy skirts and always changed into sneakers when she left the hospital after work. Usually I don't like sneakers with skirts, but on Jannie, it was somehow always an improvement. She wasn't so sexy, a slightly overweight, large-framed, bookwormy kind of person with straight brown shoulder-length hair and big flat breasts that just seemed to somehow fade into her large body, but there was something really charming about her when she walked around in sneakers beneath her brown corduroy skirt. It always made me happy if I saw her on her way home. Apparently she moved to New Orleans after she graduated.

Greg became my good buddy after Jannie brought in a shiny coffee spoon from the hospital coffee shop to group one day, so that he could talk to us about it and explain why he loved spoons so much. She said that if everyone agreed he had good reasons, he would be cured. She just loved to tell us that mental health is a matter of *proportion*. She always said it like she had read it in some book, as if she were telling a grade school class a simple fact. Children, *two plus two is four*, *whales are mammals*, and *mental health is a matter of proportion*.

I have to admit that I think she was pretty much right, though. If you want to be considered sane by all the people that get to judge your sanity, all you have to do is try to stick to doing whatever most people agree is reasonable when anyone else is around to see you.

Of course, Jannie was sure that Greg couldn't explain his love of spoons in a way that anyone would agree with. When he failed, she would have proved to him that he was, by group consensus, crazy. For her, that was a necessary step in the right direction. First, we had to admit we were diagnosable. Then we could do something about it. A lot of us in group were definitely stuck on the first step.

But Greg surprised her. He is not convinced that he has ever been diagnosable, and he has a degree in art history. Already at that time he was earning a little bit of money writing about art. He was working on a book based on his master's thesis called *Bear-Breed Spirit Depth: Duchamp, Semantic Multiplicity, and the Artistic Life*, which he is still working on today. It is coming along, I am told.

For Greg, writing a book is not so much about getting it finished; it's about taking the right kind of journey.

His title is an anagram for *The Bride Stripped Bare*, in case you didn't notice that right away.

Greg had thought a lot about the ordinary metal spoon in the context of modern aesthetic theory. In group, he told us that he had come to see his *obsession* with spoons as a piece of performance art. He assumed that we would all agree that no one sane would wish to be *cured of art*. Why would they?

Even our nanny Jannie had to agree.

Greg told us how his hero, the French artist Marcel Duchamp, had declared mundane objects bought from an ordinary store—a sink stopper, a coat hanger, a wine bottle rack, a shovel, a bicycle wheel, a urinal—to be art. These were his *ready-mades*. Greg pointed out that the international art community clearly accepted the ready-mades as real art, since they spent millions of dollars to acquire the mundane mass-produced objects that had been anointed as art by Duchamp.

And if a *urinal* or a *shovel* or a *sink stopper* could be art, then, Greg argued, there was no good reason why a *spoon* couldn't be.

∷

My real given name, *Isaac*, comes from a Hebrew word meaning "May God smile" or "laughter." I am not a reader of the Bible.

I'm more interested in things that have occurred *since* 200 AD. However, I have read a very long PhD thesis about Abraham killing or banishing his various children in various religions, so it happens that I know *those* stories very well.

So I know that Genesis says that my name sprang from the laughter of the first Isaac's mother, *Sarah*. In my mind, Sarah is a particularly *beautiful* lady. According to the actual words that are printed in the Bible, she was a very *old* lady when her children were born.

A person is allowed to have leeway in telling stories. There are facts and then there are stories about those facts. The simple truth is not always as great a story as it could be if the facts are allowed to have a teensy little bit of help (which is probably why science is considered by most people to be more boring than art). I am not a *scientist*. I think of the biblical Sarah as looking exactly like a makeup artist, also named Sarah, who I met in Philadelphia when we first went down there. Both Sarahs have long, shiny brown hair, dark brown friendly eyes, tiny perfect ears, and pretty big breasts pulled a little together by their bras, and they are forever wearing a low-cut sweater and are in their early twenties.

In Genesis, it says that Sarah was laughing at the fact that she had managed to bear a child at her advanced age, which according to *that* version of the story was 90 years. God told Sarah's husband Abraham—Isaac's dad—to cut Isaac's throat.

This story of Abraham and Isaac is pretty complicated. Greg's and my friend Kelly is the one who wrote her PhD thesis about it, and it took her 318 and a half pages to say everything. Apparently some people on her committee thought it was too long, but that's just how long it was. It definitely wasn't padded with filler. It's 318 and a half pages of solid, informative prose. It was published by Harvard University Press as *Mother, Madame, Sister, Aunt, and Angel: Depictions of the Divine Feminine at Abraham's Sacrifices in Christian, Islamic, and Jewish Traditions*. It has plural sacrifices in it because Abraham also tried to kill Isaac's half-brother Ishmael by abandoning him in the desert (though he did have God's word that Ishmael wouldn't actually die). It is hard not to wonder what God had against Abraham's children.

You should buy Kelly's book if you're interested. It's pretty good, especially given what it is. I am even going to recommend it. Personally, I found some of the feminist interpretation a bit difficult to swallow, but it did make me realize how much Sarah has been ignored in most representations of the sacrifices of Abraham. Kelly even has statistics about that. You have to have statistics even in women's studies in religion these days.

I have an inscribed hard-cover first edition.

I am also mentioned by name in the acknowledgements.

Some versions of Isaac's story say that Isaac went willingly up the mountain with his father. He trusted the old man. He admired his strength, skill, and wisdom. He venerated his age. Abraham did not have his first child, Isaac's later-to-be-abandoned half-brother Ishmael, until he was 85 years old. He didn't have the sacrificial ox Isaac until 14 years later, aged 98 (some versions say he was 100). And he lived much longer than that.

I call Isaac a sacrificial *ox* because he was no little lamb when his Dad tried to take him down (or, I guess, as he would have had it, *send him up*). He is often painted as a baby or small child by lazy artists looking to improve their version of the story (my revered Caravaggio, as well as Rembrandt, La Hire, Ligozzi, Chagall). But by the Bible's own testimony, he was 35 years old when he went up the mountain to have his father slit his throat.

When you think about it, it wouldn't be so easy for a very old man to slit the throat of a younger, stronger man, even if the stronger man were entirely *willing* to have his throat slit, as steady in his resolve as an ox. It would be very difficult, probably impossible, for a man with any passion to lie still, to resist the urge to fight back, as the knife sliced into the flesh of his throat. It would be impossible for Abraham to hold Isaac down, even if he were bound hand and foot. The young man was very strong.

In Kelly's version, there is no reason for Abraham to fight a battle he could not win with a much stronger man who did not want to fight. They were both smart guys. She says in her book that Isaac and Abraham would have negotiated an easier, cleaner, faster, more humane method for the sacrifice, which was beheading with Abraham's great sword. She gives some historical arguments for thinking so.

In Kelly's version, Isaac knew his father's sword intimately. He had used it himself, many times. He himself sharpened it on this occasion, the occasion of his own sacrifice. He sharpened it, as he had always sharpened it, with the full respect due a tool created specifically for taking life.

Of course Isaac was not carried up to the sacrificial grounds by his old man. Imagine the paintings we would have now if the Bible had told that version of the story! The subject would be pathetic and ridiculous. Imagine an old, bent man staggering desperately up a mountain under the weight of the buff, fully grown son he has thrown awkwardly over his shoulder. Isaac is lying there talking, or praying, or making suggestions to his father about how he should be carried, or maybe just begging to be let the *schlooby-pie* down so he could walk up by himself and spare his father this unnecessary ignobility.

That scene would not make a decent subject for painting until about 1955.

No. It was surely not like that. I agree with Kelly that the best story is that Isaac walked up the mountain willingly, lost in deep discussion with his father about the bewildering but wondrous mystery of God's way.

When they arrived at the sacrificial altar, the two men shared a few cups of what they had agreed on as the best wine from the wine cellar they had built together. They toasted each other and ate fresh crusty bread smeared with the best tangy goat cheese. They kneeled down in front of the altar together, and they prayed there together.

These people weren't *idiots*. Each one completely understood the position he had been assigned. It didn't matter to either of them who did the killing or who was killed. If God had not decreed their roles, they would have happily just flipped a coin for it. A sacrifice was what it was. They both had a lot of experience with sacrifice.

Abraham bound Isaac's hands behind his back, but only loosely, gently, with a soft red strip of cloth given to them for this purpose by Isaac's loving mother, Sarah. The tying was only there for show, a symbolic gesture. Isaac could have taken his hands out whenever he wanted to. He wouldn't need to be *tied up* for this. It wasn't about one person *doing something* to another. It was about two people doing something together.

With his hands bound, Isaac knelt in front of the great gray stone covered with the stain of old kills, facing away.

He looked at his father, who was as serious and calm as he was. He smiled the open, warm, accepting smile of a loving comrade. He shrugged a little as if to say: *Eh*. Then he leaned backward and reared back to drop his head down gently onto the hard stone, the best he could do for a deathbed pillow. He shimmied his shoulders back, and pushed his head far back as he did. He was going to expose his neck as much as possible. That would make it easier for them both.

With his eyes wide open, Isaac lay on the stone gazing up at the beautiful clear blue sky. A silver sliver of moon was visible. Of course Isaac had no clue what the moon was. He had no idea how the sky could stay where it was, how the sun and the moon and the stars could possibly attach themselves to it. He had no notion that a human life could be extended by willpower, knowledge, or the regular use of Sani-Wipes.

Isaac basically knew just one thing for sure: Many are born, few flourish, all die. If you didn't die as a sacrifice for God today, you would die of an incomprehensible plague tomorrow, or of undeserved starvation the day after, or of good old-fashioned senseless human slaughter before the next harvest. Life was short in those days, and people were grateful for whatever they could get. They didn't expect wireless video game consoles, fast German cars, dental insurance, antidepressants, and a pension.

Abraham walked around to the wide end of the stone and positioned himself at exactly a right angle to his son's neck. He raised the almighty sword high over his head. His face showed no pity, no anger, no doubt, no worry. He was smiling, grimly but honestly, as only someone can who believes completely in what he is doing.

They say that an angel of the Lord prevented Abraham from striking Isaac, and that God trapped a ewe in a nearby thicket to die in Isaac's stead.

Perhaps.

After all, they also say that God works in mysterious ways.

∷

OK, here's a pop quiz for you! What medical discovery do you think is responsible for saving the most human lives? Anesthetic? The vaccine? Mercurachrome? Penicillin?

If you are like my mother, the former Julia, you guessed penicillin. It's a very good guess. Penicillin has saved many millions, maybe even hundreds of millions, of lives.

But if penicillin was your guess, guess again.

You can still have full points if you get it right on your second guess.

The medical discovery responsible for more saved lives than any other is the discovery in 1847 by Ignaz Semmelweis of the importance of washing your hands. Semmelweiss insisted that nurses dealing with both the recently departed and the newly arrived should wash their hands as they walked from throwing out one body to bringing in another. This insistence drastically reduced the number of mothers dying in childbirth at his clinic. It later revolutionized many different aspects of medical care.

Dr. Semmelweis's ideas about washing hands were met at the time with scorn. He was treated as a crank. He died in an insane asylum.

Oops.

::

I was trying to tell a better story when I said that Julia died in her garden of a stroke. That was how I *wish* she died. She actually died of melanoma—skin cancer. It's not contagious, so it seems weird that she died of the same thing as my father.

That makes two parents, in case you weren't counting. It may not be contagious in the normal sense, but melanoma is definitely hereditary. It's contagious *between generations*. The average person only has a 2 percent chance of developing melanoma. But if you have one parent with the familial form, you have a whopping 50 percent chance of developing it yourself. No one really knows my chances, with two parents who may or may not have had the same form of melanoma, but they are probably higher than that.

Higher than 50 percent! That is a drag.

Of course we all have to die, and I don't expect anything else.

But I'd rather go quick, as if I were being beheaded with a great axe.

Melanoma is a slow way to die. Trust me, it sucks.

∷

Greg's artistic hero Marcel Duchamp did a lot of very weird things. You wouldn't believe half of them if I told you. Greg's favorite thing was that he made the piece *Étant donnés: 1° la chute d'eau 2° le gaz d'éclairage*, or in English, *Given: 1. The Waterfall, 2. The Illuminating Gas*. *Étant donnés* (as it is usually called) was secretly constructed by Duchamp between 1943 (or 1946, depending on whether you measure from when he rented the space or when he actually started building the piece) and 1966. After Duchamp died in 1969, *Étant donnés* was permanently installed in the Walter Arensberg Gallery at the Philadelphia Museum of Modern Art. The artist had left behind very detailed notes on the construction of the work and had instructed that it not be photographed for 15 years.

If you wanted to see it, you were supposed to go and actually *visit* it.

But if you do ever visit it, you can't actually just sit down in a gallery and *gaze* at it. You can't really contemplate it while you study it visually. You can only catch a little glimpse of it by peeking through a tiny hole drilled into a door that does not open.

Greg says that *Étant donnés* is the ultimate work of art.

After *Étant donnés*, he says, everything possible had been done in art.

You might ask (as I did): What about the all the art made since then?

Greg says that everything after *Étant donnés* is just a copy. There has been no more original art after that. Now there are only copies.

It's an odd notion.

But that's Greg.

::

In Kelly's version of the Abraham story, Abraham's hand was stilled at the last minute, but not by a ewe, like it says in the Bible. Kelly's version is way better.

Imagine Abrahram as he stood there, the great family sword raised over his head. He moved his feet over a smidge in preparation for the blow to fall. He knew he was as sure and strong as any man could be. He was old, but he was very strong.

His stringy shoulder muscles stood out in relief against the thin covering of his skin as he prepared to swing the mighty sword over his head. He paused.

Not because he saw an animal trapped in a nearby thicket.

Not because he saw an angel.

He paused because he heard an odd sound.

It started low and uncertain, almost like a waterfall tinkling in the distance.

He paused to listen. As it became clearer and louder, he was able to focus in on it, to figure out where it was coming from.

It was not in the distance.

It is right *here*, he thought.

It is right *here* in front of me.

Isaac was still lying with his neck outstretched, his arms still hanging awkwardly behind his back. He was trying hard to lie still. No man ever wanted God's will to be done more than Isaac did. But it was not working. Isaac was not lying still. He was shaking ever so slightly. Not from fear. Not because he chose to. Isaac was shaking because he was *giggling*. He was trying very hard not to, but he still was. His face muscles worked to keep a serious face showing, but it was a losing battle. His shoulders began to shake. His mouth opened involuntarily and closed voluntarily, as he tried, embarrassed, to stifle himself.

Ah ha ha ha mmm mmm ah ha ha ha mmm mmm ha ha.

He looked up at his father's bewildered face staring down at him. Isaac's smile broadened at the sight of his confused dad, which set him off even more, so he started to twist on the rock, wriggling back and forth. The stifling became more difficult, and finally impossible.

Ah ha ha ha ha ha ha ha mmm ah ha ha ha ha ha ha mmm ha ha ha ha ha ha.

Abraham stared, at first in utter disbelief, and then in growing mirth himself. His hard muscles loosened as he started to shake with laughter. His son writhed over and twisted off the stone, hitting the ground with a thud, and he knelt down and let himself go, laughed and laughed, hooting now, rolling back and forth and actually *hooting*.

Hoo hoo hoo hoo ha ha ha hoo hoo hoo ha ha.

Isaac's amazing dad pulled the family sword easily back over his shoulders and leaned it against the killing stone. He sat on the grass beside his son, not hooting, but laughing an old man's laugh. His shoulders jerked up and down. He wore a wide, open smile. You have to remember that Abraham was a very serious guy. He wasn't a big laugher. He laughed more that evening than he had ever laughed before in his long life.

The two of them laughed together until they could laugh no more, the son finally twisting over to pull his right hand free from its loving binds, and put it over his father's shoulder. The men laid easily together with their backs against the great killing stone, swatting insects away and watching the light fade from the green landscape around them.

There would be no sacrifice that day.

::

Since she died slowly of melanoma rather than suddenly of a stroke, you probably figured out that I didn't really find my mother's body in her garden. I would argue that I still *could* have. Maybe she somehow walked down from her bedroom, in her enfeebled state, after weeks of being near death, just so that she could die in that way in her garden, which she loved. Maybe she somehow sensed that death was coming at that exact moment (who knows?), and at the same time the nurse left her alone and Milly was not around, so she could drag herself down the stairs and die very quickly, before anyone else could say anything about it.

My mother definitely could have done that if anyone could have done it. She was a very *determined* person. She thought that people should decide what they were going to do and then just do it. I don't think she even cared so much about what people did as long as they did do it. This was probably one reason why she and my dad got along so well. He was a doer too.

Genetics is not everything. I am not a natural doer, even though both my parents were.

But since I have done it, I can tell you how to become a doer if you are not naturally one: You just *schlooby do* stuff. It gets easier and easier once you start.

::

The precise proportions that count as totally sane are not at all obvious. To me, that's one big problem with Jannie's favorite idea. It's great to tell everyone to act proportionally. But how are we supposed to figure out what the correct proportions are? Just telling someone to act proportionally is like telling someone to just bake a loaf of bread after giving them a sheaf of freshly scythed wheat. Once you have the most essential raw materials, I guess everything else is just supposed to be *details*.

Everyone agrees that washing your hands while walking from the dead to the birthing is a totally excellent idea.

Almost everyone agrees that washing every time you go to the bathroom and before you eat is good.

Most people agree that washing more than twice between each of the above events is marginal.

After that, you are pretty much on your own. Some people say one thing, some another. There are no actual facts to guide us.

I can definitely tell you that washing your hand soap so you can use it to wash your hands is not acceptable, and washing your soap and your hands between each mouthful of a meal is also totally *schlooby-pied*. I pinned Jannie down on those two, even though she hated to be so precise about things like that. She always told us that everyone was different. We have to be pretty much like everyone else, but we can't say how much, because everyone is different.

I used to wash my hands no less than 64 times per day. *Exactly* 64, a number that has a (hopefully) obvious beauty to it, one times two to the power of two times three.

I was diagnosable then. Now I wash my hands a less precise number of times. This is why I am not *diagnosable*, but just *fastidious*.

One pretty definite rule is: If you make sure that the number of times you do something breaks down into powers of low integers, then you are definitely diagnosable. The majority of normal people will not agree that this is reasonable.

I know that it is difficult for normal people to say what a good washing style would be like. It just seems totally natural to normal people to wash their hands, and they are all different about it, but they all somehow do it exactly right. Jannie said my washing *style* might be OK in itself, but that since my hands were bleeding, she was sure I was scrubbing too much.

One hundred percent sure.

I asked.

::

I wish I had really been at the Isabella Stewart Gardner Museum at the exact moment that Julia died. I mean, I wish I could have been there with her at her bedside, of course, if that was what she wanted. But if I couldn't have been there, for some reason, then I would have liked to have been at a precise spot in the Isabella Stewart Gardner Museum. I love that museum. I love it mainly because on March 18, 1990, thieves had stolen some paintings from that museum that had been painted by very well-known painters.

Johannes Vermeer.

Rembrandt Harmenszoon van Rijn. Yes, *that* Rembrandt.

Edgar Degas.

When she died in 1924, Isabella Stewart Gardner, heir through marriage to a pepper fortune, had decreed that nobody was allowed to add to the collection or change the way it was displayed. She also left enough money to make this wish possible.

She is one of Greg's and my heroes. She made *her whole art museum* into a work of art. Like Duchamp, she is a meta-artist.

When the paintings were stolen, the people charged with respecting Isabella's wishes were in a bind. Whether they acted or not, her decree was going to be violated. Things would be different no matter what they did. Making the best of a bad thing (and, I think, also making exactly the right decision), they just left a blank space where the paintings had been, along with notices saying that the paintings that had once hung there had been stolen.

Sometimes I would wander around the museum a bit. Eventually I would always sit down in front of one of the blank spaces. *That's* where I would have wanted to be when Julia died, if I could have chosen my spot, and if I couldn't be at her bedside, if she wanted me there.

After the *Mona Lisa* was stolen in Paris in 1911, thousands of people flocked to the Louvre to do exactly the same thing: to look at the empty spot where a painting had once hung. Duchamp said in an interview (long after the painting had been recovered) that "The poor *Mona Lisa* is gone because no matter how wonderful her smile may be, it's been looked at so much that the smile has disappeared."

Whenever I sat in front of an empty space at the Isabella Stewart Gardner Museum, I would try to feel exactly what I would have felt if the amazing missing painting were actually there.

That's what I wish I had been doing at *the exact second* that my mother died.

::

In case you wondered how I was able to afford the gold-plated spoon I gave to Greg and spend all my time in museums, it was because I am well-off. Not *rich*. Just very well-off.

I got about 260 grand after my father died that I never touched. That was more than I needed because Julia pretty much still paid for everything even after I got it. I inherited another 1 million 750 thousand dollars after my mother died. In case you don't know, that is still supposed to be *nowhere near* enough to make you actually rich. Maybe in the old days a couple of million was enough to make you rich, but these days, it's just *schlooby-pie*. That's what Mr. Salandhi told me when he explained it to me (except that he didn't use the exact word "*schlooby-pie*"). "Be careful," he said, "you can burn though that much money very quickly. It's nowhere near enough to make you rich."

That's why I don't say that I am *rich* (even though I have a net worth of $2.9 million now, if you include my real estate). I guess these days, you need like a hundred million or something before you get to actually just sit down and say to people: "*Well, I'm rich!*"

I didn't get all that money on the day Julia died, of course. It took an amazingly long time, actually. I don't really understand why. All I know is that there are a lot of laws out there that you never hear about until you have to. While I was waiting, Mr. Salandhi put me on an allowance that was actually way more than I needed. Mr. Salandhi still paid all the bills at my house, so I didn't have to spend it on much. I had no expenses. So even though I wasn't even a fact millionaire (which means: someone who actually does have one million dollars as a matter of actual *fact*), I felt like I was rich.

In case you didn't know, the average American is worth somewhere between negative 8,000 dollars and 80,000 dollars, depending on which version of the story you want to believe.

So I know I have been a lot better off than average all my life.

::

I loved Greg's Duchampian defense of spoon-gazing as art as soon he told group about it. I thought it was excellent. I told Jannie that she should let him go with a clean bill of health. It was obvious to me that he was a thinker, a philosopher, an artist, a visionary—not a crazy guy. Give him the House-Tree-Person test, and he'd draw you a classical reclining nude. Give him a Rorschach, and he would find a Rembrandt drawing outlined in inkblots.

It turned out that I wasn't normal, either. Greg and I got voted down, 12 against two. Jannie wrote something down in her notepad and told me that it didn't help us to try to normalize each other's symptoms. We were there to *be normalized*, not *to normalize*.

Then she took Greg's spoon away.

After the meeting, I told Greg that I really liked the idea that art might be being able to just see things in a certain way.

I was definitely the snappier dresser, but Greg and I had crossed paths in a mental hospital. I didn't feel like I didn't belong there. I never felt that I was better, less crazy, than anyone else there. I never thought that *a mistake had been made*. Crazy is as crazy does. I did things that were agreed by a majority to be crazy. Therefore, I was crazy.

One of the benefits of being crazy that is not appreciated by the non-diagnosable is that insanity is great for breaking down the barriers of snobbery or elitism. Since I have experienced mental illness myself, I have never felt that anyone was worse than me, have never treated anyone as beneath me, never felt that anyone I met should be simply snubbed or ignored. If you open yourself up to the crazy, it is easy to make lots of friends. A lot of your friends will be very annoying, I admit. But some of the crazy ones aren't so bad, and some of the sane ones are also going to be a total pain in the *schlooby-pie*.

::

Another trick to being sane is *to get thinking and feeling to work in harmony*. It sounds a little vague, but it's kind of like sexiness, you just know what it means when you see it. I have known a lot of obsessives who spent way too much time thinking. Greg and I once had an inpatient in our group named Dan B., who was a very intelligent displaced New York Jew. He had come to Boston to study computer science at MIT. We had to use the "B" in his name because we had more than one Daniel on the ward. We all said it like "Danby," like it was just one word.

When I first met Danby, he had created some crazy numerological system. The system was represented in two ways. Its principles, rules, charts, and diagrams, and the rationale for all of these, were scribbled in small black handwriting in a brown leather-bound notebook that he generally kept in his bedside drawer when he was not working on it. He was happy to explain it to anyone who would listen. I spent many happy hours with him, but his system was so Byzantine that I was never able to totally get it. He and I often were required in the course of going through his notes to consult tiny cribbed footnotes that seemed to lead back to rules we had already read, or to rules so similar that they could pass as identical to someone with numerological aesthetics as unrefined as mine.

Perhaps foreseeing such skepticism, or perhaps merely to speed up the tedium that was an inevitable side effect of the complexity of his system, or maybe just because he could, Danby had also written a computer program to run his system. Unfortunately, Danby's program was housed on a mainframe at MIT that could only be accessed on campus, both because he needed it to print out on old-fashioned 8-by-14-inch printouts that no one except MIT still had and because he needed a supercomputer to run it. Since he himself was unable to get to campus at all and could find no one who would do it more often, Danby had his computer access delivered to him by an old classmate, Bill, every Thursday night, in the form of a massive printout on the thin sheets of paper folded like an accordion. Since it was impossible for Danby to know precisely which parameters would be most influential on his calculation, he treated his system like we treat our favorite complex system, the weather. Every Wednesday, Danby would spend several hours frantically writing down and numerically encoding possible scenarios for the seven upcoming days. Each possible scenario was encoded, using some kind of coding involving summing powers of prime integers as a very long digit. He delivered hundreds of these digits to Bill every Thursday. Bill in turn dropped them off to a MIT secretary who entered them into the computer as instructed in return for a consideration from the weekly allowance Danby was given by his family.

As Danby was fond of pointing out to me, the fact that his program produced output was evidence that the system was not simply circular, as I sometimes thought it was. Danby was required to consult his precious printout repeatedly as events unfolded, both to see which of the prepared scenarios most closely matched current reality and to forecast tomorrow's most likely events. For this reason he carried his week's pile of computer paper with him everywhere he went.

Danby was definitely capable of thinking straight. He had, after all, won entrance to MIT. However, his thinking had grown like a kind of psychic tumor, until it came to consume all his time and energy. It had grown so much that it was impossible for him to feel anything. In particular, he could not feel, as the rest of us did, that he was totally full of *schlooby-pie*.

Most obsessives are the opposite of Danby: too strongly ruled by *feeling* without enough *thinking*. We feelers are the hand-washers, the counters, the worriers, the over-focusers. We are the bewitched. We are in the grip of a certainty that we must do something—wash our hands; count out steps; backtrack; stare at the edge of a doorway—even though we might *think* that we should not.

::

Greg received my questions about his lecture on the ordinary spoon with interest and enthusiasm. That was when I first found out that he had an MA in art history.

That was when he taught me that Duchamp had taken art to its logical conclusion.

Every act of perception is art.

So everything that perceives is an artist.

2

ADAGE OF SPONTANEITY =
THE BACHELOR GRINDS HIS CHOCOLATE HIMSELF

For months after my mother died, I didn't leave the house at all except to go to group. That was a very bad time for me. Mr. Salandhi helped me get my groceries delivered. He paid Milly to come in three times a week instead of just once, as she had been doing for years, so that she could do some cooking too. She said she didn't mind *and* she was a great cook.

She was actually better than my mother ever was.

I feel a little bad writing that down too, even though I know my mother can't read it (unless my theology is radically wrong). But it's just a fact.

There wasn't much cleaning for Milly to do anyway since I can't stand to make a mess. My mother was much messier than I am. After I asked Mr. Salandhi to cancel all her magazines, things seemed much more organized than they had ever been when she was alive.

After my mother died, I stopped going out to museums completely. I just started staying in the big house all day, every day.

It was Greg who got me going out again. He held up his hand in group one day when the therapist asked if anyone had anything to share.

"I do," said Greg, raising his hand.

"Greg?" she said. "What would you like to share with the group today?"

"If I understand your general philosophy of mental health," began Greg, "which I think I do, since I have been coming to group for longer than anyone except"—he looked around—"Samantha and Danby—"

Samantha was a large woman with pendulous breasts, an enormous nose, and absurdly straight shoulder-length black hair. She would have looked exactly like a fairy tale witch if it weren't for the fact that she was always wearing clothing that she had crocheted for herself in bright colors.

"I came after you," answered Danby. "I remember seeing you here when I came the first time. We talked about a stupid TV show, about how stupid it was. I remember that. That was one of the best times I ever had at group. Usually it's a total waste of my time."

"Longer than anyone except Samantha," continued Greg, uncharacteristically indifferent to the details. He had already heard Danby complain about how boring group was dozens of times.

Samantha confirmed Greg's correction with a subtle but authoritative tip of her head. No one in the room had been coming to group as long as she had. Unless you count her invention of the crocheted corset—which most of us did not consider to be a noteworthy achievement and which she was not allowed to wear to group anymore because it was inappropriate—being in group the longest was Samantha's main claim to fame.

"So, OK. We can agree that I understand your philosophy. A claim based in terms of *length of time*, even if that time has been spent observing things from the disadvantaged side of the mental hospital desk, as it were, if not necessarily in formal teaching situations . . ."

"Greg," said our therapist, who was actually better than anyone else at cutting Greg off when he went off on a tangent, as he inevitably did. She must have learned that in psychotherapy school.

"Yes," said Greg.

"I think we all agree that you do understand what I mean by mental health."

"Well. OK. I'll just take that as a given. If everyone agrees that I can."

He looked around at everyone hopefully, to find the expected chorus of expressions of absolute agreement.

"Good. Yes. I think that was a good decision on everyone's part. To agree. The *correct* decision. And since you have . . ."

The therapist wrote something on her clipboard, which always brought Greg back to the point.

". . . have agreed that I understand Jannie's *philosophy* of mental health, then I expect I will not find anyone among us, unless he or she doesn't understand that *philosophy*, who disagrees that sanity is—if it is actually anything at all!—*a matter of proportion.*"

Someone said "Amen," and everyone else nodded, perhaps a little disappointed, as I was, because they had been hoping for something a bit more interesting.

Greg looked at everyone one by one again. No one spoke. We were used to his style of speech. There were always pauses. You can get used to it, but it is not easy at first.

"Now, what I wanted to bring up today is a question of precisely that: *proportion*. Specifically, the proportion of time that is spent *by a person outside of the home base*, whether that home base be, for each different individual, an apartment, a whole big house, or one room in a house, or a shared room in a hospital ward, as the case may be. A question of how to proportion a person's *time*."

"OK, Greg," said the therapist. "You are not being totally clear for the group, but I think you are talking about being housebound."

"Yes. *Bound* to a house, as that word implies. Exactly. Not bound in the sense of 'going toward' or 'bound *for*,' like . . ."

Here he sang the next line, far better than I would have ever expected.

"'*I'm bound for Carolina with a banjo on my knee.*' Which is an old song written by the great Stephen Foster, people, just by the way, not some sort of *sui generis* children's rhyme as everyone I have ever talked to about this seems to think."

"Greg," said the therapist.

I heard someone else listening mutter, "Does the topic come up in conversation often?" and a few titters in response.

"I'm getting very precisely and as rapidly as possible to my point," continued Greg. "If it takes me longer than most people to get there, maybe it is because I understand better than most people that words must be used with a little bit of *care* or they may fail to *take us to where we want to go.*

"*If* words are being used to *get somewhere*, which is *not*, by any means, the *only* use of words.

"Not by any means.

"But the other uses are less relevant here, although some of them are extremely interesting. I just want to make sure everyone here understands that when I use the word 'bound,' I don't mean 'bound' as in 'my love comes *bounding* over the hills,' or 'bound' as in 'tied up like a kidnap victim or a participant in an act of consensual bondage sex play.'"

The therapist made another note.

"But—as our very good doctor, or at least our young *student* trying to act like a doctor, but not a real *medical* doctor, here has suggested—I mean 'bound to a house' in the sense of being housebound, which is an idiomatic expression with a very particular sense of what it means to bound, in the sense of a limning . . ."

"A limning?" repeated the therapist, as if she were doubtful that it was a real word.

"A limiting, narrowing, or restriction to a small region of highly regarded personal space. A domestic confinement, whether by choice or due to the pressing forces of external necessity."

"Yes. So. Greg. Please. Let's move along a little. You are complicating something simple again. You want to talk again about *getting out of your apartment more often.*"

"Yes. As we have one or two times before. I want to talk about *proportions* and how to deal in a brisk and extremely decisive and mentally healthy manner with the multitude of issues involved in frequently departing from my domicile, my *home sweet home*."

"OK. This is a very important topic, Greg. Thanks for bringing it up again. Because we know that you do have trouble leaving your apartment, don't you?"

"I don't use the word 'trouble' myself. As I think you know. In this context, 'trouble' is exactly the wrong word. I think I probably—we have agreed on this already in group so it will come as news to no one—that mathematically or probabilistically speaking, I do leave my apartment less often than the majority of people who, in virtue of *being* in the majority, get to determine the norms of proportionally proper—or what some might call mentally healthy behavior . . ."

"OK, *good*, Greg."

". . . which by the method of proportions implies that I am *insane*."

Another note.

"Or so *some* might say that, *if* they were not well acquainted with the vernacular of the mental health field in the 21st century, whether that person be educated in that vernacular formally through attending a school of medicine or clinical psychology, like one person in this room, or more directly, through unfortunate and lengthy direct personal experience with disproportionate living, like most of us here.

"But all of us *do* speak that vernacular through one means or the other, and so we all know that a person is never just 'sane' or 'insane,' but that a person might rather have developed an entirely changeable habit of spending a disproportionate amount of time limning—or *limiting*—him- or herself within one space or another."

"Like *you spending too much time alone in your apartment*," pushed the therapist, rather optimistically, I thought.

"OK. Let's go with that, since all conversation in group perversely has to center on the speaker as if there were no principles of *general* interest or *general* relevance.

"In cases of a person such as *myself*, to take just one example among many, time becomes disproportionally arrayed between a domestic space and the myriad of other spaces across which it *might* have been arrayed."

"Yes. So, Greg. You're still talking about things in a bit of a weird way. Remember when we talked about defense mechanisms? What can you do about this?"

"Yes. Absolutely! I do! I remember that, and I thank you very much for reminding me of it! Let's cut right *to the chase*! Enough *verbal behavior*! Enough *philosophizing*! I could surely adjust the way time is arrayed in my life, according to certain principles of balance and normal proportions.

"And then: bingo! I'd be normal, just like that. I'd become *totally undiagnosable*."

"As long as we don't mention the spoons," someone said.

"But it would be so much easier for me to do *that* if I could proportion the responsibility for a regularly scheduled departure from over-familiar domesticity into the greater external world which holds so many dangers that we have all agreed are *real*, even if *low probability*."

"Yes, Greg. Let's not get into that again. We have all agreed with you about this. The world has danger in it, but *any individual person has a low likelihood of encountering any particular danger.*"

"Any *particular* danger," corrected Greg. "On that we have indeed agreed! Definitely! As any logical people would! The probability of encountering *some* danger is nevertheless high because there are so very many dangers."

"Yes, yes, yes. OK. We have agreed on that, too, haven't we, Greg? So you are still trying to get around to telling us about *what you can do to find a way to leave your apartment.*"

"Yes. And I am also trying to get to reminding group that some people have the exact *opposite* problem as me."

"The opposite problem?"

"Yes. The total opposite of houseboundedness. Not actually *homelessness*, which would be a third and very radical category of domestic disproportion, but never being *at* home. The symptoms of that might be quiescent for some time, but we all know that is just how diagnosably disproportionate behavior works its misguided magic. One minute you are out at a bar having a beer with your friends, and the next day you find yourself spending endless hours of your time, say, for example, thinking about having sex with a small animal."

"What are you talking about now, Greg?!" asked Jannie, visibly alarmed, rapidly jotting down a cribbed note.

"You have sex with small animals?" said someone else with notable interest.

"Of course not," said Greg.

"You just spend hours *thinking* about doing it," the person suggested.

"I don't think about having sex with any living being, unless you count myself, since I masturbate regularly using appropriate non-exploitive fantasy material for the sole purpose of keeping my prostate gland in good health, as has been widely recommended by the mainstream medical profession."

Several people groaned. We had also already passed a lot of time in group listening to Greg's well-documented lectures on the relationship between male orgasms and prostate cancer. For him, regular masturbation was as necessary as regular flossing.

"I was just using *having sex with small animals* as an example of a behavior that fell definitely outside out of normal proportion and that I *hoped* would not offend anyone in group, since it had not been brought up here before."

"It's *illegal*," said someone.

"We've talked about Samantha stealing before," pointed out another. "That was *illegal*."

"Drugs are *illegal*. We've talked about doing drugs."

"We all agreed it wasn't actually stealing," said Samantha, looking like she might start crying soon, which was normal for her in group.

"It wasn't drugs. Pot is not even a drug," replied the one who had once confessed in group to using street drugs, in an agitated tone. "By definition."

"Soon everything will be illegal," said Danby. "The government won't even let us gather together in groups any more. Unless it's for a wedding between two people of medically certified opposite genders or the funeral of someone who has left official documents showing that he . . ."

"Or she," added Greg, quickly, loud enough to cut in.

". . . died of natural causes."

"OK, we are going way off track here now again, Dan," intervened the therapist.

We had also already spent a lot of time in group listening to Danby's views of the coming international government state. They were not as well documented as Greg's views on prostate cancer, and so they were more controversial.

"So, I don't want to name the name of any person in group other than myself," continued Greg, "but if I don't, I won't be able to convey to you that when I am speaking about this disproportion of domestic *unboundedness*, the kind of *anti-houseboundedness* that is disproportional in the opposite direction to my own tendency to *be housebound*, I am thinking inside of my own head of *Isaac*. I have to say his name since I know you aren't *mind-readers*."

We had discussed that many times in group, too: People aren't mind-readers; you need to say what you mean.

"So," continued Greg, "I have to name names or else I can't even say what it is I am actually *thinking* about."

"Greg, we aren't . . ." began the therapist.

"Of course, we aren't here *to criticize other people in group*," finished Greg with practiced fluency. "Which should go without saying, since it has already been said so often here. One might even say *disproportionately* often. Which then raises the *extremely* interesting question of whether the inmates are now running the prison, as it were, which I don't want to get into here since I find myself, by the dumb luck of biological history, occupying a chair on the opposite side of the desk than the one whose occupiers draw a paycheck.

"So when I name *Isaac*, as I just have done in order to make sensible to others the otherwise invisible contents of my mind, it is of course not to *criticize* him in any way, or to imply that he is in any way less than *perfectly* adequate or *able to become* proportionally adequate for all normal purposes just as he is, but rather to *implore* him . . ."

"To implore him?"

". . . to recognize that our situation is a perfect one from the point of view of my new *proportional therapy*."

Greg stopped here, evidently because he thought his point had now been made completely clear.

No one said anything for a beat or two, since the point was not at all clear and we were all expecting further clarification. Finally the therapist cottoned on.

"So, Greg. Very good. Today you have identified a disproportion in your life. And have you thought of any way you might address that disproportion in your life? Without disparaging others in group?"

"Yes. That is *exactly my point*. I am currently *housebound*. As you know. Isaac's disproportionate behavior is being overcompensated in the *opposite* direction, just as a certain doctor *Freud* of the 19th century, whose theories I don't, as you know, *endorse as a whole*, suggested that disproportionate behaviors would be.

"So he is *housebound* at the moment, but usually he is *unable to stay in his house*, which is the *opposite* of being housebound. He usually spends a *diagnosably disproportionate* amount of time in non-domestic spaces such as museums and other exhibit spaces."

"I haven't been to a museum since Julia died," I corrected him.

"Isaac. You know we have agreed that you wouldn't distance yourself from your mother by calling her 'Julia,'" the therapist reminded me.

"Yes. Sorry."

"We have already spent a disproportionate amount of time discussing that, too," said Greg.

"Yes. Sorry," I said, again. "I meant to say *mother*.

"*Mom*."

"No need to apologize," replied Greg. "My time is *yours*, if you want to discuss it any more. It wouldn't be *normal*, but I am still willing. I am not as convinced as some of the people in this room that everything the majority does is *necessarily* the best thing for everyone to do.

"It's not clear to me about how the utility function could possibly be unconsciously maximized by the masses."

"No. Please. I'm fine. I meant to say that I haven't been to a museum since . . . my mom kicked the bucket."

The therapist wrote a note.

"*Died*," I corrected.

"Indeed," said Greg. "But we both know that the time is going to come when you are going to go to museums *too often* again. Because that is *the kind of person that you are*.

"Which I don't mean as a criticism. To me, it is a fine way to be. And that is why I am suggesting today that you and I should go to the museum *together*."

He turned to the therapist.

"This is my new 'proportional therapy.' You, the therapist, or a person suffering from a disproportion if he or she is able to do so on his or her own—one of you, anyway—finds someone who has one disproportion and then *pairs* him, or *her* if it was a person of the female gender, with some other person who has the *exact opposite disproportion*. We can't average the two to make two proportional people—which is another design flaw in the human race, by the way; is anyone keeping notes of how many that is? Twenty-two, I think—but one person's excessive behavioral tendency should balance out the other's so that neither person would be able to go to their most disproportional extreme of behavior."

"Like a sadist and a masochist having sex?" said someone.

"Oh no! The exact opposite! That would be *summing* disproportions," said Danby. "They'd both end up worse, since each of their disproportions would encourage the other's."

"Exactly," said Greg. "As usual, at least Danby is following what I am talking about. I'm sorry if it is difficult for the rest of you to keep up. It is good to have at least one other mind here in group. As Danby has realized, the masochist and the sadist encourage each other to be *ever more disproportionate*. It's the exact opposite of mental health. Each masochist would have to be paired with *another masochist*, so each one is forced to hurt the other by refusing to give into the pleasure of hurting him . . . or her, as the case may be . . ."

"Exactly!" said Danby, showing obvious enthusiasm. "And every sadist would have to be paired with a sadist so that each would want to hurt the other by refusing to give him any opportunity to hurt anyone, so when properly balanced they would end up living happily ever after in *normal proportion* . . ."

". . . Which then suggests that the valence of behavioral disproportions might have something like a *mating assortment* to it, with some mixing *positive-positive*, some *positive-negative* (or *negative-positive*, depending on how you look at it), and some *negative-negative*. There could be male and female disproportions, some of which are, as it were, gay, combining fruitfully only with like, and some heterosexual, combining only with unlike, and some bi . . ."

"Exactly! And one can imagine there might be some disproportions that can only be made proportional by *two* or more intersecting disproportions working together," said Danby. "Some very *interesting cases.*"

"This is a very interesting extension of the idea. I am envisioning an evolving ecology of adaptive disproportions," said Greg. "I think this might be a route to unifying clinical psychology and sociology."

"Greg," said the therapist.

"Yes. This is not for everyone. I know. Danby, let's diagram this out after group. You bring the paper; I'll bring the brains.

"I'm just saying here that I think it would be helpful as a matter of simple mathematics for my own housebounded disproportion if

Isaac would take me to a museum with him, since we naturally have opposite tendencies toward disproportion."

"I'll bring brains *and* paper, buddy," replied Danby.

"I wouldn't mind except that I don't go to museums any more," I replied to Greg.

"I know! Exactly! Which is why I am speaking up here in group to ask you if you will! Start going again! For *my sake*!"

"For your sake?"

"Yes! Of course! Totally for *my* sake, man! *Obviously* so! That's exactly how proportional therapy works. *I'm* the house-bound one. Without a force to pull me away from the siren call of my apartment, it's quite possible that I might spend the rest of my life mired in diagnosably disproportionate boundedness to my domestic living space."

"Isaac? Can you help Greg with this request?"

"Do I have to?"

"Isaac. You don't *have* to. But do you remember what I told you that we should say about group?"

"That we are in group *as* a group," I cited.

"Exactly."

"I won't point out again that it is tautological to say that *a group* is a group," said Danby. "You may as well just remind us that integers are numbers."

"OK," I said. "I'll force Greg to go to a museum with me, for his own good."

"Excellent. You're gonna love the one I picked out for you," said Greg.

::

The next day I went out for the first time since Julia had died, for Greg's sake.

We went the Harvard Museum of Natural History, which is connected to the Peabody Museum of Archaeology and Ethnology. Luckily it wasn't too far away. We had to walk all the way there because Greg couldn't do the subway or a bus without considerable effort.

That museum has a totally *amazing* flower museum. All the flowers in it are made entirely of glass. They were made by two German guys, Leopold Blaschka and his son Rudolph, Duchamp's equals in terms of showing us what art is. It took them 50 years to make all those flowers. Fifty years! It wasn't so long ago that 50 years was more than an entire normal lifespan. That was all they did with their lives.

The Harvard Museum of Natural History had a stuffed dodo. It was ratty and beat-up, but that was understandable. Its entire species had been murdered.

Greg and I spent two days there together, and then he had had all he could stand. He returned to his limned domestic space. I did not. His proportional therapy had worked.

I pondered the dodo by myself for many happy months. I liked to think about the exact moment of a species' extinction. Some might say that it was the moment when the last living dodo died. But if you think about it, that is too simplistic. It can be pushed back. The real moment of extinction might have occurred when the last opposite-sex pair disappeared. Maybe there were lots of males hanging around after all the females had died, or vice versa. At that point, extinction was a done deal. In any meaningful sense, dodos were functionally extinct, even if some were still, strictly speaking, alive.

Maybe even before that, an intelligent dodo—or, say, an observing human being or a God—could have called it. Maybe there were three females left, but two were sterile and one was too young to mate. Maybe there were many opposite-sex pairs, but no two of them could stand each other enough to mate. In that case, the species was dead. Anyone who knew the facts could have called it.

What I was really thinking about is this: It is not always easy to say exactly when a life ends.

Sometimes it ends before anything actually dies.

::

After that, I decided to switch to another Harvard University Museum, the Busch-Reisinger Museum. This little museum dedicated to European (mostly Germanic 20th-century) art is tucked away on the Harvard campus, not so easy to find unless you know where to look.

The day that I first went to the Busch-Reisinger Museum, they were having an exhibit called "Rococo Religion." Rococo comes from the French word *"rocaille,"* which means "shell," and it refers to the wild, elaborate, turning, twisting ways of a shell. The exhibit was composed of art that treated "religious" (but really just Christian) themes in a rococo manner: sensuous, jazzy, pulsating, rich, complex works. I was delighted to discover this exhibit because I already loved this kind of art.

I had not been raised religious. I did not know if God existed, and I did not have any reason to think much about it. Despite my milquetoast faith, however, the great rich Christian works that started coming out at the end of the Middle Ages, in the so-called Renaissance, affected me from the time I was old enough to notice them. The paintings from this period are action-based, dramatic depictions of a seething complex world, the action hero comics of their time, fantastic works intended to excite passion in the name of some abstract Great Good.

I walked around and studied the paintings that day with interest. I was trying to get a sense of where I would return, of which among these works were to be a special part of my life for the next months. I walked up to the second floor, and I exited the stairs into a large room—a kind of enclosed landing—that housed a few objects in glass cases that were placed in front of long benches built into the wall.

The room was empty when I first stepped into it. I wandered over to the display cases, my arms behind my back. In one case, I found a small statue of the Virgin Mary holding her baby in her arms. It was amazingly detailed, carved from wax in a beautiful sumptuous creamy yellow. I had to sit down in front of the case and consider it for two hours before I could bring any attention to the next one.

The piece next to the wax Madonna was so amazing that I knew right away when I saw it that I was going to have to spend time with it.

A *lot* of time.

At first I thought it was another wax carving. It had a similar perfect beautiful creamy texture. When I looked closer, I could see that it wasn't carved in wax. It was carved in ivory.

I am ambivalent about ivory. Of course I love ivory carvings. The smoothness and detail that ivory allows and its otherworldly, too-perfect creaminess is so delicious for the eye that anyone seeing artistically has to adore it.

I hate ivory because of a picture I once saw in a magazine. The picture had been taken in the early evening. The sky low in the far horizon showed the slightest tinge of purple. The brown-green blades of straggly African savannah grass were bathed in gold and cast long black shadows. The photographer had positioned herself at the top of a dip, a slight shrug in the completely flat landscape that faded off beyond all the edges of the photograph. Because of the way the golden evening sun was glinting off of everything, the viewer of the photograph cannot immediately see what he is looking at. He sees, but he withholds judgment.

There are eight large masses sprawled out on the ground below, but it is not a viewer's first instinct to see that each mass is a dead elephant. The photographer has allowed the golden evening light to paint itself across the soft, obviously organic masses in a way that makes each one look, at first sight, as if it were glowing from within. A viewer might think that each lump was a hut, with a family huddled around a small fire inside.

But such rough, such hairy huts?! Could they be huts made out of *elephant skins*?!

The viewer who peers a little closer will make out new details: two white dots and three red dots near each mass. And yes, large ears on every mass that now seem impossible to miss. It is obvious that these are not elephant huts, but simply elephants. Elephants lying on their sides.

But something looks wrong. Do elephants lie down on their sides like that? Do they sleep on their sides?

But no. These are not just elephants lounging together on their sides. These are dead elephants. They are not glowing from within. They are lit from without.

The elephants' mighty eyes are shut. The viewer will now easily make out the two white dots below them and wonder how he didn't see what they were right away: the stumps left where poachers have sawed off the dense tusks for their beautiful ivory.

The viewer will start feeling that something terribly wrong has been caught on film, even before he understands what the red dots are. Ivory poaching is not a good thing. Ivory poachers are not good people. Red is not a good color on a dead mammal. Of course it is now too late to withhold judgment, to stop seeing exactly what there is to see. The process of seeing what there is to be seen must run its course.

One red dot on each dead elephant: a view inside their massive gaping mouths, fallen dumbly, sickeningly, unnaturally open. Each animal's lip is stretched in a way that signals the manner of its death. The edges of the mouths are twisted by more than just the meaningless pull of gravity on dead flesh. The viewer can see from the twisted horrifying mouths that these noble beasts died in anguish.

And now it will become clearer what the two other red dots are, one above and one below the mouth, the lower one not always in the same place on each elephant. Now this is completely obvious too.

The one above is a hole going into each elephant. A strangely neat, surprisingly large hole going into each elephant.

And the one below is somehow a hole in an elephant too.

But how? A hole in which elephant? Where is the *other* elephant?

Yes. That becomes obvious too.

Out of sheer laziness, the poachers sawed off the elephant's soft trunks with the same chainsaw they used to saw off those dense tusks. One quick cut gets everything off. It is possible to make out the telltale slash of blood on the ground in front of some of the nearer elephants.

The red hole above is the hole where the trunk used to be attached.

The red hole below is the edge of the trunk that has been severed from that hole, the hole at the end of each elephant's detached trunk, from where it dropped awkwardly onto the ground.

The viewer withdraws.

::

So I hate ivory for what it has done to elephants.

But this ivory carving was . . . it truly is . . . beautiful. It is as close to perfect as anything I have ever seen.

I didn't want to look at it, out of courtesy to the elephant that had to sacrifice his life for it. But I couldn't stop myself from looking at it.

The carving was of Abraham and Isaac.

::

At that time, I knew the story of Abraham and Isaac only slightly, the way any of us does. It wasn't the subject that attracted me. I only started to care about that after I met Kelly. It was the way the subject had been portrayed. The piece is a perfect compromise between the demands of the medium and the demands of the subject. The artist has taken amazing advantage of the natural dimensionality of the elephant tusk.

At the bottom stands a thick, almost squat Abraham. He raises himself up on two massive short muscular legs topped with immense powerful hips, visible through the covering of his tunic, which is carved so fine that you can almost see the weave. Following the cone of the ivory, his proportions get smaller toward his head, and he seems to stretch out vertically, as if to portray his yearning to reach up to heaven. His outstretched arms are very slightly too thin, too long for the rest of his body. In his hands, held high above him, he clutches an improbably tiny child, his unfortunate son Isaac, portrayed in the work as a doll-sized baby.

In order to keep the carving contained within the natural limits of the available medium, the artist had to have Abraham twist his magnificently muscled body unnaturally as he rises up toward

God. The fabric of his robe had to billow fantastically down from him, tight to his body because of the natural limits of the tusk, the fluttering of the rough wool cloth incredibly captured in the smooth hard cold cream.

Flat on the head of the baby-doll son held up so high in Abraham's mighty hands, almost too tiny to be believably part of the work, is another hand. It is the hand of a tiny buxom angel, carved from the very tip end of the tusk. Her tiny wings flutter out so lightly that the ivory there lets the light shine though. Tiny and nearly transparent herself, she seems hardly there at all.

::

It didn't take me long to make friends with the museum guard, a muscular young red-haired Irish Bostonian named Bobby Sheridan. He sussed me out on my first vigil in front of the ivory carving. After I had been sitting in front of it for about an hour, he came over to ask me if I was OK. I told him I was fine, very well actually, except for having a minor mental illness. I explained to him that I had obsessive compulsive disorder and couldn't touch anything, and also that I didn't have to work because my mother had died and I had inherited some money, enough to live for a while on but not really a lot. I explained to him that I was planning to spend many months in his museum, not touching anything of course but mainly just looking at a particular single piece of art, namely the carving of Abraham and Isaac that was in front of me. And I also let him know that I always wore pretty much the same clothes but that I changed my clothes and had a shower every day, and that I was very careful about cleanliness as part of my OCD. I drew his attention to some of the things I appreciated so much about the ivory carving, especially the ample bosom and translucent wings of the tiny angel.

He was perfectly satisfied with my explanation, which was a good thing since it was only the truth. After that, Bobby always said hi to me when I came in each day. He is a super-nice guy. I still see him sometimes. He isn't a museum guard anymore. Now he works at a fish counter in a grocery store in Somerville. If I phone him before I go in, he'll find a good piece of fish for me.

Bobby told me about Kelly a few days after he and I met. I was sitting quietly, resplendent in a light blue silk tie with Italian musical terms printed on it in a rich scarlet. Bobby came over and greeted me, then asked:

"Did you meet Kelly yet?"

I looked up. I never minded being interrupted during my vigil. Interruptions were a normal part of my task. I was prepared to speak to people as I undertook that task.

"Kelly Baxter?"

"Hey, Bobby!" I said, smiling. Of course I didn't shake his hand or anything. "How ya doing? No, I don't know any Kelly Baxter. Who's that?"

"Ah, well, you're in for a treat, pal, if you haven't met her yet. You will. You have to. You're going to have to share with her—she's your statue's second-biggest fan. After you, of course. Nice lady. Pretty too. She usually comes in here every week or two and always takes a look at that piece when she does. She's writing her PhD thesis on Abraham and Isaac. I think it's in art history, but it might be in religious studies or women's studies."

"Maybe she's writing about the angel," I said, pointing to her. "That angel is definitely a woman. Just look at her boobs."

::

When I began to study *The Bride Stripped Bare by Her Bachelors, Even*, I was surprised to learn that one part of the piece—one of the few elements that is unambiguously representational—is a chocolate grinder. The chocolate grinder in the piece is, like all things Duchampian, something of a puzzle. Duchamp specifies that the men grinding chocolate are not grinding for commercial purposes. They are not professional *chocolatiers*. They are specifically grinding *their own* chocolate.

We know that Duchamp liked chocolate grinders just for what they were, in the same way that Greg loves spoons just for what they are (but maybe not so diagnosably). Duchamp painted chocolate grinders several times before he put one into the *The Bride Stripped Bare by Her Bachelors, Even*. In an interview he once described standing transfixed at a store window when he saw one in action at a chocolate shop in Rouen. In *The Bride* work, the chocolate grinder is operated by the nine bachelors—a priest, a delivery boy, a gendarme, a cavalryman, a policeman, an undertaker, a servant, a busboy, and a station-master—who will strip the Bride, or help the Bride to strip herself, or who will at least (as

Duchamp seems to have had in mind) imagine that a bride would theoretically be strippable. As you might imagine, Duchamp had something sexual in mind for the bachelors' grinder. Most of the elements of *The Bride Stripped Bare by Her Bachelors, Even* have some connection to sex, or at least to the idea of sex. The piece is intended to delay us so that we focus our attention on the possibilities of male stripping female.

So perhaps a bachelor grinding *his own chocolate* is, in advance of stripping the Bride, a masturbator. Who would not think that? According to Greg's scientific documentation, 93 percent of bachelors masturbate. Greg suggested that we can conclude from this finding that 7 percent of bachelors are liars.

The reason I was so surprised to read about the bachelors who grind their own chocolate is that I myself was at that time a bachelor who ground his own chocolate.

But I don't mean to reveal anything personal by that.

I *literally* ground my own chocolate. I started grinding my own after my mother died. The arterial walls can be thickened with chocolate. Chocolate also helps the arteries to relax, which drops blood pressure and helps to prevent the buildup of arterial plaque. My problem is that most commercially available chocolate contains a lot of sugar and fat. Both of these cause the arterial walls to become *congested*, a different kind of thickening than what I want. Having congested arteries increases the probability of having a heart attack.

I wanted to be able to get the artery-strengthening benefits of chocolate without the downsides. I found several suppliers who would supply me with 99 percent pure chocolate. I have always enjoyed bitter flavors, so 99 percent pure chocolate was very much to my taste. I ate it for some time, for health reasons, before I began to worry about the fat content. Commercially available dark chocolate contains far more fat than is necessary.

I tried to find a chocolate with lower fat, but it does not exist.

I am not surprised because I know now that eating ultra-low-fat, non-sweetened chocolate is like eating dried mud.

After trying a few different possibilities, I began to order my own organic chocolate beans from a store in Boston, which bought them directly from a specialty farmer in Ghana. If you know your chocolate, you will know that most of the chocolate from Ghana is pretty mediocre, but the guy I buy from is a real devotee of chocolate, absolutely devoted to getting it right. His beans are not *cheap*, but they are very *good*. I get them before they have been adulterated in any way.

At first I ground them up the very old-fashioned way, with a mortar and pestle. When that turned out to be a lot of work, I started looking around for a *decent* chocolate grinder. These are not easy to find.

::

Dying of cancer demands patience. People don't appreciate that.

Someone they know gets a diagnosis of cancer and maybe they have only have a few months or years to live. They know that is not enough. They want more for that person.

But try *getting hit by a car*, or *dying of a heart attack*, or *falling off a mountain*, or *having a massive stroke in your garden*. You get up in the morning, eat your toast and jam for breakfast, and then you are dead before lunch.

These are ways of dying that do not demand any patience. They do not ask anything of the dying person except that he (or she) die. They do not ask anything of the living except that they mourn the death.

Cancer also asks for *patience*.

Cancer is a very demanding way for a person to die.

••

When you first look at *The Bride Stripped Bare by Her Bachelors, Even*, you may have the same reaction I did when I first looked at it: You may wonder where the Bride is. She actually has the whole top panel of the piece to herself, but she is not easy to pick out even when you know that she is there. On the left side of the upper panel is a thin outline of a mechanical-looking object that resembles an anorexic ostrich. The space to the right of this wiry object—the upper-right two-thirds of the piece—is mainly empty, except for a cloud-like object, like a thought bubble in a cartoon, with three large rectangular holes cut in it, that extends across the very top. The thought-bubble cloud is hanging from a hook just visible at the top of the piece. One is forced to conclude, as Duchamp did intend, that the mechanical-looking wiry object must be the Bride. The artist referred to the anorexic ostrich as a *pendu femelle*, or,

roughly, a hanging female thing. If you squint and have an imagination, you might convince yourself, given the wasp-like waist
above a slight rear protuberance, perhaps a bustle or an ample
bum, that the *pendu femelle* has the shape of a woman.

Duchamp called the thought-bubble cloud *the Halo of the
Bride, the Milky Way* (suggesting breasts as much as grinding ones
own chocolate suggests masturbation), or, most wonderfully to
me, *the Bride's Cinematic Blossoming*. Some believe that it may
also be an emanation of the *Love Gasoline* or *Timid Power* that
Duchamp mentions in his notes. One's imagination would have to
be very vivid indeed—diagnosably psychotic, in fact—to understand just from seeing it that this Cinematic Blossoming is part of
the Bride herself. It is Duchamp's intention that it is, somehow. If
it is not part of her physically, the blossoming/halo/emanation is at
least somehow *of* the Bride, just as a woman's scent is *of* her, but
not truly part of her.

Those hoping for titillation from seeing the Bride stripped bare
will be disappointed (but if you want titillation, you can head over
into the next room in the Philadelphia Museum of Art to catch a
glimpse of *Given: 1. The Waterfall, 2. The Illuminating Gas*). *The
Bride Stripped Bare by Her Bachelors, Even* has only the tiniest
hint of femininity. Most of the Bride's domain in the upper half
of the piece is just empty. Duchamp's notes make clear that he
had imagined other mechanical aspects of the Bride to go into that
empty area, aspects that might allow for a more complete (but still
very abstract and still unfulfilled) relationship between the Bride
and her chocolate-grinding bachelors. These are not suggested in

the piece itself. Like Isabella Stewart Gardner's paintings, they are alluded to by their absence, by a pointer to the empty space where they could go.

Duchamp's Bride has not just been stripped of clothes. She has been stripped of almost everything. She is just the slightest notion of a bride.

It is no wonder that the bachelors have to grind their own chocolate.

::

There are chocolate grinders for sale on the Web, but not as many as I was expecting there would be. If you search the Web for pages on chocolate grinders, you will get more hits to essays describing Duchamp's work than you will to pages discussing real chocolate grinders, a rare case of art trumping real life.

The chocolate grinders that were available on the Web looked boring and problematic to me. I didn't just want another incomprehensible machine slowly becoming contaminated and unusable in a corner of my kitchen. I wanted a chocolate grinder I could understand, interact with, fix, and clean. I wanted one I could admire. I wanted a *real* chocolate grinder. I wanted Duchamp's chocolate grinder.

Duchamp's chocolate grinder consists of three large grinding wheels, like drums with lines running down their sides. The drums are connected to a cross of wooden poles that might be used to turn the grinder. Halfway up the left side of the bottom panel, there are the nine "malic moulds" (Duchamp made up the word "malic," which makes as little sense in French as in English, to indicate their maleness) that represent the nine bachelors. Crisscrossed with vertical or horizontal lines, each one resembles a cloak or jacket, which is the only hint that they are human. They are standing on what looks like a wire frame on a sled. Inside the wire frame there is a wheel that looks a little like the treadmills that boys give to their pet hamsters. It is in fact a water wheel, as you can see when you look close: It has paddle-like protrusions to catch the water. The absence of any apparent water source implies that the bachelors are going to be turning that wheel themselves, though the scale is wrong for them. The malic moulds are too big, the waterwheel too small. The impression is that the whole thing is some kind of Rube Goldberg machine that has been jury-rigged from parts that do not belong together. The malic moulds are connected by thin lines to seven cones arrayed, mysteriously, around the wooden turning poles. The three grinding drums are arrayed in thirds on a short round table, which oddly has feet in the style of *Louis Quinze*. By rotating the mechanism, using rods attached above the drums in the center of the table, chocolate beans are crunched into chocolate dust between and beneath the drums.

::

In the last months of my father's life, he knew he was dying. At first he fought the cancer very aggressively, using every tool he could find.

That didn't work.

Once he realized that, he accepted the inevitable. He was ready for it. He *wanted* to die. Not because he didn't love life. He did. He surely wanted to spend more time driving his bright blue Porsche and showing people his big house and accounting for money and hanging out with us all.

He wanted to die because he could see how things were going. He would be a burden on us, and had no pleasure for himself. No one was going to win by his staying home. My father liked to win.

On his deathbed, he and I talked about euthanasia.

He thought it should be legal.

::

When I started thinking about buying a Duchampian chocolate grinder, I was still being very careful about my money. I hadn't spent much, except on my clothes. In six months, my net worth had increased by about $82,000, due either to luck or to the skill of the broker chosen by Mr. Salandhi. Although I wanted to delay the inevitable dissipation of my million and change for as long as I could, I felt I should risk splurging on this so that when I was out on the street, broke, I could honestly say I knew what it felt like to just buy whatever you wanted, no matter how outrageous your want was. *That* was what it meant to be rich.

Somewhere, there had to be someone willing to sell me a working antique chocolate grinder.

Of course the first person I called when I decided to buy the chocolate grinder was Greg. I didn't think that he would know where I might buy one, but he was the only person who might at least understand why I wanted one. He met me at what had become our usual meeting place, a Starbucks in Somerville. I explained to him about how chocolate could strengthen your arteries, how sugar and fat were bad because they might give you a stroke, and how pure chocolate tasted of a mixture of ash and dirt. I told him about how I was buying my own Ghanaian chocolate beans, and how difficult they were to grind.

Then I asked the question: "So, I want to buy a chocolate grinder like Duchamp's *Chocolate Grinder*. Preferably exactly the same, but I am willing to compromise on the *Louis Quinze* legs, which could be a figment of Duchamp's imagination. I'm not saying that I *want* to compromise on that, but I'm willing. So: How can I do that?"

Greg looked at me warily, as if he was doubtful that my words could possibly mean what he thought they did. He repeated them, as is his habit.

"So, you want to buy an antique chocolate grinder?"

I looked at him the same way he had looked at me.

"Yes, Greg," I said. "I do."

"An antique chocolate grinder as much like the one Duchamp painted as possible?"

Pause.

"Yes, Greg."

I was obsessive myself, but I did find Greg's conversational style to be maddening.

"It's also in the *Bride Stripped Bare by Her Bachelors, Even*."

"Yes, Greg. It is. I know. That's the one I want to buy."

"It's French," he said.

"Yes, Greg. You're right. Duchamp was *French*. He saw the grinder at a candy store in *Rouen*. It's a *French* chocolate grinder."

"Yes."

"Yup."

Pause.

"It is," I said, hoping to move the conversation forward just a little.

"So you would prefer to buy a genuine antique French chocolate grinder. OK. I can understand that. Of course that would be the best. But would you be willing to settle for a good replica?"

"Yup." There really didn't seem to be much more I could say.

He sat silent for a few seconds, looking up into the white ceiling as if he was expecting a message to appear on it.

"I've never seen anything like that," he said, finally. "I never thought about it before, but I have never seen anything that looks like Duchamp's *Chocolate Grinder* except Duchamp's *Chocolate Grinder*."

He was silent for a few more moments.

"This is a really cool idea!" he said. "I'm gonna have to look into this."

⁚⁚

Greg called me back a few weeks after we had met in Starbucks.

We met at the same Starbucks.

"So," he said, when we had sat down. "It's not so easy as you might have hoped to get an antique French chocolate grinder."

"No?" I said, wondering how easy he thought that I thought it would be.

"No," he said.

I waited. He shook his head.

"No."

I sighed, and thought about my beloved ivory angel's breasts to distract myself.

"You really can't get one," he said. "I phoned everyone I know in the Duchamp world to ask if they had ever seen a chocolate grinder exactly like Duchamp's *Chocolate Grinder* anywhere, and no one has.

"Everyone agrees there must be some somewhere, but no one knows where."

Pause.

"I even had a Belgian friend of mine call *Gamelin's* in Rouen. Because I don't actually know anyone in France. Maybe there are no Duchampians in France any more. Duchamp has been Americanized," he said. "Anyway, no luck. The guy who answered the phone there didn't even know what we were talking about."

He looked into his Americano, and stirred it. With a brown plastic stirrer. Luckily.

"But you still want one, right?"

I nodded.

"OK. Well, there's only one way to get one. We have to go to Philadelphia."

"We have to go to Philadelphia?" I repeated.

Both the word "Philadelphia" and the word "we" threw me off.

"Yes," he said, "I know a guy in Philadelphia who can make you an exact copy of Duchamp's chocolate grinder. I'll have to send him a letter. He doesn't have a phone."

I looked at him questioningly.

He looked at me questioningly, too, before he continued.

"He thinks they emit rays that hurt your brain. Which for all I know they *do*. I don't like phones that much either.

"And you know Arensburg's collection is there, of course? The biggest collection of Duchamp's work in the world."

"Yes, I know. I guess we could go and see that while we are there."

Another pause, and then Greg continued.

"Yeah. You're rich. Right?"

⁝⁝

Three weeks later, Greg had a curt mail reply from his contact. The man in Philadelphia could and would make a working copy of Duchamp's chocolate grinder, even including the *Louis Quinze* legs, for a not inconsiderable sum in five figures. The price was what I had expected and was still only a fraction of my $82,000 in recent profit.

And a splurge is a splurge.

I wrote an equally curt reply to accept the terms, enclosing a check for 50 percent of the cost. The rest was to be paid upon receipt of the work, if I was satisfied with it. If I wasn't, he would start again.

While we waited for word on how long it would take to create, we set about planning our trip. Philadelphia is only about 300 miles from Boston. During the day, there is a flight nearly every hour between the two cities. Under normal circumstances, a fact millionaire with time on his hands could decide at lunch in Boston to travel to Philadelphia with a companion and get there in time for happy hour at the hotel bar.

Greg and I met at Starbucks seven times over the next seven weeks before we finally agreed that the combined probabilities of germs and aircraft disasters were more than either of us could willingly take on. We expected, in any case, that the chocolate grinder would be too bulky and heavy for transport by plane. We spent several meetings discussing what we would need to know to calculate the weight of grinder before we agreed that there were so many variables that it would be hard to estimate the weight with any certainty. We met to discuss the Greyhound bus only once, dismissing it in 15 minutes as both more contaminated and more dangerous than an aircraft. Greg presented me with a thick folder of documentation about the Greyhound passenger in Canada whose head had been chopped off in the bus by another passenger.

After that, we passed seven more Starbucks meetings talking about what kind of private vehicle would work for us. It needed to be clean, safe, and large enough to hold a life-size, possibly heavy replica of an antique chocolate grinder.

Finally, we came to an agreement: I would rent a *Winnebago* to drive to Philadelphia on the conditions that we could rent one that had never been rented by anyone before, that we had it immediately cleaned for chemical contamination after we got it, that Greg could stay in it for three days before we left so he could get used to it (his demand), and that Greg would wear new plain white shirts with a collar, new blue slacks, and a new jacket, all provided by me, and would change his shirt every day (my demand). I gave in on getting him to wear a tie. In part, I admit, this was because I wanted to retain my position as the snappiest dresser. Greg braved the alleged waves from the phone and put in the calls. He managed to find a rental agency that agreed to call us when they had a virgin Winnebago to rent.

We were almost ready for our trip.

All we needed was someone uncontaminated with a driver's license.

DESCRIPTION OF THE NECKTIE:
1. RESPLENDENT IN COLOR
2. PROVIDED AT THE 4 CORNERS
WITH VERY SHARP POINTS (LIKE ALL NECKTIES)

The chocolate grinder splurge was my second splurge. Unless you want to count my parents' huge house—which I don't, since I didn't actually buy it and only kept it for tax reasons—my first splurge was on my clothes. Even though I knew that I wasn't *really* rich, I already felt that I should do something to mark my new status. I was, after all, a fact millionaire, however tenuous the position might be for me. If I really was destined to lose a million, it only made sense to act like a millionaire while I still was one.

I decided to mark my new status by wearing a suit and tie every day. Before that time, I had worn a suit just a few times in my life, for a few weddings and two funerals. I decided that I would henceforth wear the same clothes every day. Some kind of clean white shirt with a button-down collar and (my favorite detail!) French cuffs, to be worn for one day and professionally dry-cleaned each week until I ran out of money for such a luxury as dry-cleaning. A few cheap sets of very simple, very similar steel cuff links. Always unremarkable blue slacks, pressed sometimes but with less fervor than the shirts. Always the same brand of 100 percent cotton gray socks. Always a generic blue blazer.

I had to buy the shirts new. French cuffs are almost impossible to find secondhand. That cost me quite a bit because I bought 10 identical, high-quality, Italian, 100 percent cotton shirts. The Italian guy who sold me the shirts said they were called *Italian* cuffs. I guess they are so great that everyone wants to say they were their idea. Those shirts were a splurge. I was going to buy just seven so I could change every day of the week, but then I thought that one might lose a button or be worn out before I had time to get a new one. So I bought three spares and rotated them with the other seven so they were all worn an equal amount of the time.

I bought my unremarkable slacks and blazers secondhand, which is one reason they were unremarkable: They were what was easiest to find. It was very easy to buy 10 of each, not absolutely identical but very similar. It didn't cost me much at all.

Again, it comes down to proportions. To wear pretty much exactly the same thing each day, like Greg and Danby used to do, is undeniably crazy. It often smells terrible, it looks ugly, and it displays poor taste. It makes the person who hardly changes his clothes stand out as diagnosable. To wear exactly the same *slacks*, *socks*, *shirts*, and *shoes*, but to change each piece daily, is undeniably less crazy. It is not in the slightest bit offensive, it is completely invisible to undiagnosable strangers, and it looks sharp. So it is perfectly acceptable. It would pass as merely eccentric even if someone noticed the regularity.

Changing my tie every day pushed my wardrobe into the category of *total sanity*.

After all, many undeniably sane—even very successful—men pass much of their adult lives wearing more or less the same suit and shirt every day, changing only their tie. We think nothing of it when they do. I was completely indistinguishable from the average businessman, stockbroker, accountant, or lawyer.

My look was simple, inoffensive, and standard, as well as being very clean and crisp. I looked the best I had ever looked. I liked the way I looked in a suit.

Ties quickly became my indulgence, especially as my bank balance grew rather than shrank as it was supposed to. A nice tie is a simple luxury. I saw no reason to deny myself one simple pleasure when so many pleasures that normal people spent money on did not attract me at all. So I bought a lot of ties. I made them my *signature piece*. I always wore the same slacks, always the same shirts, the same socks, the same simple metal cufflinks, the same generic black polished shoes. But you never knew what crazy colorful tie you might find me wearing! I soon had a lot of ties, both new and used, in a vast range of colors and patterns. Unless you spent many days with me, you were not likely to see me wearing the same tie twice.

Familiar as I was with Duchamp's notes, I thought of my ties as "resplendent in color, and provided at the four corners with very sharp points (like all neckties)." That colorful description came from Duchamp's description of the ties worn by the nine bachelors portrayed in *The Large Glass*. I thought it was a very fine line when I read it in Duchamp's extensive notes for the piece. I still do. I love the phrase "resplendent in color"! So unnatural a phrase, and yet so noble sounding!

I like to shout out the last phrase. *"Like all neckties!"*

I also love the idea of specifically describing the tie corners, only to admit that they were really just the same as any other tie corners. It is like saying that the woman you love is beautiful. In fact, she is no more beautiful than any number of other women. But she is your love. Her beauty is special to you for that reason.

My ties have sharp points.

They are no sharper than any tie's points, in fact.

But I still love my own points.

::

I met Kelly for the first time when Bobby brought her over to me just for that purpose. She is half Japanese and half Canadian/American—more American than Japanese in her attitudes, but more Japanese than American in her looks. The day that we met, her lips were, as they usually are, painted very red, very strong, with a tight line outside the red. She had black mascara that made her eyelashes curve way up. Her long black hair was up in a bun, held with a glossy black chopstick. She was wearing swishy black pants, red pumps, and a very fine ivory-colored silk shirt printed with a colorful sushi motif. She was carrying a faded black leather backpack with an also-faded Mandela painted on it.

Bobby reminded me about having mentioned her to me before, introduced us briefly, and then said to Kelly: "He can't shake hands with you, but I'll leave him to tell you why not." He winked at me, and left.

So I told Kelly the whole same thing I had told Bobby: that I had OCD and that I wore different clothes every day even if they looked the same and that I couldn't touch many things and that it didn't really matter because I had a small amount of money, hardly anything really and not enough to retire on, but enough so that for a while I could afford to just spend some time in art museums not touching anything. Including other people's hands.

I didn't tell her that if I were ever going to touch anyone's hands, hers would definitely be my first choice. She has very beautiful skin, of an unusual orange-brown tone, darker than most Japanese. Her fingers are long and delicate and are usually adorned with several silver rings. Her fingernails that day were painted bright shiny red (as they often are) to match her lips.

Kelly sat down beside me on the steel and fake black leather sofa, which was the only good place to sit if you wanted to sit down when you were looking at the carving. When she sat down, I got a whiff of her perfume: an exquisite rich, fresh mixture that smelled of lemons and fresh sawdust.

She reached into her backpack and took out a gray notebook with a crude homemade painting of the ouroboros, a dragon devouring his own tail, on the front. She opened the book to a fresh page. The paper was a wonderful clean cream, the color of the ivory and the background of her blouse. Later on, she told me that this was because the paper was made of bamboo. She took out an expensive-looking fountain pen decorated with a purple and pink peacock feather design.

She didn't seem put off by my confession. I think she had been tipped off by Bobby.

All she said was, "I'm really sorry about your having OCD. That must be a drag."

I shrugged and said it wasn't so bad. I was used to it, I knew no other life, and I hardly ever thought about it. People adapt.

After a second, she said, "Anyway, Bobby tells me you really love looking at this statue. I love to look at it too. Let's look at it a while together."

She sat close beside me, emanating her delicious sweet and intoxicating odor, without writing or saying a word, gazing at Abraham, Isaac, and the busty angel. At first I was nervous about her, but she was so quiet and smelled so good that after a few minutes, I started to feel very happy she was there with me. I was surprised to discover that it felt good to have a companion with me.

I wanted to look at Kelly too because she also was very beautiful, she also drew my attention. She was also buxom.

But I understood that people didn't like to be stared at, so I kept my eyes on the statue.

∷

After about 15 minutes—which is a good long stretch of time for a person without OCD to look at anything that doesn't have a car chase or naked people in it—Kelly said: "We have to admit it's good. It's very good." She put her pen back in her purse and flipped her notebook to a page where she had pasted in a series of photographs of the statue we had been admiring together. There were six photographs, taken from four sides, and then two views of each side from a slightly higher viewpoint, highlighting the tiny angel. Because they were taken from above, they gave a good view of her tiny but proportionally magnificent cleavage. All the photographs were in black and white, taken against a matte black background. There was no reflection from the glass, so I knew that they had been taken somewhere else.

"Wow!" I exclaimed. "Those are great photographs! Where'd you get those?"

Everything this woman did made me like her more.

"We took them last year. I know the woman who does the photographic work for the galleries around here. They already had some good pictures of this one, but I managed to convince her to re-photograph all the depictions of Abraham and Isaac, and to let me be there when she took the pictures."

"So did you actually get to touch it?" I asked. I was quite excited about that possibility.

"Well, yes. Sort of. We have to wear cotton gloves when we handle the artwork. So I couldn't actually touch it directly. But I did lift it up and move it around. It's heavier than it looks."

I felt sad about the cotton gloves. To me, wearing cotton gloves to touch art is like wearing a condom to touch female flesh: Even if you can understand why it's a good idea, you still want to feel what it would be like without it. I wanted to feel the smoothness of the ivory, to run my fingers over the billowing ridges of Abraham's robe, to touch the angel's face and caress her perfect translucent wings between my fingers. I felt sure that the ivory of the carving was pure and uncontaminated.

"So why this one? Why do you like it so much? Is it art appreciation, or is it OCD?"

It was a fair question. I told her about Greg's spoons and how he had told me about Duchamp, and how reading Duchamp had made me think more about what art was, and how since I couldn't touch anything and was well-off, I had spent a lot of time in art museums. I told her about the months I had passed looking at the stuffed dodo and the glass flowers that had taken two lifetimes to construct and then at the empty spaces where stolen paintings had once hung.

And then I continued.

"But I don't really know yet what it is that grabs me. I'm trying to figure that out. It's not just something simple like the curve of a spoon, obviously. It's something *like* that, though. Maybe it's a bunch of different things like that. Or a bunch of things like the *idea* of the simple curve of a spoon, anyway.

"In this one, right now, I love the luscious texture. And the idea of the extreme outrageous sacrifice. And the way the piece is constructed, going from gigantic to tiny. And the fact that the angel has such great breasts.

"And also the fact that it's about *Isaac*, because that's my name. You know where it comes from?"

She smiled and riffled through her notebook to another page. She turned the book to show it to me. In large print in the middle of an otherwise empty page, she had written: "Isaac = laughter." I was very surprised to see that written there.

"Sarah laughed because she was so old when she had a baby—you know?" she asked.

I didn't know yet.

She continued. "Sadly, *Kelly* doesn't have such a great meaning as *Isaac*. It means either 'church' or 'warrior,' depending on who you believe."

Then she told me her idea about Abraham and Isaac laughing together that I already told you about.

"When I wrote that, I was thinking about this possibility that Isaac might have actually been laughing when he was about to be done in by Dad. It isn't a *funny ha-ha* situation, but you have to admit there is a certain crazy, almost joyous, absurdity about it, isn't there? You know how human beings who are totally cornered, completely stuck by circumstances beyond their control, can sometimes reach a time when all they can do is laugh? They see their lives reduced to a single point of inescapable fate, they see all that they tried to make of themselves shrunk to that single point, and the fact that it all comes down to a forced move seems so outrageous, so crazy, that all they can do is laugh.

"And I was also thinking that maybe if Isaac did laugh, that was what saved him. Because think about it: If you were about to kill someone and they started laughing, wouldn't that make it tough for you to kill him? Wouldn't it be hard to kill someone who was laughing? Wouldn't that suddenly bring the whole situation down to such a human and personal level that it might be harder to go through with it?

"Anyway, that's what I was thinking.

"I'm doing my PhD thesis on representations of women in the story of Abraham and Isaac, so I'm always looking for some new angle. Wouldn't that be totally great, to be the first to see the humor in the situation? It's usually all so dully serious, isn't it? Always all about men. Always all about killing and power.

"But there's definitely a kind of comical Beckettian futility in the story. Something almost sweet, almost funny.

"Beckett's whole idea that *we can't escape, we can't go on, but we must go on.*

"No matter how crazy it seems to be."

⁚⁚

Kelly paused and then continued.

"Do you know about Ishmael?"

I didn't know who Ishmael was. I didn't know *anything* about the story of the sacrifice. I thought that it was just a very short and simple story.

I just thought that Abraham had been told to kill Isaac and had killed a ewe instead.

"Well, Ishmael was Isaac's older half-brother. His mother was Sarah's personal servant, Hagar, who Sarah gave to Abraham because she couldn't get pregnant herself. That was a custom at

CHRIS F. WESTBURY 79

the time. According to the Koran, it is *Ishmael*, not Isaac, who was supposed to be sacrificed.

"And in the Koran, God says that Abraham doesn't have to go through with the sacrifice because *he already fulfilled God's vision just by agreeing to do it.* It's not about knives and blood. It's entirely *conceptual*. It's all about *right thought.*

"If it's Ishmael instead of Isaac, there might be a different story about the laughter. But I've also thought that there might *not be.* 'Ishmael' is Hebrew for 'God will hear.' Maybe what God hears is laughter in either case, no matter if it was Isaac or Ishmael he was having killed.

"Maybe it is *always* laughter that softens God's heart."

I looked at the statue again. It felt odd, uncanny, to consider that this person I had been meditating on for so many hours might not be who I thought he was. I looked at the boy depicted in the statue and tried to think of him as both Isaac and Ishmael, as the laugher and the listener simultaneously. I tried to think of him as a more general thing than just a person.

I tried to tell Kelly how it made me feel and what it made me think of.

Duchamp, of course.

"Wow, that's weird for me to hear," I said to her. "Because I've spent so much time looking at the child thinking it was Isaac that now it freaks me out to see him as Ishmael instead. But this is good! It's very good for me! Because one of the things I am trying to work on here is this *concept* of Duchamp's . . ."

Kelly smiled. I continued.

"Well, maybe you know that he said that a work of art is a 'delay.' In his notes to *The Large Glass*, he said we should use the word 'delay' instead of the word 'painting.'

"And to me that had two meanings for him. One is that a piece of art literally *delays* you—it *stops* you and keeps you standing in one place, at least for a few seconds. That delay wasn't necessarily a *good thing* for Duchamp, because the other thing is that when art *delays* you, you are also delayed from *moving beyond* art. You are delayed from understanding that art is not a thing that you look at in museums, but a way of seeing everything in the whole world."

"Yeah. It's not about *paint* and *ivory*. It's all *conceptual*," said Kelly, smiling and nodding.

"Right! Exactly! But the other meaning, kind of related I guess, is that a piece of art—anyway, Duchamp's art, which was *made* to be hard to understand—can delay you from making a judgment, from reaching a decision about what you're looking at. You stop, you look, you *withhold judgment*. For Duchamp, you were supposed to stay in that state. Rest delayed. That was his goal.

"So I have been trying to take advantage of the fact that I have OCD and money to see how far this delay can go. I seek out the best object for obsession. I stop, I look, and I withhold judgment. For a long time. For as long as I can. I see this as my duty, somehow. Or my need. Or maybe just my symptom.

"But now I can see that I *failed*. To withhold judgment. All this time I have been looking at this child held in Abraham's hands. Without ever thinking about it, I have been assuming that *I know who he is.*

"But that was a judgment! Of course I don't actually know who the people in this statue are! As you say, maybe this is not Isaac, but Ishmael. Maybe I don't really know who Abraham is, or if this is really him. And maybe this isn't even *supposed* to be a real angel because probably there aren't any real angels.

"But now I can see.

"I can start to see this thing without reaching any judgment about what it is supposed to be. I can withhold a judgment I had been automatically making. Which is excellent progress for me! So, thanks!"

Kelly smiled again, and looked at me, hard, for a few seconds without saying anything. She was processing the fact that I truly was crazy. I didn't look crazy. But now I had confessed that I did things in public that no sane person would do. I looked and withheld judgment. For months and months.

Crazy.

This is how I know what she was thinking: because she told me.

"Well, I have to say you were right: You're crazy, all right.

"But I guess there are worse ways to be crazy than to give your attention entirely over to art. It's really a form of devotion, right? Even if you don't think so yourself, I know that it is. A devotion to something bigger than any of us, and to something that maybe even *deserves* devotion.

"What you are doing is definitely crazy. But it's not really much crazier than spending six years writing a PhD thesis on some minute aspect of the world. A PhD in women's studies in religion is no path to greatness either. I do what I do for the same reason you do what you do: because *that is what we like to do*.

"Well, I'm gonna go and get a cup of coffee. I'd invite you for coffee, but I'm guessing that going out for a coffee is not your thing?"

Of course I did go out for coffee, but with Greg to his local Starbucks.

"Right? OK. I won't shake your hand, Isaac.

"But I'll tell you what: I'll salute you."

And she stood up absurdly straight and saluted me, just like they do in the army, her gorgeous flat palm held outward against the right edge of her forehead, smiling all the while.

"I'll see you again, OK? I'll be back sometime. And I know you aren't going anywhere."

And she took up her bag started to walk away.

As she left, I called out, "Hey, by the way!"

She turned to look at me, and I told her: "You really smell great!"

Kelly stared at me again, laughed, and said thanks.

Then she was gone.

::

I think of Duchamp's description of a tie's points every time I buy, choose, put on, or take off a tie. Sometimes, if I was at home and I was sure that no one would hear me and think I was crazy because I talked to myself, I used to say the words aloud as I looked at a tie lying across my hand.

"Resplendent in color," I would say, as if I were speaking directly to my tie, as if I were giving it a compliment, as if the tie were a favored old cat.

"And provided at the four corners with very sharp points."

And then, always more loudly: "(like all neckties)!"

If you only talk to yourself when no one can hear you, it doesn't count. No one knows if non-crazy people talk to themselves when no one else can hear them. Talking to yourself may be normal. Insanity is acceptable in isolation. This is why you are allowed to think crazy thoughts, but not do crazy things. Crazy is as crazy *does*. Not as crazy *thinks*.

Now you can imagine my resplendence! I am not just being vain when I tell you that I am pleasant looking. I got lucky that way. I have average looks, or probably, I would have to say, better than average. In those days, I kept my black hair cropped neatly short, but not so short that anyone could suspect that I might belong to some worrisome and unclear subculture. Despite my diagnosis, I was not anxious or troubled. I was happy, as I am constitutionally prone to be. Being crazy was not bad for me. Since I was a fact millionaire, I could afford to sit around not touching anything.

And I never felt any shame for being what I am. I didn't ask to be born obsessive compulsive. I didn't ask to want to look at art. I was just made that way.

To me it was just like having blue eyes or being farsighted.

::

The day after I first met Kelly, I thought about *With Hidden Noise* as I sat in front of our ivory. I had begun my day by ruminating again about whether I had been looking at Ishmael all the time I had been thinking I was looking at Isaac. That made me think I thought that my ivory was not just what it seemed. It also had *hidden noise.*

Duchamp made a piece called *With Hidden Noise* that is displayed near *The Bride Stripped Bare by Her Bachelors, Even* at the Philadelphia Museum of Art. *With Hidden Noise* consists of a ball of boric twine secured with bolts between two plaques of brass. Boric twine is twine treated with boric acid, a flame retardant. The twine used to be used in candles or just as a kind of safety twine, less likely to catch fire than untreated twines. Some people say boric acid is very unhealthy for you. It can lead to damage in reproductive and neurological organs. It can cause genital or brain damage, anemia, infertility, birth defects, or death. Anyway, it might at least irritate your skin.

Duchamp made the piece in 1916, the same year he declared that a mass-produced typewriter cover was art. When he was putting together *With Hidden Noise*, Duchamp invited his friend and collector Walter Arensberg to add a small object inside the twine, which can be heard when the piece gets shaken. Clearly, the essence of *With Hidden Noise* is the hidden object. It is important that nobody knows what it is. It is important that it remains unseen and unseeable.

At first I was thinking of the hidden noise in my ivory purely conceptually. I did not know what I was seeing when I looked at it, in the sense of not having any ideas about what it meant that were definitely true. I didn't know what the people were really named, what story was really being told, whether or not angels could really exist, and if they could really have nice boobs if they did.

Then I began to ponder the idea that maybe there *literally* was something hidden inside the statue. Something tiny, hidden inside so carefully that there was no evidence of it. *Hidden* hidden noise.

By lunchtime I was pondering the possibility that the sculptor had so loved his subjects that he had actually carved their entire bodies in ivory, inside and out, in exquisite detail. I imagined an artist like Lorenzo Ghiberti, who spent most of life making a single cathedral door in Florence, or like Duchamp, who spent twenty years making his final piece of art, *Given: 1. The Waterfall, 2. The Illuminating Gas.* I thought about Kelly spending so many years writing a PhD thesis on such an obscure topic.

I imagined that inside the tiny ivory Abraham and his tinier son and the even-tinier angel, there were still tinier ivory skeletons. Within the tiny ribs were tinier ivory livers, kidneys, bladders, intestines. I imagined that all this was jigsaw-puzzled together so tightly that no one had ever suspected it could actually separate. I imagined how the artist might have devoted months just to constructing the specialized tools he needed to put the pieces together. A long, elegant, flexible pair of tweezers made from bird feathers, wax, and black thread, created just to delicately place the child's left kidney into his body cavity. A dark rococo hardwood pick, curving around like a scythe specifically so the angel's womb—or whatever a buxom angel may carry in place of a womb—could be pushed down into its proper place. I imagined tiny brown glass bottles of home-brewed organic glue, to be placed onto the work with a single horse's hair, each tiny drop intended to last only long enough to get the blocking piece into position, before it evaporated and disappeared completely.

••

Kelly came back to see our ivory about a week later, striding off the stairs in jeans and a T-shirt with a colorful Ganesh printed on it. She smiled at me in the corner, took two steps toward me, and saluted.

"Hey, Isaac! Good to see you haven't given up the devotion. Stick with it, buddy! Good things come to those who wait."

She walked over, swinging her handbag: bright red leather with a wavy blue leather strip sewed across that looked like a gash into the sky. When she sat down beside me, the smell of lemons and fresh sawdust delighted me again.

She reached into the bag, took out her notebook, and opened it up for me to look at it, careful not to hold it too close to me.

"Check this out."

There were images, mostly old photo reproductions that seemed to have been cut from books, of people, mostly Indian, sitting in front of religious icons and deities. Above them, across the top of the page, Kelly had written: *Ishta-deva*. She pointed to it, as if she were reading a storybook to a small child.

"'Ishta-deva,'" she read, "you know that word?"

I didn't.

"You gotta learn it! Because that's what you have! Like all these guys!"

She pointed to all the pictures, like a waitress in a restaurant waving her hand across faded 1970s-style pictures of the day's cocktail specials.

"Ishta-deva. Hindu. It means 'cherished divinity.' Literally. But it refers to whatever is a chosen reminder of the Divine. If you look, you can see they are all different. Because they're Hindus, so for them, God comes in different forms. *Many* forms. In Hinduism, representations of God are really just there to entertain you, until you come to focus your attention on that aspect of God that can never be represented, which is true Divinity.

"So this piece"—she pointed to our ivory—"is your Ishta-deva."

As far as I knew, the motivation for my task had never been in any way religious. So I just said, "OK."

Kelly turned to another, earlier page, covered entirely with a reproduction of an antique etching of an old woman wearing what looked like a nun's habit, closed high up her neck. Oddly, either her naked belly is protruding from her clothes or she is wearing a largish metal stomach plate with a belly button carved into it. Two tiny angels in the background appear to be fighting each other in the street. Above them, two wise-looking men stand, apparently talking to each other, each pointing to the exit, stage left.

"This is the thing that I think is missing from our piece: Sarah. Isaac's mom, right? And even if it was Hagar who actually gave birth to Ishmael, Sarah would have been the one to raise him as her son. Hagar was given to Abraham by Sarah as a servant, and a servant she remained.

"So Sarah is Ishmael's mom too, in every sense but the biological.

"But you know who else Sarah is? This is the kicker: She's also Abraham's half-sister! Look, I copied it down below the picture."

She held the book closer to read her note.

"*Genesis 20:12 And yet indeed she is my sister; she is the daughter of my father, but not the daughter of my mother; and she became my wife.*

"It gets a little more complicated than that if you really look into it. Some people say she wasn't actually his sister; he was just saying so. But it doesn't matter. It's not about whether she was *really* his half-sister; it's about why saying that she *was* is part of the whole story. Think about it! Sarah has at least associative relations of mother, sister, aunt, wife, and madam to these guys! She has all these crazy ties to this story, but she's never actually *in it*! Every time you see Sarah, she's either off by herself or standing around somewhere with Isaac and Abraham talking in the background.

"Can I keep talking for a second? Yeah. I'm not boring you too much?"

I enjoyed her company equally whether she spoke or not, so it was easy to assure her that she was not boring me at all. My attention span is not short.

"Ok. Thanks. I'm almost done.

"Because you know what Sarah means? It comes from a word that literally means 'a high-ranking woman.' But it gets translated as 'princess' or 'high holy one' or even sometimes 'goddess.'

"Goddess! So here's my new angle, which I started thinking about after you pointed out the angel's excellent boobs the other day; tell me what you think: Sarah *is* in the depictions. She's *the angel*!"

And then she went on to explain about how the angel at Abraham's sacrifice is *Malak Yahweh*, the Angel of Jehovah, basically a kind of super-angel.

"So I'm not saying that every sighting of the Angel of Jehovah was really *Sarah*. *Of course* she's not the Angel of Jehovah who appeared to Moses in a burning bush or to Abraham in a dream. But, here, in this statue, and in all the depictions of Abraham's sacrifice, she's an Ishta-deva, the specially chosen feminine representation of the unportrayable Divine.

"And that's why I think the angel is always a woman, even though the Bible clearly says elsewhere that the Angel of Jehovah, this super-angel, has to be a man, or at least manlike . . . maybe without all the man parts. But that's why she can *be* a woman: the Angel of Jehovah is an Ishta-deva, not *a Divine One*, but a pointer to the very idea of Divinity."

It was a lot to think about. Luckily, I didn't have to say anything about it because Kelly closed the book, smiled at me, and said: "OK, end of the lecture, let's look a while."

So we did.

::

As we looked, I began to think about Kelly's idea that the tiny buxom angel touching the child's hand was a divine aspect of Sarah.

I disturbed her from her meditation on our ivory. Interruptions were part of her task, too.

"Hey, Kelly. Does the Bible say anything about what the angel actually looked like?"

Kelly smiled, as she seemed to do before answering any question. Her nose crinkles a little when she smiles. It is delightful to see.

"Nope, it doesn't say anything. In fact, it doesn't even say that the angel actually had any visible body at all. In the Bible it just says that the Angel of Jehovah *called to* Abraham from heaven."

"And did the kid hear it calling too?"

"It doesn't say. No mention of the kid interacting with the angel at all. The kid is very much a bit player in the story. In fact, Isaac never gets a lot of mention in the Bible, even though he eventually went on to become one of the great patriarchs. The only thing he got is that he is the only patriarch in the Bible who didn't have to change his name—not surprisingly, with such a great name, huh?"

"Right! So," I continued, "it's possible that Abraham just *thought* he heard an angel, that the angel was inside his head? That he was hearing voices that weren't really there?"

"Yeah! For sure. It's totally possible! Just like it's totally possible that Abraham might have just been hearing things when he heard God demand the sacrifices. We don't have any way to know if Abraham *really* had a direct line to God. Do we? All we have is stories written by people who weren't actually there. And even if they were people in Abraham's circle, they *still* couldn't be sure that Abraham actually did hear God. All they had was Abraham's word for it. He *said* he heard God. That's all we know."

"So," I went on, "even if angels do exist, this one probably never actually appeared physically on this scene. So the angels are definitely the artist's addition."

"Definitely. There's really no strong authority for how angels are supposed to look, especially the Angel of Jehovah, who is a shape-shifter anyway. Which is why I am thinking that the angel is not really just a single thing. The female Angel of Jehovah symbolizes the need for a feminine aspect of the Divine."

"So you're saying it's just a figment of our imaginations?"

"I'd never say something was *just* a figment of our imaginations! What does that mean? That whatever we think up in our own heads is for that reason just *nonsense*?! I don't believe that! *Love* is in our heads, and *joy*, and *inspiration*, and a sense of perfected beauty that goes beyond the most beautiful realities ever actually experienced by anyone! So I wouldn't disparage the Angel of Jehovah because it was *just an idea*. Ideas matter! Most important, aspects of the Divine can *only* present themselves to us as ideas.

"If you look at a baby, say, and feel overcome with love and concern and hope for the future, it isn't because that *baby* has been charged with the ability to make us feel those things. It is because we have been charged with the ability to let the baby make us feel those things. The baby is just a catalyst of those feelings of Divinity. It is we who actually feel Divinity into the world.

"There are always people around smashing babies' heads on rocks because they don't like the babies' parents, or drowning babies in toilets because they don't like the idea of a baby, or shaking them until they die because they don't like babies' crying. If a baby was Divine *in itself*, that would never happen! It would be *impossible*. It does happen because the baby-smashers and the baby-drowners and the baby-shakers have not seen a baby as a source of the Divine Idea."

I had never met a major in women's studies in religion before, so I didn't know what to think. Maybe Kelly was just crazy like the rest of us.

"Do you think the angel is maybe just Abraham and Isaac's *thoughts* about Sarah?" I asked Kelly. "I mean, do you think that the artist was trying to show that they were both *thinking* about Sarah? So the angel is like a thought bubble in a comic book—a way of showing you what was in the character's heads?"

"Yeah, exactly!" she exclaimed. "That's just what I've been thinking about! That's actually *the perfect way* to put it! An angel is an empty comic book thought bubble. The content has to be filled in by the viewer. The Angel of Jehovah is just the idea that turns people's minds toward Divinity! And here, in this story"— she gestured to the ivory—"it was Sarah that did that! It was Lover, Mother, Sister, Aunt, and Madame. It was Woman!"

As you know, Kelly did end up writing her thesis about exactly this idea.

::

I was starting to like Kelly by then. You know what I mean. I was really starting to like her a lot. Too much, already, by then. So early on.

I liked to look at her. I liked her hands and her clothes. I liked the shape and color of her long, thin body. I liked her shoes. I liked her smell. I liked her lipstick. I liked her lively brown eyes. I liked her crinkly nose. I liked to see her smile. I liked to make her laugh. I liked to listen to her. I liked her notebook. I liked her salute.

When she left, I turned again to the ivory statue.

I thought of the stolen paintings, and how I had imagined what it would be like if they were there.

I thought of Kelly's perfume and tried to re-create its scent, as if it still hung in the air.

I thought about the mutilated elephants I had seen in a magazine. I wished that I could see this ivory carving illuminated under that same golden light of an African evening. I imagined the long shadow it would cast if it were set down on the wild savannah.

I thought about how the mountainous dead flesh looked when it seemed to have been lit from inside.

I let my focus go loose, not really looking at the carving so much as feeling what it might be like. I felt that this piece of carved ivory had some of that same magical illumination. I felt that it too was shining with a light that came from within.

A RESERVOIR OF LOVE GASOLINE
(OR TIMID POWER)

Another guy that Greg and I met in group was David Renard, "Daver," we called him, for "Dave R." His wife divorced him after she discovered how disproportionate his behavior was.

Daver had married his high school sweetheart young. At the time of his divorce, he had never had any girlfriends except his wife. Nevertheless, in group he revealed that after his divorce, he had figured out the best way to pick up a woman very quickly. A devout Christian (who believed that his diagnosability was a test from God), he called his pick-up approach the Bible Method, because he followed advice in Mathew 7:7: "*Ask and ye shall receive.*" He was really just following Jannie the nanny's advice to say what you mean. He told us that he had a high success rate by telling women that he found them attractive and wanted to have sex with them. He said that he only said it when he really meant it, to women he knew at least slightly, and never insistently. According to Daver, not one of them had ever taken offence, and several had just said yes. That amazed us. He wasn't an especially good-looking guy, and he didn't lie about being diagnosable. But he didn't look crazy, he was sincere, and he was really a nice man. I was glad to hear that women liked him. Not only for him, but also because it gave the rest of us some hope.

I had not had a chance to try the Bible Method as a pick-up method myself. I wasn't very good at dating and have always had trouble asking people for things. Jannie always said it was because I was raised in a wealthy family, because a lot of rich people believe that everyone could be rich if only they worked hard enough, so they don't think anyone should help anyone else. She may be right.

I think that my dad did believe that. He didn't meet too many diagnosable people until I came along, I guess.

∷

Kelly came by a few days after Greg and I had first put in the call for our Winnebago. She sailed in with her hair up high in a complicated asymmetric arrangement held together with three large industrial-looking clips. She was wearing a long black skirt below a silky white blouse with large ivory-colored buttons. A hint of a lacy red bra was visible at the top of her blouse. She stopped to salute me as usual, said, "Hello, sir!" then turned to the ivory statue, bowed low, and said, "Hey, Ishta-deva."

I had been looking forward with such longing to her next visit. When I saw her, I was overcome with the desire to smell her scent. I could hardly wait for her to sit down beside me. When she did,

I was very surprised. She did not smell like lemons and fresh sawdust. She smelled like cinnamon and cloves on fresh apples. It was a glorious smell. But it was not Kelly's smell.

"Hi, Kelly. You changed your perfume, huh?"

She smiled.

"Not permanently. But yeah, I'm wearing a different perfume than my usual one today. Thanks for noticing! Like it?"

Of course I didn't. What could I say?

"I guess so. I mean, I do like the smell well enough. It smells really great. But I love that other one you usually have. I really love that one. When you have that one, you smell super-great, fabulous, unbelievably amazing."

I was embarrassed at my unexpectedly strong outburst but forged ahead after a pause.

"I think about how you smell *all the time.*"

I was feeling ever more uncomfortable. I had been expecting Kelly to smell one way, had been anticipating that smell. When she arrived and smelled differently, I was bewildered. It had thrown me off. I had a growing feeling that something was wrong. I had stepped over a line of intimacy with my confession. Some part of me understood that. I was embarrassed.

Kelly missed a beat or two, but then recovered herself and smiled.

"Do you really?"

Another beat.

"Well, so do I. I like to think that I smell good. And that perfume really is great, isn't it?"

I smiled and told her, "It smells like lemons and fresh sawdust. You know that sweet, earthy smell that sawdust has when it's new? Like that. Mixed with lemons. I think so, anyway. I do think so."

I could feel a pressure welling up inside me, an itch I knew I would need to scratch. I was feeling increasingly anxious. My stomach was starting to burn. My mind was slipping a little. I was being taken somewhere I did not want to go, being dragged by something more powerful than me.

I needed to wash my hands.

∷

It turns out that one part of the cure for a compulsion is to speak truth to it. Speak truth to power.

"Hey, Kelly? You remember how I told you that I have this medical disorder, or some would say 'disease,' OCD?"

She nodded, and looked at me closely.

"Well, I'm having a compulsion right now. I dunno why, because I usually don't have them in the museum. Which is why I come here so much. I think I told you. But now I have to tell you that I do need to go and wash my hands. I need to wash them."

"OK," she said. "Do you need me to do anything?"

Now it was my turn to look at her, as she slid over to let me out of the bench.

"What do ya mean?" I said. "To do anything for what?"

"Well, you know. I dunno. I don't know what we are supposed to do in this situation. I don't know if I am supposed to do anything. Like, to help you or something. Or maybe try to talk you out of it. But I don't do anything? You just go off and wash your hands, is that how it works?"

I couldn't quite see where she was coming from.

"Well, yes. I guess so. Yes, I just go off and wash my hands."

"So should I just wait right here then?" she asked.

I looked at her again.

"Wait here for what?" I asked.

"For you!" she said. "I mean, you are going to wash your hands compulsively, right? The rest of us, who don't do that, are we supposed to just treat that as if it were a normal hand-washing? I mean, is it supposed to be just like you said, 'I gotta go and take a leak'? Because if it is, then I'll just wait around. Because that's what you normally do if someone just goes to take a leak, right?"

"Well, yes, I guess so," I said. The people I spent time with made the distinction between normal and compulsive behavior less than clearcut. I could only imagine what people normally did.

"But if compulsive washing is some different kind of thing, more like *going to a movie*, say, than going for a pee, then we may as well just say goodbye and go our separate ways for today. Just as if everything was normal and you just had something else you had to go do. So you'd go off to do that and you wouldn't have any expectations about whether I'd still be there when you came back. Because it would be a totally different activity. There would have been a definitive end to the first meeting. Instead of saying, 'Oh, are you still here?' or 'Ok, I'm back,' when you came back, you'd say, 'Oh, wow, you're back here again, huh? Me too!'

"So, I was just asking if this hand-washing would be more like taking a pee or more like going to a movie."

I understood.

"Um. Well. Let's see. I guess. I'd say it is like taking a pee. I guess. Like, I'll be maybe two minutes. Or three or five minutes at the most. So if you want to wait here, I'll be back soon and see you then."

I paused.

"And I hope you do stay. So I can. See you then. If you don't mind."

"Well, if it's just like that, I'll just go to the bathroom too while you're at it," she said, smiling again. "Powder my nose.

"For an estimated one to two point five minutes," she ended.

And then she swept up her beautiful bag and followed me out of the gallery.

::

When I got back eight to 12 minutes later with extremely clean hands, Kelly was still there looking at our statue. I sat beside her, drew a breath, and took courage in Daver's Bible Method: Just ask.

"Hey, Kelly," I just asked. "Do you have a driver's license?"

I won't say she agreed instantly. I had to explain to her all about the fat content in commercial chocolate, and how much my chocolate grinder might weigh, and about Greg's OCD, and how the guy in Philadelphia might also be diagnosable, and about the Winnebago, and more about Duchamp, and all that sort of stuff. I wasn't embarrassed anymore. My hands felt fine. I felt like I didn't even have OCD. It was just like talking to Greg. Like talking to a friend.

After about 45 minutes, I finally got to the part about our little problem with the lack of a valid driver's license, and how it would take a certain kind of person with a tolerance for OCD to drive for us, and how she seemed like she might be that kind of person.

"So you want me to drive you and your friend Greg to Philadelphia in a Winnebago?" she said.

"Yes," I said.

"You know that Philadelphia's only a couple of hundred miles away from here, right?"

"Yes," I said.

"So you know you could just drive there and back in a day, right?" she asked.

"No. We can't," I said.

And then I explained the whole deal with the Winnebago to her, and how Greg had insisted it had to be new and cleaned and how we had to rent it three days early so he could break it in and how I had insisted he had to wear a suit (but not necessarily a tie) and how we had finally agreed that we would go as soon as we got a Winnebago and a driver.

Kelly looked at me.

"So, would I have to stay in the Winnebago too?" she asked.

Good question.

"We didn't put that in. I guess you wouldn't have to. I don't see why. We have to stay in it, but you don't."

"And I wouldn't have to be part of the breaking-in period?"

"The three days?! No, definitely not. Those are totally Greg's days. We'll just leave him to it."

"Is this a paid position?" she asked. "I only ask because I'm a little broke right now. I don't have a lot of extra money for traveling."

So I explained to her again about all the money I had inherited, and the allowance I had from Mr. Salandhi, and the $82,000 I had just made, and how I knew I wasn't really rich but I was living large anyway, wearing suits with Italian shirts, buying expensive replicas of antique chocolate grinders, and renting brand-new Winnebagos.

"So, we need a driver, and I don't see why you should have to spend your own money to drive us. So we can either say the trip is free for you, or I can pay you some kind of chauffeur's wage, whichever you like. I like the idea of having my own chauffeur. After all, I am a fact millionaire. I *should* have a chauffeur."

I had to explain to her what a "fact milllionaire" was. After that, Kelly sat in thought for a second.

"OK," she said. "Here's the deal. I drive, and you pay all my expenses. I sleep out of the Winnebago, in a motel or something. You pay for that."

She paused.

"We spend a day together at the Duchamp museum, and you and Greg have to tell me what you love so much about him.

"I don't get treated like a chauffeur, but just like I'm hanging out with you."

She paused.

"And you guys have to ask my permission before you wash your hands. Or do anything else like that. You know. Something compulsive. You have to discuss it with me."

We both paused.

"And I get to take notes and pictures."

I would have to check with Greg.

∷

I met Greg at Starbucks. Of course.

Four times.

The first time he was very nervous about the fact that he didn't know this woman Kelly. I pointed out that he hardly knew anyone who he hadn't met in the hospital and that most of those people were definitely usuitable candidates for a driver.

He thought she might not understand him. I assured him that she would not.

He wondered if she would be prejudiced against us because we were diagnosable. I told him about how she had asked me whether she should just wait, and how she seemed pretty cool with my hand-washing and that was why I decided to ask her to drive. That, and the fact that she smelled great.

He insisted she had to be OK with us having Sani-Wipes available in several places in the Winnebago. I agreed that she would have to, or she couldn't come.

He worried that she might not like Duchamp, since her interest was religious art. Also, that she might not like that he was an atheist. Or that he had some very particular food preferences. Or that she might not get the spoon thing. I sighed.

He said she would have to accept that he wasn't going to wear his shoes in the Winnebago, and he hoped she wouldn't either.

I met him the next time with a pad of paper and a pen, and started writing.

I left him after that meeting with the 13 pages of notes I had written, so he could edit the text. He brought back as many pages of addendums, caveats, and edits.

The final document I took to Kelly ran to 31 double-spaced pages.

Kelly surprised me.

Her counter-document ran to 58 pages.

::

"What the *schlooby-pie* is this?" said Greg, pointing to an item on page seven stipulating that one of us had to pop a chocolate truffle from a specific Boston *chocolaterie* into Kelly's mouth every 90 minutes while she was driving.

I pointed to his own item on page three insisting that the Winnebago had to be oriented due north in a Walmart parking lot at night. To me, it seemed like a wash when it came to the insanity of the requirements. At least chocolate tastes good (if you sweeten it).

Kelly wanted an agreement that hand-washing had to be limited to two minutes and 22 seconds. Greg pointed out that she didn't specify why it was two minutes and 22 seconds and complained that it seemed totally arbitrary. I knew that it was, although 2:22 is

certainly an attractive number. I pointed out that he had not specified any reason for why the Winnebago had to be oriented north,
and suggested that it probably seemed just as arbitrary to Kelly.

He wanted a particular brand of toilet paper stocked in sufficient quantities to last three weeks, in case we got stuck somewhere.

She wanted to have complete control of the radio station and/
or CD player while the vehicle was moving. Greg countered that he
wanted control just when we went in to Philadelphia.

He wanted to be subsidized by me to dispose of one pair of 100
percent cotton boxers at the end of each day.

She wanted me to provide good maps to everywhere we had to
get to. Which Greg also thought was an excellent idea. He wanted
lots of maps. "Redundant maps," as he put it.

I added up all the demands on a calculator. They were easily
within the reach of a fact millionaire on a spree. I accepted them
all, and then, getting into the spirit of the thing, I added a few
choice demands of my own.

Greg and Kelly tussled a little more on a few points, but six
weeks after I had first broached the topic, I delivered 55 typed
pages to Kelly, plus a $250 advance for her miscellaneous expenses,
as specified by her, plus an additional $80 for a new bottle of the
sawdust and lemon perfume, which she was obliged by *my* stipulation to buy and wear in generous quantities every day and which I
was obliged by *her* stipulation to pay for.

Kelly signed the last page, which had already been signed by Greg
and me. So she agreed that we were going on a road trip together.

All we needed was an acceptable vehicle.

⠒⠒

Vehicle rental offices do not buy new vehicles every day. I stopped phoning our guys every day after they agreed to send me an e-mail every day saying that they hadn't forgotten my needs, so I would know that they were still waiting for a suitable vehicle.

I got 42 e-mails before they phoned me to say they had a candidate on the lot waiting for us. Greg and I took a cab to check it out. After a couple of hours, we were able to accept it as long as it was shampooed inside once at our expense. I signed the papers and paid, and I phoned Kelly to let her know she could pick it up whenever she was ready. She was the only one on the trip who had real-world commitments to schedule around.

⠒⠒

The first time Kelly ever phoned me was to say that she was going to get the Winnebago the next day and was wondering where Greg wanted her to park it for his habituation period. Greg had written into the contract that it would always be parked at a Walmart because the Walmart company had a policy of tolerating long-term parking of recreational vehicles on their property and because a lot of Walmart parking lots were the same. Kelly duly delivered the vehicle to the agreed Walmart, and she delivered its key to me at the museum. I had a prearrangement with a key maker of Greg's choice to make a copy of the "Do Not Copy" key without touching it with human hands. I had to provide gloves for the key maker. The key he made was delivered to Greg at Starbucks, inside a pre-supplied black silk bag.

::

The first day of Greg's habituation period was not too hard for me, but I could feel a growing tension in my body, and I had to rely more heavily than usual on my Sani-Wipes.

The second day I was definitely symptomatic. I washed my hands on seven occasions that I deemed unnecessary by normal standards, and my average wash length exceeded the normal average length by many minutes.

When Kelly came by around noon of the third day, I was in dire straits. My symptoms had reached an intensity I had not felt for many years. I had spent more than an hour in the bathroom preparing to go to the museum, and more time in the museum bathroom than in front of my Ishta-deva. My hands did not chap after such a short time, but they itched and burned with a desire to be slathered with soap and warm water.

"I salute you, sir!" she said to me when she saw me, saluting me. This boded well for my requirement that she would greet me with a salute on every day of the trip. I loved it when she did that.

"Hi, Kelly," I said. "I'm glad you're here."

She looked at me, sitting down. The delicious familiar smell of raw sawdust and lemon juice wafted across me.

"I don't know exactly when the agreement about the judging begins, but I'm ready for it to begin today if you are."

She looked at me and replied slowly, a little uncertainly: "OK."

"So, the last three days my OCD has just gotten worse and worse just when I thought I was getting better, so if you want to keep me on a normal schedule while you're here, just so long as you were planning to be here anyway. . . it might . . . it possibly could be helpful for me. Quite possibly. You know, in controlling myself. In acting normal."

"Yeah, OK. So you want to wash your hands right now?" she asked.

I nodded, a tight smile on my face.

She ascertained by questioning me that I had left the bathroom only seven minutes earlier and had peed and washed my hands 26 minutes earlier. For her, that meant I couldn't go back to the bathroom for at least another 34 minutes without being disportionate from normalcy, and therefore diagnosable.

"So" she said. "Let's look at our Ishta-deva for 35 minutes."

::

In her thesis, Kelly wrote a whole chapter about how the Angel of Jehovah is "Malak Yahweh," while common angels are "bene elohim," the sons of God. The word "malak" is usually glossed as "messenger," but its root means both "to be or become a monarch" and "to counsel." "Yahweh" is a more personal name, a title, for God, and a complex word that a lot of people have been arguing about for a long time. The Bible attests that the word "Yahweh" derives from the verb "to be," and therefore means something like

"I am" or (using an even more torturous etymological argument) "I am that I am." Kelly says we should translate "Yahweh" only a little more loosely as "What Is."

If you put it all together, the Angel of Jehovah is a big shot who counsels What Is. There is a lot in Kelly's thesis about the theological implications of an angel, especially a clearly *female* angel, who advises God. It's a weird concept.

In my statue, the hand of God's buxom advisor hardly touches the child's head. But the delicate piece would not have held together if she hadn't made solid contact with it. Her fingertips are not stretched out in a desperate attempt to reach the boy. They are flat on his head. It was not a *stretch* for her to touch him. She is touching him the way a mother might rest her hand on her child's head: naturally, openly, easily, hardly even thinking about it. For her it was not a duty, not a command, not a requirement, not even a need. She is touching him in a way that says she is doing it just because he is there.

I thought about this as I sat basking in the comforting cloud of Kelly's scent. My own hands were aching to be washed, were tingling with need and the responses to that need.

I thought about what it might feel like to have the hands of Malak Yahweh, hands so free and easy with their blessed touch, hands that made no demands of their own. Hands that took a stand about how to act. I thought about what it might be like, if I were an angel, to tousle the hair of a boy as he was about to be killed by his father simply because I chose to tousle that hair. I thought about what it must be to feel uncompelled even in that horrific situation, to be able to look on with such indifference that touching the child or not was entirely a matter of chance and circumstance. I tried to feel what it would be like if washing my hands were like an angel tousling the condemned child's hair, a pleasant moment if the chance happened to arise, but hardly worth working for.

The combination of Kelly's perfume and my meditation on the angelic hands had a definite effect on my symptoms. By the time 35 minutes had passed, my compulsion had subsided somewhat.

I told Kelly I thought I could hold a while longer and thanked her for helping me reduce a need to a desire.

"Let's try for 45," I said.

::

My mother always tried to get me to stick to my guns like she did. She wasn't so concerned about what it was that a person decided to do. All she cared about is that they *did* whatever it was they decided to do. Whether I decided to take up skydiving or checkers was less important to her than that I did it after I had decided to do it. As soon as possible after I had made a decision, I should either be hurling myself out of airplanes or moving plastic markers around on a piece of cardboard. That was what mattered.

::

The Bride Stripped Bare by Her Bachelors, Even is over nine feet tall, consisting of two glass panels joined together. The lower part is for the bachelors and depicts mainly automatic responses to unavoidable causes. The mis-sized waterwheel (powered by water that is alluded to by its absence) drives the chocolate grinder that in turn causes a pair of giant scissors to open and close.

The Bride's emanations cause the bachelors to inflate and release their own pent-up emanations into a sieve, where they are conflated and deflected away from the Bride.

Many other unavoidable obstacles, including the scissors, are placed in the way of the stream of the emanation from the chocolate grinders.

The Bride's upper panel shows less constraint by the forces of necessity. Although the *pendu femelle* is a kind of machine and the Bride's *Cinematic Blossoming* includes three rectangles that are supposed (perhaps) to be pistons, the Bride is not *just* a machine.

For one thing, the pistons are not *normal pistons*; they are not used simply to turn an engine. They were intended by Duchamp to be a communication device by which the Bride could speak to her bachelors, mainly, it seems, so she could boss them around.

For another thing, the Bride's parts branch out into an organic set of tentacles that are, like *the Cinematic Blossoming* itself, decidedly un-machine-like.

And for another thing, she is not even a bride. She is *the idea of a bride*, existing outside the hard mechanics of reality in which the would-be suitors are inextricably mired.

::

I was thinking of this as Kelly and I continued to look at our ivory.

Abraham and his son were also mechanically reacting to forces in the world, driven like puppets to do what they must do. They made no choices because they had no choices to make.

Above them the *merest idea* of a female, a mere *notion* of an angel ungrounded in anything, was free to tousle the hair of the child (or not) while the drama unfolded in whatever way it might.

She didn't care.

She wasn't trying to *get* anything.

She was just *doing what she does*.

I thought that maybe it was the angel putting her hand on his head that caused the child on the sacrificial altar to start laughing, breaking the spell of the moment.

I got another whiff of Kelly's wonderful perfume, and it brought me a deep peace.

I turned to look at her, and she smiled at me the way she does. She raised her eyebrows and looked at me sideways in question.

Forty-five minutes.

I no longer had any desire to wash my hands.

I smiled back at her.

5

A SORT OF WATERSPOUT COMING
FROM A DISTANCE IN A HALF CIRCLE

The next Friday, Kelly came to get me in a black pickup truck she had borrowed from a friend. We needed a truck because there was a lot to carry: several boxes of chocolates, a case of Spanish sparkling wine, 24 rolls of toilet paper, a compass, a battery-operated radio, 14 extra pairs of underwear for Greg, a medium-sized library of books on Duchamp that Greg and I wanted to have along in case we needed to consult them, 20 Italian shirts for Greg and me, a suitcase full of ties so that I could have a good selection to choose from and so there would be plenty for Greg to choose from, if he decided to wear one. We were leaving on a Friday with the understanding that, while it was possible we would be back as early as Sunday, we probably wouldn't return until a few days after that. To help us through our uncertain adventure, we were taking generous quantities of both the luxuries and necessities of life.

I felt both embarrassed and proud when Kelly drove up to my house. Mr. Salandhi had it set up so that I rented my house from my incorporated self, who is identical to me except that he pays less tax. I had to pay my incorporated self rent each month for the nine-tenths of the house that was rented to my unincorporated self. I liked to sit alone in my office and write the check, and then solemnly hand it from one hand to the other. That always made me laugh.

Kelly drove up in the Texan-sized pickup, jacked up high on its wheels. We would have to climb it just to throw stuff into its bed. She smiled.

I didn't.

She was not dressed according to the agreement.

Since Greg and I were wearing suits, Kelly had agreed to dress *business casual or better*.

But she had arrived at my house wearing an oversize gray *Carpe diem* sweatshirt over a pair of pink cotton sweatpants with the manufacturer's name stenciled in white on the bum. She was wearing running shoes.

This was not *business casual*.

This was just *casual*.

I felt a panicking energy rising inside me.

Kelly must have seen it rising because she looked up at me from the curb, saluted, and explained, "Don't worry, boss; I didn't forget the dress code. I have to take the truck back afterward, so I'm gonna change at home. Don't forget that I get to take cabs between the Winnebago and my accommodation as a billable expense. I'm not going to give that up! I will arrive by cab."

She was right. I should have remembered about the cab rides.

"Is that all of it?" she asked, running her eyes over the teetering pile of supplies on my porch.

"Almost," I said. "I just have a couple more suitcases inside."

"Good!" she said, smiling and flipping her long hair back with a twist of her head, "Because we are going away for, like, a long weekend. I wouldn't want to attempt a trip like that with just one small suitcase."

Loading up the truck was not bad. In fact, it was fun. Kelly was cheerful about it, and I felt happily excited.

I worked hard enough that I had to take off my jacket, which I had not taken off outside my house for a long time.

::

I had printed some notes for Kelly for us to consult when we got to the Winnebago. Greg had specified in our agreement that our first entry into the Winnebago, in particular, be very sterile. We were supposed to change our shoes, wash the soles of the new shoes in a bleach solution of a specified strength, and then leave the old shoes behind. We also had to wash the key we had and pass it to Greg through the window in a silk bag. He would return his original, illegally copied key to us in the first silk bag.

Kelly loves ceremonies, so she had no trouble accepting this arrangement. Greg and I accepted all requirements. We knew we might have to give up something ourselves if we made anyone else give anything up.

Along the way, Kelly and I realized that she wasn't going to be able to come in right away since she had to take her friend's truck back and go home to change. She couldn't go into the Winnebago, since she didn't have her new shoes with her and was underdressed. After discussing it, we both agreed that we couldn't start unpacking until we knew how we were going to deal with this unexpected deviation from our plan.

I walked over to the Winnebago and knocked at the window. Greg peered out from behind the curtain but didn't make a move to open the window or the door. I pointed to Kelly, hoping that would somehow make everything obvious. He just shooed us away with his hands and closed the curtains.

I tapped on the window again. There was no response.

I walked over and knocked on the door. I heard garbled human sounds that meant nothing to me. I knocked and called out.

"Hey, Greg. Hey, open up. I need to talk to you for a second."

There was no response for a few seconds, and then the door opened, a hand poked out, and a sheet of lined yellow paper torn from a pad wafted down to the concrete parking lot.

I picked it up.

"WHAT IS THE USE OF AN AGREEMENT," it said, in beautifully printed block capital letters, "IF YOU DON'T FOLLOW IT?"

I took it over to Kelly and showed it to her.

"Well," she said. "He does have a point. The whole system will break down if we don't all honor the agreement, and without an insane system of arbitrary constraints on our behavior, we won't have nearly as much fun. So, we do need to honor it. You'll just have to wait with all the stuff while I drop off the truck. When I get back we can do it the way we are supposed to. What do you say? OK? I'll be quick."

It was a plan, which was more than I had. So Kelly and I unloaded all of the packages, bags, boxes, and cases from the truck, all life's luxuries and necessities, and I sat down on the case of cava to wait for her to get back.

From inside the Winnebago, there was silence.

••

It was not so much thirst as boredom and a sense of occasion that made me decide to open up a bottle of the cava. Sparkling wine seemed fit to the occasion. This was, after all, a spree. The deal only specified that I had to bring seven bottles, one for each day of our maximum foreseeable time away, but I had brought a case of 12 because a full box always looks tidier. I only needed the front nine bottles for a seat, so I could take a back bottle out. I did.

I somehow managed to coax the cork out. I had never opened a bottle of champagne before.

Kelly says I shouldn't call it champagne.

I have to admit that the first swig was good. The wine had been stored in my parents' basement wine cellar, which was usually just empty, so it was cool. Tasting it was like smelling perfume. I had a few more mouthfuls to appreciate how the flavors melded together.

I thought about my parents and their empty wine cellar. I wished they were not both dead. I missed them.

I finished the bottle a while later, and then I desperately had to pee.

I rose unsteadily to my feet and knocked on the door.

"Greg," I said, in an extremely reasonable holler. "I havta take a leak now."

No response.

"Greg, I really mean it. I really havta pee. I'm gonna *burst*."

No response. I sat down again on the bottles, feeling annoyed. Five minutes later, the door opened and another yellow sheet of notepaper floated gently down onto the asphalt.

It contained a six-panel cartoon that Greg had drawn to illustrate how Kelly and I were supposed to go into the Winnebago. The first panel showed a dishpan lying in isolation on the parking lot pavement, casting a shadow like a huge stone in a Japanese Zen garden. In the second panel, we see water and bleach being poured into the same dishpan, with a small annotation specifying the quantities of each. In the third panel, Kelly (wearing an evening gown) and I (wearing a bowtie and tuxedo) are shown approaching the dishpan, which can now be seen lying in front of the Winnebago steps. In panel four, we are shown removing our shoes when we are three to four feet (as helpfully annotated) from the dishpan. We are clearly displaying the shoes we each hold in our hands, with cartoon dollar tags still on them to symbolize that they are brand new. In panel five, we are kneeling to dip those shoes into the disinfectant. In the final panel, Greg watches with a smile on his face as we ascend the stairs holding our unworn shoes in our hands, still dripping. In place of a signature on the lower right, Greg had sketched a small spoon.

Underneath that panel, in neat small capital letters, he had written, "AND DON'T FORGET ABOUT THE KEY EXCHANGE."

In the first panel, Greg succeeded in making the dishpan look *lonely*.

"Greg!" I yelled again.

Schloobies.

I couldn't really leave all our baggage to go and pee in Walmart. There was a lot of valuable stuff piled behind me. I knew Greg wasn't going to leave the Winnebago to protect it.

I sat down once more on the case of wine.

Schloobies!

I really did have to pee. I was going to have to do something.

::

After just a few seconds of sitting, I resolved that immediate action was required. I looked around. The only thing I could see that looked like a vessel suitable for peeing into was the blue dishpan we had bought for the sterilization ceremony. I had purchased it myself, from Walmart. Since we were actually *at* a Walmart, I reasoned, I could just replace it with another when Kelly got there. I could empty the original one into the toilet inside the store and discard it. It only cost $4.99.

I was by now very happy to pay $4.99 for a piss.

I moved to the back of the Winnebago, to the left of the rear window so that Greg wouldn't see me peeing into the sterilization vessel. I wouldn't mention it. I placed the dishpan as close to the vehicle as I could, leaned against the vehicle, held my jacket back with my arms, unzipped, and relieved myself with a sigh.

The police arrived five minutes later.

::

The car contained a single officer. He parked beside our pile of stuff, pulled himself out of his car, and walked to where I sat on the box of wine.

I heard the window on the Winnebago slide open a little.

"Hello, sir," said the policeman.

"Hello, offisher," I answered.

It had not occurred to me that I had done anything wrong. I had no idea that the officer had been called because of me. I thought he was just friendly and curious, just come to visit.

"What's that?" he said, pointing to the empty bottle at my feet.

"It's Freixnet," I said. "It's Shpanish champagne. But we can't actually call it champagne. Because it's Shpanish. Champagne has to come from Fransh. We call it cava."

I paused, then continued.

"We could call it *Sham*-pagne, though. S, H, A, M. Get it?"

"Have you been drinking that wine, sir?"

"Yes, I have. Officer. I did. Very nice wine. Quite a flavor. A nice flavor. More complicated than I expected. But I don't think I should have drunk the whole thing myself."

"So you just drank this bottle yourself?"

"Yup. I drank it right from the bottle. It was like perf—"

"Sir, you know it is illegal to have open liquor in a public place."

I didn't know that.

"No, officer. I did *not* know that. I most *certainly* did not. If I had known that it was illegal, I most certainly would never have . . . would not have opened that bottle. I'm very sorry. It was wrong of me. Very, very wrong. Ekshtremely wrong."

"Saying you're sorry is not good enough, sir. An open bottle is a ticketable offence. I am going to have to write it up."

"I'm getting a ticket?" I said, laughing out loud at the thought of it. As far as I knew, tickets were only given for traffic offences. "But I'm not even driving! Kelly is driving!"

"I can assure you that you will not be driving anywhere any-time soon, sir. Not after consuming an entire bottle of wine by yourself. You are now far over your legal limit. You will not be getting behind the wheel of any vehicle."

"I most shertainly will not!" I heartily agreed, smiling. "No *way* will I be getting behind the wheel of any vehicle!"

"No, sir. You are intoxicated after drinking in public. However, I am here to investigate a different complaint. A lady called in to say that she had seen a man urinating in public. Have you been urinating in the parking lot, sir?"

My knowledge of law was as limited as my ability to lie.

"Yes, officer, I *have*. I have been . . . urinating. I am guilty of *taking a pish*. Thank God I did too, because I was gonna pee my pants after drinking that whole bottle by myself. I pished into that tub that was sh'posed to be . . . for the shoe shter . . . shoe sher . . . shoe sterilization ceremony."

"Sir, do you mean the plastic washing pan by the edge of the Winnebago?"

"Yes, officer."

"Urinating in public is a ticketable offence. You were observed by a woman shopping with her two young children. Families do not expect to go to Walmart to see men urinating."

"I sure hope not!" I said, laughing again in spite of the growing gravity of the situation. "I mean, if families went to Walmart to see men pissing, I bet they'd be disappointed almost every time. Do they really do that now? Go to Walmart for that?"

The officer said nothing, but he took out a notebook and started writing in it. He walked over to the rear of the Winnebago to look at the license plate, glancing down with clear disgust at my pee as he passed it. He walked back.

"Sir, I see that this is a rented vehicle. Did you rent this vehicle, sir?"

"Yes, officer. I did rent this vehicle.

"It's a Winnebago," I added helpfully.

"I'm going to have to see your license, sir."

"My license?"

"Yes, give me your driver's license please, sir."

"I don't have a driver's license!" I explained.

He looked at me threateningly, or maybe just angrily.

"What has happened to your driver's license, sir?"

"Nothing has happened to it. It is alluded to only by its absence."

I was thrilled to be able to use that phrase in conversation. But the officer just looked at me blankly. I wanted to explain about the Duchampian idea of allusion by absence, but I thought better of it, and continued.

"I never had any driver's license."

"Sir, did you drive this vehicle here?"

Again, I could not help laughing out loud, louder than ever. The question struck me as absurd.

"Of course not, officer! I mean: No sir! I am not the driver! At *all*. I am *never* the driver. I don't even know *how* to drive!"

"Who drove it here?" he asked.

"Kelly drove it here!" I said. "Kelly is my excellent driver. I am a fact millionaire, which means I have at least a million dollars, in case you couldn't guess, which is why I am wearing this excellent suit and tie, and I am going on a trip, as you can see, in this Winnebago I have paid for, and I have my very own excellent driver. Kelly. She's not *hired*, she's just coming for *fun*. And to *drive*. So actually *she* rented the Winnebago. I just *paid* for it. Because in case you didn't know, you need a driversh license to rent a vehicle. So. Yup. My good friend Kelly."

"Where is Kelly?"

"She went to change into business casual. Or better. I dress *better*. Because I'm the boss, I guess." I stopped, surprised at my own use of the word "boss." "That's part of our agreement. Business casual or better," I said, holding my arms apart to make sure he could clearly see my jacket and tie. I wanted to point out that the shirt was a specially made Italian that had French/Italian cuffs, but he went on before I could.

"Where does she live?"

"I don't know. I've never *been* to her house. She came to *my* house today, though. My very big house. Mainly for tax purposes. For the very first time *ever*. To help me with my luggage."

"So, all this is yours?" he said, gazing across my pile.

"Well, no, officer. Not at all. I cannot say that. Not all of it. It's mine and Greg's and Kelly's. It's our supplies. I mean, I bought it all because I'm the only *fact millionaire* on the trip. You don't see too many of those!

"But I bought some of it for them. Because Greg and Kelly don't have much money. Like all the chocolate over there is really for Kelly, because she *loves* that. Chocolate. It's way too sweet for me. I don't like sweetened chocolate, do you?

"And most of the Spanish champagne is really hers, but I did buy extra bottles, so some of it's mine. Which is why I drank one.

"All the underwear over there and all the toilet paper are Greg's. Well, I guess he has to share the toilet paper, but it was his special choice. It's very soft, but it really doesn't tear easily. Like some toilet paper does, at the least convenient time. Which can *very* unhygienic. You know?

"Some of the books are mine, but some of them—"

"OK, sir. I understand. Where can I find Greg?"

"Greg?"

"Yes, this man Greg. Where is he?"

"Greg's in there," I explained, pointing to the Winnebago. "But we can't go in!"

"Why can't you go in?"

"We have to *shterilize* ourselves first! Here, take a look at this," I said, and I handed him Greg's comic. The officer studied it for a moment and then looked at me levelly for several seconds.

"I'm going to need to see some kind of ID, sir."

So I gave him my wallet and told him he could look at anything he wanted, but that he couldn't take any of the money because it was all mine. He copied a few pieces of information from a few different cards and handed the wallet back.

None of the money was gone. I checked.

He walked over to knock on the door of the Winnebago.

Nothing happened.

"What's Greg's last name?" he asked.

I told him. He wrote it down.

"Mr. Zipf?" he called.

Nothing.

"Are you sure someone is in there?" he asked me. He tried the door, but it was locked.

"Yes. Greg is in there." I tried yelling from where I sat. "*Greg!* Open the door! This policeman is here and he wants to give me a *ticket*! They're not just for people who drive anymore!"

The door opened just wide enough to slip a folded piece of yellow paper out, and then it closed again. The lock clicked.

The officer reached down and picked it up. He slumped slightly as he read it.

"Seems to be for you," he said, handing it to me.

I read what Greg had written. In perfectly proportioned block capitals it said, "GET A SHARPIE SO WE CAN SIGN THE *PISSOIR*. OUR OWN FOUNTAIN! A GOOD START!"

::

I knew what he meant, but I didn't try to explain it for the policeman.

In 1917, Duchamp bought a Bedfordshire model urinal from the J.L. Mott Iron Works on Fifth Avenue in New York and submitted it as a piece of art to the Society of Independent Artists exhibit. He submitted it signed as "R. Mutt." The Society had agreed to show every piece that was submitted. They did not show R. Mutt's signed urinal, which would later become known as *Fountain* and be valued in the millions of dollars.

Duchamp and his collector friend Walter Arensburg resigned from the board of the Society of Independent Artists in protest.

Chaos and modern art ensued.

⁜

When Kelly arrived back a few minutes later, the officer was in his car on the phone, having obtained my assurance that I would not leave my position on the wine box. Kelly stepped out of the yellow cab behind the Winnebago. She was wearing a pair of dark blue pants with a matching cloth belt tied in front and a flowing white linen blouse. Her hair was up in a bun, with a black chopstick in it again as when I had first met her. She carried a tiny red suitcase and a large black purse.

"What's happening?" she said, looking as much amused as worried.

So I explained about the "Shpanish shampagne," and about the joke of "*sham*-pagne" and how I had needed to pee, and how

Greg wouldn't let me in and I couldn't go to the toilet anywhere else, and how I had bought the purification vessel at Walmart anyway, and how a whole family came to Walmart to look for men peeing and found me and then called a policeman. I gave her Greg's two notes.

"Ha! Oh yeah, this is totally excellent! We're off to a great start! You stay there; I'll go deal with the popo. I'm going to leave my bag here."

So she put the bag down beside the front door and walked over to the car. The officer saw her and got out. I watched her hand him a card, presumably a driver's license. The policeman disappeared back into his car and returned a few minutes later to give back the card. He and Kelly started talking. I couldn't hear what they were saying, but I was starting to be worried. I was trying to figure out whether the police actually held the power to stop our trip.

Maybe he was just going to tell us we couldn't go at all.

Maybe I was going to be arrested.

Maybe I was going to prison.

After a few minutes, the policeman took a notebook from somewhere on his body and ripped off two pages that he handed to Kelly. I heard her apologizing for the trouble as she walked away. The policeman watched her walk all the way back to the Winnebago. Not for purely professional reasons, in my opinion.

Kelly stopped a few feet away from me.

"Well, you got one ticket for having an open bottle and another one for pissing in public." She waved the papers in her hand like it was a big wad of money she was showing off.

"It could have been worse. So, let's get ourselves together. I think that under the circumstances, it might be best if I go and buy us a new, uh, purification vessel. You're looking a little unsteady there. Can you sit there for a few more minutes?"

I assured her I could.

"*Do not pee!*"

I nodded.

She walked over to the original purification vessel.

"Well, I dunno. I don't see how I can walk into Walmart with a container full of ripe pee. It's gonna have to stay here."

And she picked it up, walked a few feet behind the Winnebago, and poured my piss onto the pavement.

"I'll be back in a second," she said, with a deliberate note of daintiness in her voice.

::

Kelly came back with a Sharpie and two vessels—my original one, sterilized, as she assured me, with soap and hot water, and a new one that was identical except for being green and never urinated into. Luckily, there was nothing in the notes about the *color* of the purification vessel.

Kelly and I reread my notes and checked them against Greg's comic. We poured bleach and purified water in carefully measured proportions into the new purification vessel. Kelly knocked at the window, behind which Greg had evidently been waiting. The exchange of silk bags was made. Kelly put hers in her handbag.

We carefully submerged the soles of our brand-new shoes into the bleach mixture, stepped on the stairs of the Winnebago, and kicked our used shoes off. Kelly unlocked the door. Greg stood beaming a few feet inside.

"Welcome to our home sweet home away from home!" he said.

Kelly saluted him. I glared at him. He just smiled at us both.

::

I was glad to see that Greg had not undertaken any obvious eccentric remodeling of the interior during his three days in the vehicle. It looked exactly as I had last seen it. Greg moved back and sat down on a bed in the rear of the vehicle. Kelly and I sat in two swiveling captain's chairs at the front, behind the driver's and front passenger's seats.

"Did you get the Sharpie?" Greg asked.

Kelly reached into her bag and brought out the permanent marker.

"Excellent," he said. "Did you guys totally sterilize all Isaac's piss? 'Cause I don't want to catch cooties from him. I have enough problems already."

Kelly assured him that she had cleaned it using a lot of soap and very hot water.

"Well, OK, hand them over then, the Sharpie and the *pissoir*."

Kelly handed them over to him, looking slightly bemused. With startling fluidity, Greg took the marker and expertly copied Duchamp's "R. Mutt" signature from a book he had open, onto the outside of the vessel.

"There!" he said. "We're on our way! We already have our very own *Fountain*! And we haven't even left! This is so good! This is gonna be such a great trip!"

::

Our agreement did not foresee that we would need a plan to load the Winnebago with our supplies, so we were delayed while the three of us discussed the pros and cons of various possible plans. Eventually we all agreed that it would be best if Kelly went out in her new shoes and brought the items to the Winnebago. Greg and I would stay inside, without shoes, and load them into their proper places inside. Kelly would resterilize her shoes as before, dump the bleach solution on top of my spilled urine to sterilize it, and enter the Winnebago with the purification vessel and her new shoes in hand.

This plan worked perfectly. The vehicle was soon loaded, and we were able to close the door and get into our assigned seats: Kelly driving, me beside her, and Greg on the chair directly behind mine, which he claimed was safer than being behind the driver because of the decreased risk of being impaled on the steering wheel if there was a collision.

I did not express my doubt that there had been a sufficient number of impalings on steering shafts by passengers in Winnebagos to draw any statistically reliable conclusions.

We snapped on our seatbelts.

Kelly looked at me and Greg.

"Ready?" she said.

"Ready," I said.

"Ready," said Greg.

::

There is an ambiguity in what it means to "get a chocolate every 90 minutes." To Greg and me, it meant that Kelly should have to drive for 90 minutes before her first chocolate. To Kelly, it meant that she should have one before she turned the ignition key, and no more for another 90 minutes after that.

This ambiguity became apparent when Kelly asked for her first chocolate just before she turned the ignition key.

If chocolate is understood as a payment, then obviously it must come at the end of the work period. No payment without work.

But Kelly pointed out that chocolate is not best understood as a payment for 90 minutes of driving. It is best understood as a peace offering. As an inducement to drive.

If chocolate is understood as an inducement, then obviously, as Kelly explained, it must come at the start of any period in which peace and/or driving was desired.

::

Kelly turned the key, sucking with evident pleasure on her chocolate. She smiled, a wide, soft, genuine smile.

"Ready?" she said.

"Ready," I said.

"Ready," said Greg.

She slipped the Winnebago into gear and eased it forward through the Walmart parking lot.

We were off.

FAR FROM BEING IN DIRECT CONTACT WITH THE BRIDE, THE DESIRE-MOTOR IS SEPARATED BY AN AIR COOLER (OR WATER)

Duchamp deliberately pushed (I won't say "painted") himself into a corner from which he could not escape. His criticism of art, of popular aesthetic, of painting, of being an artist at all: All of it applied as much to him and his work as it did to anyone or anything else.

After Duchamp, nothing more could be done.

As Greg had told me: Art was finished.

When you can see what art is, he implied, a shovel is as good as a Rembrandt. A urinal is as good as Caravaggio.

To Greg and me, the question was always: To make them the same, do you raise the *pissoir* or do you lower the Caravaggio?

Is *schlooby-pie* art or is art all just *schlooby-pie*?

::

"So," Kelly said shortly after she had swung out of the parking lot, "you've got a thing for spoons, is that right, Greg?"

Another thing about Greg's obsession is that he loves to talk constantly about it.

"I do, indeed! I have a 'thing' for spoons. As you put it. I have quite a thing! A huge *thing*! Always have! I find them totally fascinating."

"You do, huh?"

"Yes. *Always* have! Almost always. I loved spoons when I was 11 years old. I don't remember the very first day. I do remember my mother discovering that most of the kitchen spoons were in a Crown Royal bag my dad gave me because I thought it was pretty. It was purple with a gold drawstring. I used to lie in bed at night with a flashlight under the covers, watching a beautiful reflected purple light play off the spoons.

"There was something so quiet, so peaceful, so beautiful, so soothing about that. Something so lovable.

"And everyone wants that, don't they? Isn't that what everyone is always chasing after in this world? Something wonderful that brings them peace?"

::

Soon I started to fall asleep, the effect of the alcohol and overexcitement. I didn't want to sleep before I got what I had been waiting so patiently for.

Just a sniff of her perfume.

Just one sniff.

But the car was blowing air backward.

All I could smell was the scent of the city outside, wafted at low concentration but at high speed into my face.

The moment I had been looking forward to for so long had arrived. I was sitting by Kelly's side on an adventure.

And I couldn't even smell her.

::

I drifted back into the conversation I had drifted out of. It had carried on, and I didn't know how much of it I might have missed.

Kelly was speaking.

"I remember when I was a kid, maybe about the same age as you were when you first started in with the spoons, sitting in a church with my parents and having a sudden revelation that *peace* was a form of evil, the work of the devil.

"Did you ever read the Grand Inquisitor scene in *The Brothers Karamazov* by Dostoyevsky? No? Well, in a nutshell, it's a parable within the story, told by some guy to his brother. Jesus comes back to earth in Seville during the Spanish Inquisition, performs a couple of miracles, and gets taken in by the authorities to see the Grand Inquisitor, the local Big Scary Powerful Guy. The Inquisitor says that Christ is not good for the Christian Church because he has set up his church to give too much freedom to human beings. The Grand Inquisitor explains to Christ that his people don't *want* to be free. He explains that the Church has become better than what Christ ever intended it to be because it has relieved people of the freedom they cannot endure.

"So he basically tells Jesus to bugger off.

"OK, that's . . . time!

"Another chocolate, please."

::

I drifted off again, really falling asleep.

I started dreaming.

In my dream, Kelly is sitting beside me, in front of the fireplace in a large dark room. She is dressed like my mother used to dress before she got sick, in a yellow dress that no one under 65 normally would ever think of wearing.

Maybe it is not Kelly in my mother's dress but my mother in Kelly's body.

This woman and I are sitting side by side, staring into the flames. She is segmented bizarrely, like a magician's assistant or a woman in a Dali painting, her middle pulled out sideways as if it were a drawer.

"Gasoline vapors," she explains in an exaggerated slow tone, as if explaining it to a small child, "are explosive."

I do not understand what she means, why she is telling me this. I am straining to understand, as if she is speaking a language I am just beginning to learn. Perhaps this is why she is speaking to me so deliberately.

"The piston," she explains, waving her hands to pick out a long imaginary object, "only moves when the gasoline explodes."

I sense that I know what she must be talking about, even if I don't understand why she is using those words. She isn't talking about sex. Even in my dream, I am sure of that. In my dream, I *think* that. This is not sex.

It's something *like* sex, though. In my dream, I'm totally sure of that too.

"The piston is constrained inside the cylinder."

She unrolls a roll of parchment that has appeared in her hand.

It is a print of *The Bride Stripped Bare by Her Bachelors, Even*, beautifully reproduced on thick archival paper at poster size.

And suddenly the Kelly/Julia woman is wearing a huge beautiful white wedding dress, Victorian in its proportions, covered with pearls. She is standing over the poster with a large pair of scissors that she has opened up so that she can use its points to pick out the nine malic moulds and the chocolate grinder simultaneously, with a great flourish, like a game show host's beautiful assistant explaining the day's prizes.

"The bachelor grinds chocolate himself!" she intones in a new loud, artificial voice, now speaking as if she were a TV advertisement announcer shilling for a new product.

"*An adage of spontaneity!*"

::

I opened my eyes with a start, strangely affected by the dream, and realized where I was. The steady rhythm of the Winnebago washed over me, pushing me down again. I closed my eyes and drifted back into the ongoing conversation.

Kelly was speaking.

"The Devil offered Christ the ability to turn stones into bread. Then he offered him the chance to test God, or His angels actually, by throwing himself off a cliff. Which I have always thought was probably not a very tempting temptation. To see if the angels would rescue him, right? Christ says no, like any sane person would if you asked him if he would like to jump off a cliff.

"Finally, the Devil offered to make Christ the Ruler of the World. *Much* more tempting than jumping off a cliff, definitely.

"But Christ rejects that too.

"He rejects everything for what he cannot know. The Great Unknown. He chooses to take"—she shrugged her beautiful slim shoulders to underline how little it seemed—"*whatever. Anything.* He is saying that *what is unknown* is better than *anything that is known*. That the freedom to go through life without even ever knowing what is going to happen to you is the best possible thing that can happen, better than any miraculous gift could ever be."

"So," said Greg, apparently referring back to a part of the conversation I had slept through, "you're saying that freedom and peace are mutually exclusive, and we can either have one or the other, but never both?"

"Yeah, sort of," said Kelly. "Freedom terrifies people.

"If you are like Christ and you choose freedom, you don't have any idea what it is you're choosing. You're basically choosing not to choose. Or, anyway, choosing to trust in what you cannot know. You can say 'trust in God,' if you want to call it that. Or in *yourself*, if you don't.

"And putting your trust in what you cannot know freaks people out."

::

When she said "God," I was reminded of Daver's Bible Method. I opened my eyes.

"Hey, Kelly," I said. "I can't even smell your perfume. Which, you know, I do like to smell. I do wanna smell. Can I borrow the bottle?"

After the usual questioning to make sure she understood what I was saying, Kelly told Greg where to find the bottle I had bought for her. I took the handkerchief from my shirt pocket, gave it a liberal dousing, and handed the bottle back to Greg with my thanks.

I leaned back, waved out the handkerchief, and placed it over my face. The first sniff was absolutely delicious.

In seconds, I fell into a deep, dreamless sleep.

::

I woke up because I felt the rhythm of the drive change, as we first slowed and then turned.

I opened my eyes. I had a headache and a dry mouth.

"What's happening?" I said, sitting up, suddenly worried.

Kelly looked at me and smiled, her usual beautiful calm smile.

"The Winnebago's making an odd sound. We have to check it out."

Greg spoke up with his usual enthusiasm.

"Isn't this fantastic?!" he said.

"Fantastic?" I was still groggy from sleep and alcohol but was feeling a rising sense of panic. "Doesn't it mean that something's wrong with our brand-new, never-driven, expensively cleaned Winnebago?"

"Maybe!" said Greg. "Maybe it does! It could be something unbelievably *terrible*!"

"I know," I said. "I know. That's what I mean. It's terrible."

"Who knows? It *might* be terrible! It *might not* be terrible! We don't know for sure yet. But don't you get it?" said Greg, almost jumping out of his seat with excitement.

"Get what?" I said. "What? What's so great about our Winnebago breaking down?"

"It's great! We're living our very own *With Hidden Noise*!"

He smiled with what seemed like too much enthusiasm.

::

I saw a sign that said we were not far from Chicopee and almost did a double take.

"Chicopee?!" I said. "Did that sign say *Chicopee*?!"

Kelly looked over and smiled again. She seemed to smile whenever I addressed her.

"Yes," she said.

"Chicopee?! Oh no! You guys are lost!" I complained. "I shouldn't've slept! We're on the wrong road! Boston's on the coast!

Philadelphia is practically on the coast! The road from Boston to Philadelphia runs along *the coast*! We should be going south, right? But you must be going north or west. Are we on the 84?"

"No," said Kelly. "We're still on Highway 90. Sorry, boss, while you were sleeping we took a vote and we decided by a majority that we'd go through Cranston."

"We did!" affirmed Greg. "We both agreed!" He was still smiling with what seemed like too much pleasure.

"Cranston!" I said. "Where the *schloobies* is Cranston?! Do you guys means *Scranton*?! I hope not, because Scranton is definitely not on the way from Medford to Philadelphia. Scranton is way north!"

"We're not going to *Scranton, Pennsylvania*, man. There's no reason to go all the way up *there*. Who goes to *Scranton*? That's nowhere. We're going to *Cranston*, Connecticut," said Greg, very calmly, as if that explained everything.

"Cranston, Connecticut?" I said. "I've never even heard of Cranston. What's in Cranston?"

"We don't know yet," said Kelly. "That's why we decided to go there."

This sounded bad.

I needed to wash my hands.

::

Greg handed over a set of stapled Google maps that made it obvious to me that he had *always* planned that we should drive through Cranston, a tiny town a few miles north of Hartford on Highway

91. We turned south on Highway 91, which made me feel a little better. Greg was totally insistent that we had to have the Winnebago looked at in Cranston, which was about 15 minutes away.

I could still hear the noise. It was a kind of mechanical beat, but it was a complicated beat, not just a repetitive *tick tick tick*. It had a structured rhythm.

Tick biddle tick tick. Pause.

Tick tick biddle biddle tick tick. Pause. Pause.

Tick tick biddle biddle tick tick biddle biddle.

"That's a weird sound," I said, worried about what it might mean. I could not believe we were having trouble with the Winnebago after all our efforts to get one that was brand new. It seemed like terrible bad luck. For the second time in only a few hours, I began to worry that our trip was going to come to an end before we could make it to Philadelphia.

"It is!" exclaimed Greg, with considerable enthusiasm. "It's a really *super-weird* sound! It doesn't sound anything like an engine! Does it, Kelly? Engines don't usually make a noise like that, do they?"

"Not that I know of," said Kelly. "But it sounds like it is coming from the engine. So I guess they can sound like that. I dunno. I'm in women's studies in religion. I'm no mechanic."

Cranston has one gas station, and not much else. We pulled into the gas station, and Kelly parked the Winnebago, engine still running.

"I'll stay here," said Greg. "I have to use the *pissoir* anyway."

"Wouldn't you rather use the toilet inside?" said Kelly.

Greg and I looked at her like she was crazy. Or rather, I suppose, like she was sane. Only a sane person would prefer an unknown public toilet used by strangers to a brand-new, carefully sanitized private toilet used only by friends.

"Oh yeah, that germ thing, right? I'm going to risk it myself. Wish me luck. Then I'll see if I can find a mechanic."

Kelly turned the key and left the vehicle.

Greg was still smiling.

"Notice anything?" he said.

"Like what?" I said, still feeling pissed off at him for ignoring me at Walmart and for changing the route while I was sleeping, still worrying about what wrong with the Winnebago.

"That hidden noise?" he said.

Tick biddle tick tick. Pause.

Tick tick biddle biddle tick tick. Pause. Pause.

Tick tick biddle biddle tick tick biddle biddle.

It was still ticking.

"It's still going!" I said. "How can that be? Isn't the engine turned off?"

"Yeah. It's a mystery, isn't it? A very mysterious hidden noise."

He looked at me pointedly, but I did not know why.

"Oh," he said, as he snapped his seatbelt undone. "It's stopped."

And it had.

::

I got up myself and used the toilet, wiping it down after I was done using Sani-Wipes from the packs that Greg and I had stocked in the bathroom, as we had agreed we would do. Then I washed my hands, very carefully, several times, drying them between each wash. I was feeling very nervous about what was happening with the Winnebago.

For some reason, when I came out I felt less clean than I had before I had gone in. I was still anxious. Despite having undone his seatbelt, Greg had not moved from his seat. I walked back over and sat back down in my seat, the front passenger's seat, so my back was toward Greg again.

"So is Kelly your *girlfriend*?" he asked.

I hoped I didn't know where this was leading. I was rubbing my hands with a Sani-Wipe, to try to get to feeling that they were clean.

"Well," I said, slowly, pointlessly, rubbing, "she's my friend, and she's a *girl* . . ."

"Obviously," he said. "But is she, like, your *girlfriend*? Do you two kiss and stuff?"

I hesitated before admitting the truth that I knew he already knew.

"No."

"Does she have a boyfriend?"

It had never occurred to me that Kelly could have a boyfriend. I half believed that she only existed when she was in the museum, or with me, now, on this trip. I never thought about how she fitted into the rest of her life.

"I dunno. Not as far as I know. But I don't really know. We never discussed that."

We sat in silence for a few moments.

"I'm not planning to make a move for her, in case that's what you're thinking right now," he said.

I didn't know whether to laugh or sigh with relief. Of course he wasn't. Of course he *couldn't*. Of course he *wouldn't*, even if he *could*.

I just said: "OK."

There was another pause.

"But she's quite a *delay*, isn't she?" he said, smiling.

I had never thought of Kelly as a delay before, as if she were a piece of art. But if a shovel or a urinal or a spoon was art, why not a beautiful perfumed lady?

"Yeah," I said, after a second thinking about it. "She's quite a delay."

⁞

Then I told Greg about how I had thought about *With Hidden Noise* when I was looking at my ivory a few months earlier, about how I thought that the angel could be composed of tiny hidden carvings of her real guts without anyone alive knowing. He liked my idea of *hidden* hidden noise a lot. I knew he would.

He is probably the only person I knew who would appreciate that.

He is a good friend.

⁞

Kelly came back a few minutes later, with a mechanic from the garage in tow.

"Guys, this is Terry. Terry, this is Isaac and Greg. They both have some weird obsessive-compulsive disorders so they get pretty freaked about a lot of things for no really good reason. So don't be weirded out if they kind of just huddle together in a back corner. Just act like it's normal.

"I'll start the engine."

Kelly understood us perfectly. I had jumped out of my seat and scurried back as soon as Kelly opened the door, and Greg and I were both near the back of the Winnebago by the time she finished introducing us.

"Hi, Terry!" we both yelled, waving in an exaggerated fashion, like shy children trying to do what they had been taught by their mothers to do when they met a stranger.

The mechanic looked at us warily, grunted hello, and stepped out to the front of the vehicle. Kelly started the engine.

Greg looked at me.

"Do you think he'll hear it?" he asked.

That reminded me that we had heard it after the engine was off.

"Hey, Kelly!" I yelled up to the front. She looked into the rear-view mirror to let me know she was listening.

"We *heard that sound* after you turned off the engine!" I yelled.

"After I turned off the engine?" she said.

"Yes!" I yelled.

"Stop yelling!" said Greg.

"Sorry," I said. It was true that I didn't need to yell. It wasn't that noisy and we weren't that far away.

"Yes," I continued in something closer to a normal tone of voice. "Greg and I heard the sound after you left."

"That's really weird," said Kelly.

"That's what I thought," I agreed. "That's why I wanted to let you know."

Greg didn't say anything.

∷

"So, what's the deal with Cranston?" I asked Greg, while Terry knocked around in front and Kelly revved the engine whenever he told her to.

"Cranston, Connecticut?" he said.

I looked at him the way I do. He was Greg. What could I do?

"Yes, Greg," I said, playing my role in a script we both understood. "Cranston, Connecticut. This very place where we now find ourselves parked, thanks to your directions."

"Well," he said, "you do know how *art* works, right? According to Duchamp?"

"I don't know, Greg. Do I?"

I knew he wanted to explain it to me. Greg's questions were almost always rhetorical.

"I think you do," he admitted. "But let me tell you anyway."

"OK," I said. "I'll just let you tell me then, Greg."

"Thanks. I appreciate that. So, the artist wants us to *stop*, right? To stop in front of the art, and *look at it*, right? Focus our attention on it? That's the *delay* part."

"Yes . . ." I said, a bit hesitantly, in case I wanted to take it back.

"So, would you agree that art is a type of *constraint*?" he asked. "Would you agree that art, any delay, initially *constrains* our attention to a small framed section of the universe to which we have sensory access?"

"Yes, Greg," I said. "I would have to agree. A delay is a kind of constraint."

"And you know what happens after that," said Greg. "But just let me tell you anyway."

"OK, Greg," I said. "I'll just let you tell me."

"Thanks. OK, the next thing that happens is that we *connect* to the object, right? We stop and are delayed in front of a piece of art. We look at it. And in doing so, we *connect* to the artistic creation that is in front of us."

That didn't seem too controversial, so I just agreed and waited to find out where he was going with this.

"OK, well, so there you are. But what does Duchamp say we have to do after that? If we just *connect* to the art, we're not finished. We haven't heard the full lesson. Because he says that after that, we need to *disconnect*, right? We have to *cut* the connection that ties our attention to that particular delay. Because in the end, a delay is just like a kind of a *decoy*. Right? Do you see that? We stop, we attend, and when we do, we eventually come to realize that *we didn't ever need to stop at all*. Right? That's Duchamp's *point*. Because he says that in the end, we have to *overcome* the urge we have to stop, to be delayed. We need to go beyond being stopped to get to the state in which we withhold judgment. We have to *stop* stopping so we can see shovels and spoons and *pissoirs* as art. But not just shovels and spoons and *pissoirs*! Right?

"Because even spoons and *pissoirs* are *still* a delay. If we could truly find our way to see how things are, we wouldn't stop just at *spoons*! Why would anyone limit themselves that way *by choice*? We would see everything as being the same, everything as if it were a Rembrandt."

"Or hopefully a Caravaggio," I suggested.

"Or a Caravaggio!" he agreed with enthusiasm. "Whatever! Non-art as art! Art as non-art! Everything as art! Art as an error! However you want to put it.

"The point is that after we have been stopped, we need to *cut* the link between our attention and the delay in order to go beyond being stopped only by traditional art objects, OK? So we can come to appreciate the whole world with an aesthetic sense?"

"OK," I said.

"So we *constrain* our attention, *connect* it to what delays us, and then we *cut* that connection?"

"OK," I said again.

"Well, so, *that's* why we had to come to Cranston, Connecticut!" he said, in his usual way, as if his point should be completely obvious when he has actually just left you confused.

"Is there some Duchamp collection here?" I asked, confused, unable to imagine how a one-street town like Cranston could have any pieces by Duchamp.

"No," he said. "Don't you get it? 'Cranston, Connecticut' is an anagram of 'Constrain, Connect, Cut'! That's why we had to come here! This whole place is a secret, *possibly* totally unconscious, monument to Duchamp's philosophy of art!"

I laughed. I had to admit that was a pretty good reason.

It really was an excellent reason.

I would definitely have planned to come to Cranston, Connecticut, if I had been told that it had this secret meaning. As Greg knew perfectly well.

"Did you tell Kelly about this?" I asked.

"Of course I did!" he said. "I told her that was why I wanted to come here. She thought it was a great idea. That's why we decided to come."

I noticed that I was no longer wiping my hands.

I had totally forgotten that they had been feeling dirty.

::

Terry had to admit that he couldn't hear anything wrong. Kelly agreed with him—she wasn't hearing any more ticking either. Greg and I both listened, and we couldn't hear anything ticking anymore. The sound had disappeared. Terry suggested we keep driving and stop at another garage if it started happening again. I was a little nervous about this idea, in case the ticking really meant something bad, but I didn't say anything because I didn't want to just give up on the trip.

When Terry was gone, Kelly sat back down in her seat.

"Kind of weird how that noise started just outside of *Cranston, Connecticut*, isn't it?" said Greg.

"Why is that so weird?" I asked.

"Well, because of Cranston, Connecticut being a shrine to Duchamp. Weird that we would have *a hidden noise* just as we entered Duchamp's shrine, isn't it?"

"You mean because of *With Hidden Noise*?" I asked.

"Exactly! Here we are driving along on the highway, and just as we enter the land dedicated to 'Constrain, Connect, Cut,' we are suddenly hit *with hidden noise*."

He emphasized the last three words pointedly.

"Greg," I asked, "what are you trying to say?"

"Oh!" he said. "Listen! It's started up again!"

And so it had.

Tick biddle tick tick. Pause.

Tick tick biddle biddle tick tick. Pause. Pause.

Tick tick biddle biddle tick tick biddle biddle.

"You hear that?!" I said to Kelly. "Just like we told you! The engine's not even on, and there's that sound again! Should you go and get the mechanic guy?"

Kelly sat where she was, listening for a second.

Tick biddle tick tick. Pause.

"It's very rhythmic, isn't it?" she said.

Tick tick biddle biddle tick tick. Pause. Pause.

"It sounds almost too rhythmic. Too perfect. It doesn't sound like a mechanical sound. It sounds like something electrical."

Tick tick biddle biddle tick tick biddle biddle.

Greg started laughing.

::

What dollar value can we put on the ball of faded boric twine known as *With Hidden Noise*? It is impossible to answer. Duchamp made the only copy of the piece for his friend Walter Arensburg. Arensburg donated it to the Philadelphia Museum of Art, where it remains today. It has never been put on the market. In the normal sense of the word, the piece has no value at all. Only market price determines the value of art. *With Hidden Noise* has never had a market. It is art that does not act like art.

When Duchamp was asked if he knew how much Arensburg had paid for his fabulous painting *Nude Descending a Staircase* (which was $240, in case you are wondering), Duchamp replied, "No, I wasn't interested. I never knew the price." He went on to add: "It's the same for *With Hidden Noise* . . . what's secret is the price!"

It pleased him to be unable to say what anything was worth.

If it went on the art market today, would *With Hidden Noise* be worth as much as one million dollars?

Oh yes.

C'mon.

Man.

Let's be serious.

Oh yes.

I am definitely sure that *With Hidden Noise* is worth much more than a million dollars. I can be definitely sure because, if it went on the market today for just a million bucks, I would sell my house so I could buy it.

And my pockets are not so very deep. I'm just a fact million-aire. That doesn't matter. I'll guarantee the low bid and be happy if I get it so cheap. But I am sure that many others would pay much more than just a million dollars.

With Hidden Noise is *priceless.*

::

Kelly picked up on what was going on before I did. Greg was still laughing. I guess that she realized, as I did not, that this was not just ordinary laughter. This was meaningful laughter, communica-tive laughter. Greg was trying to convey some information to us.

She looked at him, and I recognized the tolerant, amused, accepting smile.

"Greg."

He looked at her, trying to stifle his laughter.

"Greg," she repeated, "what's going on here?"

He looked at her, and, still trying to stifle his laugher, he stam-mered: "You . . . ha . . . you . . . ha ha ha . . . you . . . ha, mmm . . . you notice . . . you notice the sound has stopped again?"

Kelly was laughing at Greg's laughter.

It was true. The sound had stopped.

Kelly composed herself, the way I did when I talked to Greg. She spoke in almost the same tone I had practiced with Greg for so many years.

"Yes, Greg. Can you maybe tell us why that is?"

"Maybe . . . Yes. Yes . . . yes, Kelly . . . I . . . I can," he sputtered, laughing.

Kelly was looking at him, smiling the same way she always smiled. She was enjoying herself.

"Pray do," she encouraged him.

Greg composed himself.

"Now you don't hear it . . . now you do!" said Greg, and he was right.

Now we did hear it.

Tick biddle tick tick. Pause.

"Greg," said Kelly, "this is an amazingly constant and complicated sound for an engine that is not even turned on to make."

Tick tick biddle biddle tick tick. Pause. Pause.

"It sounds a little too perfect to me."

Tick tick biddle biddle tick tick biddle biddle.

"Greg. What can you tell us about this?"

"And now you don't!" Greg roared, collapsing into giggles again.

Kelly and I looked at each other, and we both understood at once what was going on.

"Greg!" we both yelled, looking at him.

"Greg!"

::

When he had finished giggling, Greg told us how he had created the sound himself and showed us the little clicker in his hand, a

garage-door opener he had modified for the purpose of controlling it. Kelly got down on her knees. She could see the little black
plastic box he had duct-taped below the dashboard, which held the
receiver and the electronic circuits that played Greg's sound.

But she didn't tell us that she could see it. Because Greg had
made her promise she wouldn't.

Just as Greg had asked her to, she sat down in her seat and
looked at us both.

"I dunno what's making the sound," she said, smiling as she
looked over at us. "We're just going to have to travel *with hidden noise.*"

Greg held up his hand to give me a high five. I hesitated. I had
never touched Greg before. Then I slapped his hand with mine and
laughed.

Kelly took the Winnebago out of the gas station. We passed a
beautiful rundown five-and-dime store, a beautiful crappy Chinese-
American restaurant, a beautiful decrepit motel, and a couple of
beautiful little houses that were little more than shacks, and then
we were out of Cranston.

"Cranston, Connecticut, rocks!" exclaimed Greg.

I just smiled happily.

7

CONDITIONS OF A LANGUAGE:
THE SEARCH FOR PRIME WORDS
(DIVISIBLE ONLY BY THEMSELVES AND BY UNITY)

G reg had mapped out the location of every Walmart between Medford and Philadelphia. He had also already decided that the best place to stop for the day was in Newark, which was about three hours away, about an hour and a half out of Philadelphia. One main reason he wanted us to stop there is that he had found out on Google maps that the layout of the Newark Walmart parking lot was almost exactly the same as the layout of the Medford Walmart. It was a bit eerie. Kelly was therefore perfectly able to fulfill one of Greg's travel requirements, that she make every possible effort to park in the same location at every Walmart as we had parked at the first one. Kelly had originally parked far from the entrance so as to maximize the likelihood that she would be able to get the same spot. As far as I could tell, she parked in Newark in the identical spot where I had peed with such gratitude in Medford.

It was like we had traveled for hours without moving at all.

Kelly got her final chocolate of the day and called a cab on her cellphone. She had a map from Greg that showed the location of the nearby motels, each one marked by a sticker whose color, ranging from blue (bad) to bright yellow (good), signaled his best estimate of a rating. She told Greg she would go to the one he rated most highly, which made Greg very happy.

While we were waiting for her cab, Greg went back into it.

"Hey, Kelly?" he said, with an innocence that he alone did not have to feign. "Isaac and I were wondering. Just because. You know. Do you have a boyfriend? Because we really think you're very beautiful and smart and kind. *Really*. So we definitely assume you must have a boyfriend. You must have had tons of boys after you. Men, I mean. Right?"

Kelly turned around in her seat to look at him.

"I do have a boyfriend," she said.

"What's his name?" asked Greg.

"Shaw."

"Shaw?" said Greg. "Isn't 'Shaw' a last name? Is that his last name?"

"No," said Kelly. "It's his first name. As it happens, he does have a first name for a last name, though: Bradley. Shaw Bradley."

"Shaw Bradley . . ." repeated Greg, slowly and a little reverently, as if the name were a gift with which he had been entrusted. "Shaw Bradley, eh? Does Shaw Bradley have to keep washing his hands all the time?"

"Greg," I started, feeling exasperated and embarrassed, "you do realize that not everyone on the entire planet has OCD, don't you? Just because everyone you know does. It's only like 8 or maybe 10 percent of the population. Or maybe 4 percent, if you use really strict criteria. Leave Kelly alone."

Kelly smiled at me.

"I don't mind," she assured me, before turning back to Greg. "Nope. He's not a hand-washer. He has a lot of annoying habits, of course, like all of us do."

"Oh, too bad!" exclaimed Greg. "*Schloobs*. That's really too bad. 'Cause you know, 'Shaw Bradley' is an anagram for 'Badly Rewash.' So I was thinking that it would be totally cool if he was a hand-washer, wouldn't it? So cool! In fact I wish *my* name was Shaw Bradley. That would be so awesome!"

I don't know how that guy does it. Mixes the letters in words up so fast. Kelly was laughing, and so was I.

"Nice one," she said.

"You know what 'Greg Zipf' is an anagram for, don't you?" he asked.

I tried to think what 'Greg Zipf' could possibly be, with two "g"s, the troublesome "z," and so few letters in all. I couldn't think of anything.

"Nothing! I have a *prime name*. That's what I call it when the letters have just one order. That's something I've always loved about my name. I *love* that. That was really good luck. Proper names should be prime. It just confuses matters if they aren't. If Shaw Bradley doesn't badly rewash, then we really can't know what's what.

"So long as you spell 'Grey' with an 'e,' which I think we should, European-style, and call me by the full name on my birth certificate, which nobody actually does, then 'Gregory Zipf' does have 'Grey Frog Zip,' which isn't completely terrible as a piece of Dadaist poetry. You guys can call me Grey Frog Zip, if you want to. It doesn't seem to have the slightest real meaning, so it doesn't actually make my real name more complicated. It's like a meaningless factor of a number, like '1.'

"Or you can just call me '*Zip*'! Just the one name. So I'd be like *Bono* or *Barbie*. Just *Zip*. That'd be a super-cool name for me. My travel name.

"What's Shaw Bradley do, Kelly? Besides, I hope, making lots of money so he can buy you wonderful presents?"

Kelly laughed.

"Nope. Not that either. Although he does give me some pretty nice presents. He's a soldier. In the Canadian army."

Greg butted in. "A soldier?! In the *Canadian* army? Isn't that an oxymoron? If he's in the *Canadian* army, he's not a soldier. Right? By definition! Because Canadians don't have soldiers; they have 'peacekeepers,' right? I'm right! That's true! Isn't that right?" He looked at me.

"Are you Canadian?!" I asked Kelly, ignoring Greg, who was once again going on a bit.

"You're right," she said to Greg, then she turned to me to say, "Yeah, I'm Canadian. I grew up in Montreal."

"Home of the Montreal Canadians!" yelled Greg, with surprising enthusiasm. I didn't know he even followed hockey.

"Yeah. Home of *les Canadiens*." She pronounced it like a French speaker. "Among other things."

"My favorite team! I've always loved the Canadians. Because they *are* very Canadian. A truly Canadian team. That's what hockey should be. Canadians, Russians, Finns, and Swedes. That's who should play hockey! Period. That's almost everyone that actually *does* play decent hockey, isn't it? There aren't any really *great* American hockey players. All the *great* players on American teams are actually Canadians, Russians, Finns, or Swedes.

"So, where does your peace-loving man keep the peace?" finished Greg, as usual switching topics with a disorienting fluidity. "If it's Canada, he's masterful! A totally peaceful country. Hardly anyone ever even shoots anyone up there. It's crazy."

"He's actually in Egypt right now. At the Canadian consulate in Cairo. Not keeping the peace. Although they do have peace there, so maybe he is. I've never been exactly sure what it is he does. I don't think he's allowed to let me know, exactly. Something political. He travels around the Middle East talking to people who *aren't* in Canada, and then he comes back and talks about those talks to people who *are* in Canada. He's a lawyer. Was trained as a lawyer, anyway. At the Canadian army's expense. So he owes them five years of service for that. He's in his third year."

"Where'd'ya meet him?"

"I met him here," she said. "In Boston, I mean."

"How'd you meet?"

"I used to be in the Canadian army too," she told us. "I met him on a training exercise."

I am sure Greg and I were both dying to ask more, but the taxi had arrived.

"Hard to believe, huh?" she said, deliberately flexing the slender bicep muscle of her left arm and squeezing it down with the fingers of her right hand. "But I'm tougher than I look!"

She smiled, stepped out to get into her cab, and turned back to salute us both as snappily as always.

"Thanks for a fun day, boys! See ya tomorrow!"

⁑

"She's got a boyfriend," said Greg, as soon as the door was closed.

"Yup," I said. Of course she did. I wasn't at all surprised. I wasn't disappointed. I just felt a bit numb.

We were silent for a minute.

"She used to be a *soldier*," said Greg.

Jannie always said we should try to figure out what purpose a symptom serves. She probably read that in a book somewhere too. She said that most of what we called "symptoms" exist because they get something for the person who has them. Usually it was attention or sympathy. I wondered what purpose Greg's repetition of the obvious served. I decided that Greg needed to have someone agree with him. I thought about how solitary his life must be because I knew he didn't have a lot of friends, and I thought it made sense. It's nice to be acknowledged, to know people agree with you.

"That's right, Greg. Apparently she was indeed in the Canadian army."

We were silent again for a moment.

"Are you gonna call me *Zip*? Do! OK? 'Cause I really do like that idea. A lot. *Greg* seems so boring, right? Like *Joe* or *Sam*. Or *Mr. Smith*. Everyone is called *Greg* or *Joe* or *Sam* or *Mr. Smith*. I really wanna be called just *Zip*! OK?"

It's nice to be called what you want to be called. When you have a nickname, every time someone says your name you know they *really know you*. Using a nickname is like telling a person you love them every time you say their name.

"OK," I said. "I'll try. It seems a little weird to me right now, but maybe I'll get used to it. *Zip*."

"It has no anagrams either. A good prime name. What do you wanna be called?"

I didn't stop to think about it. It just came out.

"Call me Ishmael."

∷

Ishmael, as you might remember, was Isaac's half-brother. He was 14 years older than Isaac. He was conceived by Abraham (with his wife Sarah's consent) as a result of what is delicately referred to as a "matrimonial allegiance" with Sarah's maidservant Hagar. Abraham was about 85 years old at the time.

According to the Koran, almost as soon as Ishmael was born, he and his mother were abandoned by Abraham in the desert because of course God told Abraham he should abandon them there because God chose Abraham to do all the dirty work.

After they had burned through the few dried dates and little water left them by Abraham, Hagar (*Hajira*, in the Koran) and Ishmael (still suckling) became understandably frantic. Hajira ran out far into the desert seven times to look for water, returning exhausted each time, with increasing fear and horror and motherly love, but always without water. When she returned the seventh time, she couldn't think of any possible solution to her problem. She was stinking of sweat and poo and pee and her baby's dried vomit and spit, unkempt, utterly exhausted in body and mind, mad with thirst, unable to think straight or to imagine why her life had been reduced to these final days of wholly undeserved torture.

She no longer thought that God might yet save her. She no longer believed she would be saved. Hajira had not lost her faith, but she was not able to find comfort in it any more. She believed that God had chosen her and her son to die. She did not want to die. She did not want her son to die. Her eyes burned and teared up as she stared out over the desert, trying to think of just one more trick she could try, ignoring the frantic unceasing wailing of her dying baby.

In his panicked thirst, baby Ishmael kicked against the ground and *Lo!* water gushed forth from the place where he had kicked.

That place has been revered ever since as the wonderfully named Well of Zamzam. It is located today in the largest mosque (3,840,570 square feet!) in Mecca.

Hagar drank from beneath her child's feet and was able to restore the two of them to health.

As Kelly points out, the Bible tells a different story.

::

I wanted to just say that my mother fell in the garden and leave it at that because that would be quick and easy. I wasn't planning to *dwell* on it here, get into all the gory details. My mother died. OK. That's true. We don't all need to *wallow* in it.

You just eat breakfast one day, and before you have finished your second cup of coffee, your mother is *dead*. You mourn, of course. It's totally terrible that she just upped and died, but at least you can skip directly to the mourning without having to go through a lot of stuff between the beginning and the end of dying.

A lot of that stuff is really just as bad as mourning. Not *worse*. But just as bad.

And the thing of it is: At the end of all that, you still have to mourn anyway.

It is better to just be sad about death, period, than it is to be sad about the poor quality of life first and then have to be just as sad about the same death anyway.

That's just like saying that it's better to be whipped with a branch than to be whipped with a branch and have the backs of your hands burned with cigarettes. One bad thing is better than two.

::

"Ishmael!" exclaimed Zip. "Like in *Moby-Dick*, huh? You know that's the first line, right? 'Call me Ishmael.'"

"I dunno about that name.

"You know why the sailor said we had to call him Ishmael in *Moby-Dick*, don't ya? Even though it obviously wasn't his *real* name?"

I did not.

"Because it's an anagram for 'I lash 'em.' Most people don't get that.

"But there's no way that Ishmael will work as a good *travel name*. There's a million anagrams for Ishmael! OK, maybe 'a slim he' is appropriate enough for you. Since you are actually pretty slim. But do you really want to be known as 'male-ish'? Or 'lame-ish'? Or as some guy's boyfriend, 'his male'? Do you really think of yourself as an ineffectual thin gay effeminate sailor? No! Because obviously you are not that. It would be very confusing to take such a complex name as Ishmael! It's not going to work.

"Anyway, it's way too long for a nickname. If you want a travel name, it has to be monosyllabic. One syllable. It has to be super-snappy, totally easy to say. It has to roll off the tongue.

"Like *Zip*.

"I say you just go for 'Ish.' Short, simple, sweet, and essentially prime. Closed class words don't count. They're way too common."

I liked the notion of not quite being anything fully. I felt like I was not quite fully anything. I was *–ish* many things. It felt right.

"OK," I said. "Call me Ish."

∷

In the Bible, Sarah and Hagar get into a disagreement while Hagar is pregnant with Ishmael. Either Hagar has become too proud, as the Bible suggests, or Sarah has become too jealous, as later events and other narratives suggest. In either case, Sarah treats Hagar so unkindly that the pregnant woman runs into the desert. Beside a spring there, she has an unexpected meeting with Malak Yahweh, the buxom angel who counsels What Is, who tells Hagar that she will have a son who will become 'a wild donkey of a man' and will leave many descendents. The angel says that Hagar should return to her mistress, Sarah.

So she does. Of course. When the advisor to What Is tells you what to do, you just do it. You'd be *definitely* diagnosable if you didn't.

The Bible does say that Hagar and Ishmael went into the desert together eventually. But it says it was a lot later than what the Koran says. According to the Bible, after my namesake was born, beautiful Sarah became angry with Ishmael for making fun of his younger half-brother Isaac. She demanded that her husband expel Hagar and Ishmael.

At first, Abraham did not agree because like any father, he loved his children equally. Perhaps he was even attached equally to their mothers. However, after God assured Abraham that He personally would look after Ishmael, Abraham had his mistress and son sent into the desert of Paran carrying only a few supplies.

Eventually, just as they had in the Koran story 13 years earlier, Hagar and Ishmael found themselves dying of thirst together. Ishmael was again close to death. His mother laid him under a bush and went to sit some distance away. She did not want to watch her son die.

Malak Yahweh, despite her job of counseling What Is, was not *au courant* with What Actually Was. When she showed up, *she had to ask Hagar what the problem was.* That kills me. This seems like a really dumb question for an Angel of What Is to ask Hagar when Hagar's son is dying of thirst at that exact moment only a few feet away, after many long days of suffering. It must have been a very busy time for God's advisor. She must have been distracted.

Anyway, she did suss out the situation. Without further ado, she told Hagar to close her eyes. When she was allowed to open them: *Lo!* Hagar saw a well, which she used to save herself and her son.

Hagar and Ishmael lived together in the desert. Ishmael became a fabulous archer, a wild donkey of a man, exactly as foreseen, and the great patriarch of the Arabian people.

Rabbinical sources tell the story with angels appearing to protest against giving the boy water, since his descendants would destroy the Israelites by thirst. That sounds like editorializing to me. We don't think of angels as the kind of things that stage a protest. Imagine them holding up their handwritten protest signs for God: No water for Ishmael! Let the bastard die! Angels against mercy!

Given the way he was favored by the Angel of Jehovah, it is not surprising that anyone who sees Ishmael in a dream will have his [or her][2] prayers answered.

---

2. Greg's addition.

::

As Zip knew, *Ish* is not strictly prime, with "his." But he felt I could own that, and we both agreed that the name was philosophically, if not perfectly, prime. So *Ish* it was.

Neither he nor I wanted to leave the safety and comfort of our Winnebago, so we heated individually wrapped frozen burritos one at a time in the microwave for supper and ate them while we practiced using our new prime names. Zip reminded me of the enigmatic lines in Duchamp's notes to *The Large Glass* where he defined prime words as "*divisible only by themselves and by unity*" and advocated the creation of a new language for describing *The Bride Stripped Bare by Her Bachelors, Even*, in which each letter stood for an abstract word. If you want to spell a simple concrete word like "cat" in this language, the word will also contain the three abstract meanings that go with its three letters. Essentially, Duchamp's idea turns all words into compound words that consist of abstract elements, like the English word "artless." The word "cat" would not simply refer to a domesticated feline, but would also allude, say, to *joy*, to *love*, and to *hope*.

After we had eaten our individually wrapped burritos (I had two), I went to my bed to continue rereading Duchamp's biography, which I had assigned myself as a task for the trip. It was even written into our agreement, by me, that I would read 20 pages each day, to make sure I couldn't weasel out of the task.

After washing his hands for long enough to confirm that he was still diagnosable, Greg sat on his bed, on the other side of the vehicle, where he unrolled his "travel spoon collection," a small subset of his total collection. He kept the spoons in a long roll of soft cloth that had individual pockets for each spoon, which he felt offered them the best protection. I watched him over the top of my book.

He treats his spoons with such gentle reverence that it is a pleasure to see him with them.

∷

Greg snores.

∷

We were awakened by Kelly's arrival, as agreed, at 8:30 AM. She unlocked the driver's door and climbed into the seat, raising a large paper coffee cup in her right hand.

"Wake up, boys! I'd have brought you some coffee, but I presumed you'd be making your own using distilled rain water and coffee beans picked by virgins and ground by high priests, filtered through sterile medical gauze, so I didn't."

"Hey, Kelly," said Greg, sitting up in his bed with the covers still over him. "You have to call Isaac 'Ish' from now on, OK? And call me 'Zip'."

"Ish?" repeated Kelly.

Greg told her that it was short for Ishmael and then spent quite a bit of time explaining why the full name made him think of a thin gay ineffectual sailor.

"So I need a new name too?" asked Kelly.

"Sure! But you have to say 'Call me . . . whatever' when you tell us what it's going to be. Like in *Moby-Dick*, you know?"

"Yeah, yeah, I got it," said Kelly. "Let me think for a second." There was silence.

"So it can't have any anagrams, then?" asked Kelly.

"It's better if it doesn't. Unless they're good ones."

"OK, if he's gonna be Ish, then call me Hajira. Let's say Haj, for short."

"It's got Jah," pointed out Greg.

"I know," said Kelly. "That's why I like it! It's a sign of feminine power and God at the same time!"

"You can own that," admitted Greg.

"I can *totally* own that," said Kelly.

::

I knew that the Rastafarians called God "Jah," but that was all I knew about Jah. I didn't even know that Jah was the exact same God as the God of Abraham, Isaac, and Ishmael. I thought the Rastafarians were Hindus like the Hare Krishnas. I thought that because I knew they smoked pot, which I associated with Nepal.

As we pulled out of the parking lot, Kelly told us that "Jah" was short for "Yahweh," a Jewish name for God. The word was never supposed to be spoken aloud except by a high priest in the Holy Temple, which was unfortunately destroyed thousands of years ago.

The four-letter Hebrew words for the name was rendered by early English translators as either JHVH or YHWH because the Hebrew did not include vowels and Latin does not distinguish "y" from "j" or "w" from "v." In the eighth century, helpful monks added vowels in to make the texts easier to read. They gave JHVH and YHWH the vowels from "Adonai" to remind early readers that they were supposed to say "Adonai" when they came to that word. However, later translators transcribed the word just as it appeared on the page, as if it really were a name instead of a pointer to a symbol of a name that cannot be spoken.

So English names for God are a way to incorrectly say what we cannot speak about.

"And of course 'Hajira' is the Arabic name for Abraham's concubine, who is called 'Hagar' in the Bible. So, *Haj*."

"So you're calling yourself by my own name's mom?" I said. I didn't like that very much. It made me want to wash my hands.

"And by your own name's God too!" she reminded me. "Don't worry! Just think of me as your God and attend to my every whim. But you still get to be the boss. It'll be just like praying: You say what you want and I try to make it so. Within reason. You know. As long as it's written somewhere in the agreement."

::

Greg, Kelly, and I pulled over at a diner only a little later because Greg and I had not yet eaten anything. Although she thought we should go hungry as a punishment for sleeping in so late when she had to get up early to come and get us, Kelly agreed to pull over at the diner as long as we agreed that we would all leave the Winnebago to eat.

She had taken us both a bit by surprise with the speed at which we had taken off. Greg and I weren't really finished getting out of bed when Kelly had started up the vehicle and told us we had to strap in. I was wearing blue pajamas and yesterday's black socks, and Zip was wearing ratty gray sweatpants, his Canadian parliament buildings T-shirt, and a pair of slippers that were made to look like Sigmund Freud, which his mother had given him, much to his delight, for Christmas a few years earlier.

Kelly was impeccably dressed in something that was maybe a little showy for business casual: wide soft red slacks that caressed themselves across her legs when she took a step, a white cotton blouse with a dragon scrawled on the back in black like a piece of graffiti, and expensive-looking embroidered red slippers. Her hair was hanging straight down except at the front, where she had swept it back with a thick red ribbon of a hairpiece.

She looked great, and she still smelled delicious too.

::

Greg and I sent Kelly in ahead of us to get a table while we washed and got dressed. Each of us pulled a clean Italian shirt from the dry cleaner's plastic wrapper. There is a great pleasure in putting on a crisp clean Italian shirt fresh from the dry-cleaning wrapper, but it is nothing compared to the even greater pleasure of putting on a brand-new pair of socks. We each had over a dozen new pairs, so it was a pleasure we could expect to have every morning for some days, whether or not we were still traveling, as I had agreed that Greg could keep the clothes I had purchased for him.

I opened my tie suitcase, a small case filled with about 150 ties from my collection. I chose an abstract red-and-green tie that had been designed by the deceased lead singer of the Grateful Dead, pulled it out, and draped it over my hand.

"Resplendent in color," I said, "And provided at the four corners with very sharp points (like all neckties)!"

Somewhat to my surprise, Greg came over and quickly pulled out a tie himself: a sky-blue tie with diagonal yellowish-orange stripes. He draped it over his hand, repeated my words as if they were an incantation, and held up his other hand for a high five again. I hit his hand with my own.

"Today I'm going formal," he said. "Can you tie it for me, please?"

::

The Russo Brothers Gas & Truck Stop was a large and busy place, with a small grocery store and gas cashier in the front and a surprisingly cavernous restaurant stretching out behind it. I could not help noticing as we walked in that very few customers were wearing a shirt with a collar, and no one except Greg and I was wearing a tie.

Kelly whistled appreciatively as we strode up to her table.

"Looking good, boys!" she said. "Zip! A tie! I thought we had all signed a contractual agreement that said that you wouldn't wear any ties!"

"Actually, we all signed a contractual agreement that I would not *have* to wear a tie," said Greg, quite correctly. "There's nothing to say I couldn't wear one if I felt like it."

"Well, I'm glad you wanted to," replied Kelly. "It looks great."

"Yes," said Greg, looking over at me as my cue. We both said it at the same time: "Resplendent in color, and provided at the four corners with very sharp points (like all neckties)!"

Kelly looked at us both quizzically, so Greg explained how it referred to Duchamp's description of the ties of the malic moulds as we took our seats at the table, which was covered with Formica flecked with pink tear-like lines and looked like it was authentically from the 1950s. I pointed out the beauty of the Formica, and then our waitress was at the table holding a carafe and asking if we wanted coffee.

"Do you know where the coffee was grown?" asked Zip.

The waitress, an ample-bosomed motherly woman just past middle age, laughed.

"No, honey, I don't. Coffee's coffee, right?"

I could see Greg formulating an enlightening answer for her, so I kicked his shin to shut him up.

"I guess it is!" he said, instead of launching, as he had no doubt been planning to, into his standard diatribe about the importance of soil, angle, and amount of sunlight, altitude of growth, and varietal of coffee bean. "It must be! Right, Haj?!" he said, looking over at her. "Because that's a tautology. So it has to be true. By definition, right? Coffee is coffee. Each thing is what it is.

"But no thanks, I won't have any. Maybe just a Mountain Dew if you have one, please."

"OK. You, hon?" she said, turning to me. I looked at Kelly, who held up her cup as if to toast me before throwing it down her throat.

"Yes, please," I said, holding out my cup.

A smell like BBQ briquette ashes mixed with turpentine rose from the liquid as she poured it.

"Thanks!" I said, lifting the cup to my mouth and taking a large sip.

"Mmmmm," I said, raising my cup to Haj. "Now that's coffee!"

When the waitress was out of earshot, I continued: "Because coffee *is* coffee!"

::

When she came back, Greg and I asked for two orders each of plain toast, me first and then him. Kelly had already eaten breakfast, but she ordered a strawberry Danish.

"Weird to be in a place owned by Italians named 'Russo,' huh?" said Kelly. "Since 'Russo' means 'Russian' in Italian."

Neither Greg nor I replied. I am sure that we both had the same idea of what we wanted to talk about, but neither of us quite knew how to broach it. I didn't, anyway. I was counting on Greg to start. We all sat in silence, Kelly looking at us slightly quizzically. By now she was beginning to understand us. She just waited.

"So," said Greg.

Now that Greg had started the thing, Kelly and I waited together. Eventually she realized what I already knew—that a response was required—so she repeated "So!" more emphatically, to encourage Greg to continue.

"You were in the army, right?" said Greg.

"Yeah, I was," said Kelly.

"The *Canadian* army," said Greg.

"Yeah. The Canadian army. 'Action from knowledge!' That's our motto."

"Cool," said Greg. "Ours is 'Shoot 'em all; let God sort 'em out.' Which I think is actually a better motto for an army since the first action of any army with any actual *knowledge* would be to stop fighting, wouldn't it? Oh yeah, that's right, I forgot: You were in the *Canadian* army. They *have* stopped fighting. At least, as far as I know. Are you guys having any wars these days?"

"They're in all of our wars," I answered. "Right?" I continued, looking over at Kelly. "Isn't the Canadian army in Afghanistan and Iraq?"

"Yeah, we are," she said.

"'Action from knowledge'!" said Greg. "Because you guys have the knowledge that we will kick your scrawny Canadian butts if you don't fight when we tell you to, right?"

Kelly smiled. I couldn't tell if she agreed or not.

"But I'm kind of amazed that you were ever a soldier!" continued Greg. "I mean, you don't seem much like the soldierly type. As far as I can tell. Not that I know a lot of military personnel. I don't know any, in fact. So no offense intended about you not being soldier material. I don't know what I am talking about. I am not the soldierly type either. And I think that's a good thing. I don't think I'd be useful in a combat situation. I'm a man of peace. How does a beautiful sweet lady like you ever get into the army?"

"I needed the money," she said. "I went through school on an intelligence operator training program. They paid for me to go to school, and I worked for them while I was at school, and then for four years afterward."

"Intelligence operator?! Does that mean like a spy?!" asked Greg.

"Sort of. Not really. I was essentially a translator for them. They took me because I speak Hebrew and Arabic."

We looked at her. She was smiling as beatifically as ever. I think that Greg and I both had the feeling that she was pulling our legs. I did, anyway. But if it wasn't true, I couldn't see what her angle was. Finally it was me that spoke.

"You speak . . . Hebrew and Arabic?" I said, tentatively, as if I hadn't heard, so I wouldn't seem too much of a fool if it was just a joke.

"I do," she said. "Believe it or not, I have a Jew for a mother, and a Palestinian for a father. Well, a half-American Palestinian."

She paused.

"I speak French too," she said. "Being as I grew up in Quebec and all."

We all paused.

"You have a Jewish mother?" I said.

"Married to a *Palestinian* father?!" added Greg.

"Well, not actually *married to*. But *mated with*, anyway. *Lived* with. *Raised a kid* with. Wacky people, my parents."

When I asked her if she wasn't in fact of Japanese descent, as she seemed to be, Kelly explained. Her mother was indeed Japanese—a Japanese Jew. Apparently such a hybrid existed. Some even say that the tiny Japanese Jewish minority is descended from one of the Lost Tribes of Israel. Jews settled in Japan and built the first synagogue there a century and a half ago. At the beginning of the last century, the small Japanese Jewish community was strengthened by the arrival of Russian, Middle Eastern, and European Jews. In World War II, Japan was, bizarrely enough, regarded as a safe haven for Jews, though not many made it there.

Kelly was descended from an early Middle Eastern Jewish settler whose descendants had, over generations, increased their percentage of Japanese blood. Her mom was raised a Hebrew/ Japanese bilingual.

In her late teens, Kelly's mom had fallen in love with a rather brilliant foreign student who was taking Japanese lessons from Kelly's grandmother while he studied Zen Buddhism. He was a Lebanese Muslim by upbringing, a professor of religious studies by education, and a lover of God in all manifestations by inclination. Faced with disapproval from all sides for reasons that spanned generations, the couple had jumped at the chance to move to Canada when Kelly's father was offered a position at Concordia University in Montreal.

Kelly had been born in Montreal, attending Catholic French day-cares and schools, studying Hebrew on Saturday, speaking Japanese and Arabic at home, and watching English TV and movies.

Like her parents, Kelly had a gift for learning languages. She mastered all five languages, and in the course of doing so, she mastered the basic tenets of three major religions: Islam, Judaism, and Christianity. Her father liked to say to her that to believe that there was just one true church was to tie oneself with false rope.

Though Kelly is always vague about the details, apparently governments find it very useful to have Arab/Hebrew bilinguals on their staff. Since Arab/Hebrew bilinguals who are politically unaffiliated with either an Arabic- or a Hebrew-speaking state are rare, she found her skills highly saleable. She was able to get herself a linguistics BA at the Canadian taxpayer's expense, in return for her summers and the first four years of her postgraduate life.

Kelly was in the middle of explaining all this when the waitress arrived, bearing a large set of plated food on a tray carried on her right shoulder.

"Plain toast for the gentlemen in the lovely suits and ties," she said, placing the plates delicately in front of us, as if she were serving in a restaurant in Paris.

"And something sweet for the beautiful lady," she said, placing a preternaturally bright red strawberry Danish on a white plate in front of Kelly. She stood up and smiled, heaving the tray back up as she surveyed the three of us with the simple acceptance of someone who sees a lot of odd people passing through.

"Enjoy."

THE 1ST FOCUS OF SPARKS
(ELECTRICAL STRIPPING)

We stayed a while in our seats, discussing the day's route, even though we were only 90 minutes out of Philadelphia now. Greg had printed out three copies of the Google directions and wanted to discuss some of the details with us. For example, there was a toll road along the route suggested by Google. Greg assumed they would make change, but just in case, he had contractually obligated me to place several rolls of coins and $20 in small bills inside the Winnebago. I was able to assure him I had done exactly what he asked. He wanted to tell us about an alternate route that would allow us to avoid the tollbooth. Kelly and I flipped to the page with that route on it and listened to many convincing reasons why we should not follow that route. And so on.

The gist of it was that we had 90 minutes of driving ahead of us.

::

As Greg's briefing came to its long-anticipated close, a curiously small redheaded child, perhaps 11 or 12 years old, walked with purpose toward our table. He was wearing a red apron that was too large for him and carrying a gray plastic bin. His face was very freckled and his eyes alarmingly blue. Our eyes met and he smiled, an open easy smile of happiness.

"Do you mind if I take the rest of this away?" he asked.

"No," I said. "I don't mind. Anyone else mind? Zip? Haj? No. It's all yours."

He reached his hand over to take my coffee cup. His thin hands were red around the knuckles. He had clearly been on the job for some time. He moved the cups and plates with the fluid grace of a master. He was weaving, grabbing, sliding, lifting, all with amazing grace and precision. He seemed to not so much take things off the table as simply shoo them into his plastic bucket.

His bussing was mesmerizing.

When he was gone, I looked across the table at Kelly.

"Who gets the tip in restaurants, Haj? I mean, does the waitress get it all, or does she have to share it with the busboy? I wanna tip that kid. Because he was a true master at bussing tables. Did you catch that, Zip? How *smooth* that kid was?"

Greg smiled and moved his head almost imperceptibly to one side, a half headshake, to signal that he had missed it but wasn't too broken up.

"It depends," said Kelly. "Usually the waitress gets most of it. She shares with the busboys, but how they do it is just up to the restaurant. Sometimes it's a percentage of tips, sometimes it's a fixed amount, sometimes it's just whatever she feels like handing over. I guess you could directly tip a busboy, but I've never heard of anyone doing it."

"So it wouldn't be normal if I gave him, like, a hundred bucks, huh? Because I really feel like doing that. The guy's a real artist."

"That would not be normal," Kelly agreed. "I think it could look a little weird."

In the end I just left a tip at the high end of the normal range and hoped for the best.

The philosophical waitress was OK. But man, that busboy could bus.

::

When we were back inside the Winnebago, Greg opened his suitcase and took out a small black velvet bag, cinched at the top with a bright yellow ribbon. He walked to the front of the Winnebago and dangled it between his fingers.

"This," he said, "is today's *objet d'art*."

He turned toward Kelly and asked, "Haj? Would you like to do the honors of unveiling the piece?"

Then he turned back to me and said, "As long as that's not problematic, Ish."

I laughed at the unintentional word play.

"It's problematic-ish. But only *-ish*. Thanks for asking. But no. It's OK. It's all hers."

Kelly took the small sack from Greg, looking at the two of us a bit suspiciously.

"OK," she said, slowly, undoing the ribbon and pushing the bag open by spreading her fingers out. "Today's art object is . . ."

She reached two elegant fingers in to grab the thing and brought it out.

I did not look at the object as much as I looked at the brilliant red fingernails that cradled it.

". . . a small black ball!" she ended, holding it above her head as if she were showing it off to a gathering crowd of onlookers.

::

A small black ball.

I have to admit, I was stumped.

A small black ball.

I tried saying it in my minimal French in case that might jog a memory of any Duchamp piece involving a small black ball.

Une petite balle noire. La petite balle noire. Une petite balle foncée.

No memories were jogged.

"A small black ball?" I said, reaching out to take it from Kelly's hand to be sure.

Greg looked at me with satisfaction. He was enjoying himself.

"Yup. That's *exactly* what it is. It's a small black ball.

"Now, for 10 points and the grand prize, can you tell us, Ish, which of Duchamp's pieces could be referenced by such a ball?"

I kept repeating what it was to myself, as if saying what it was were an incantation that would reveal the truth.

A small black ball. A black small ball. A black ball that's small.

I looked at Kelly, who shrugged and flipped her hands out to let me know I was on my own. I looked at Greg, who was still beaming.

"Zip, I must tell you that I cannot win those 10 points or today's grand prize. I don't have a clue."

"Sure you do," said Greg. "I'll give you a clue. An easy clue. It's a large piece. Very large. One of his largest."

"OK. So it's either *The Bride Stripped Bare by Her Bachelors, Even*, or *Given: 1. The Waterfall, 2. The Illuminating Gas*," I said, looking at him for confirmation.

He nodded.

"OK," I said, thinking. "OK. For 10 points, and today's *grand* prize, Zip, I'm going to go with *The Bride Stripped Bare by Her Bachelors, Even*. I don't actually know what the connection is, but that has to be it. That's my final answer."

It was the obvious bet. Where would you be more likely to find a black ball: playing some role in a complex machine or lying in the tall grass near a naked lady flashing her coochie?

Greg's smile and eyes opened wider.

"That's right! Lady and gentleman, we have today's grand winner!"

He took the ball from my hand, stuck the yellow ribbon into it with a thumbtack, and hung it from the front mirror.

∷

I had to get Richard Hamilton's typographic notes to *The Bride Stripped Bare by Her Bachelors, Even* from Greg's portable library to find out more about the small black ball. I don't apologize for that. It is not a major element. From Duchamp's writing, we only know that:

i.) One property of the *Bride Stripped Bare* is "flair," a sense that "receives *the waves of unbalance from the black ball*" (his emphasis).

ii.) The Bride has a mercurial "blossoming Barometer," a sensitive filament that extends from within her, like a butterfly's tongue, subject to her "storms and weathers."

iii.) When the blossoming happens, the Barometer must, like a flame, lick "the ball of the handler [the Tender of Gravity] displacing as it pleases," which creates a need for a "[stabilizer] (a ball or anything)."

iv.) [There is possibly a destabilizing Juggler of Gravity, who may be juggling balls. However, the Juggler is alluded to only by its absence, mentioned in Duchamp's notes but not appearing in his sculpture.]

It is hard to know if the unbalancing ball, the stabilizing ball, the ball of the Tender of Gravity, and the possible balls of the Juggler of Gravity are all the same. Greg explained that he believes it is all just one ball, consisting of multiple balls in one in the same way that the Holy Trinity is three in one. The black ball stabilizes an unstable state. It does not do that by calming down the instability so things can return to normal. It does it by creating a different kind of stability, something entirely new.

"So it's as if," he said, flicking the ball gently with his finger, "this thing could turn a hurricane into a bird."

::

A person dying of cancer is like a species going extinct.

I suppose that there must be a specific millisecond before a car hits you when that hit is mathematically inevitable, a moment at which you are not yet dead but are now guaranteed to die, but the time span between that moment and the hit is so short you can't notice it. Maybe you stare at the car as it bears down and you just have long enough to think: "*Schloobies*, it's going to hit me!" Maybe you almost have time to scream. Then you get hit.

Cancer is like a really *slow* car bearing down on you. You also want to scream, maybe, when you see it coming at you. But there's no way you can keep up the screaming for months and months, maybe even years. You might even *want* the car to hit you, maybe, so you can just get it all over with. The speed at which death bears down on you eventually becomes almost as unendurable as the certainty that it is going to hit you.

My mother told me not long after she was given a terminal diagnosis that she had asked Mr. Salandhi to make up a living will. She had watched my father die, and she wanted to avoid his mistakes. There was to be no heroics, no experimental drugs, no visits to shamans from the world's undervalued cultures. If the car was going to hit her, she had decided she was just going to let the *schlooby-pie* thing hit.

But it didn't hit her. It just got closer and closer, but it never actually made contact. First she stopped going off the property. Then she stopped going out of the house. Then she stopped leaving her room. Then she stopped reading. Then she stopped watching TV. Then she stopped listening to the radio and just lay there in bed all day, waiting with increasing impatience to die.

She wasn't against painkillers. She took those.

I think she eventually just got *bored* of dying. It had gone on too long.

∷

Kelly asked Greg to tell us about the guy we were going to see in Philadelphia. He had not wanted to say much to me when I had asked him before the trip but seemed happy to talk about the guy now.

"Well, his name is . . . well, let's just give him a prime name. Whaddya think? Kelly?"

"I'm only going to give him a name if he is going to say 'Call me X' when we see him."

"OK!" said Greg. "Definitely! He has to! Of course I can't speak for him. But I'm going to anyway. I'm pretty sure that he'll be up for that. Possibly he will. Very possibly. I'll tell you what I'll promise: I promise I'll *ask* him to say 'Call me X' when we see him. I'll even try to *convince* him that he should say it. OK? And you tell me what X is? OK?"

"Deal," said Kelly. "We have to write it in the addendum though."

We had left several blank pages at the end of our rules in case we had to add any new ones in the course of following the ones we had.

"We do. Definitely!" said Greg, and he got the rules and wrote it in with his beautiful handwriting.

"OK. So, we have Ish and Haj," said Kelly. "Not to ignore you, Zip, but I'm working with the Abraham theme here, you know. Seeing as that's my own obsession these days, at least until I finish my damn thesis."

"He's in the Abraham story!" I said "'Zip' means 'nothing,' right?

"So he is alluded to by his absence."

Kelly and Greg laughed.

"All right," said Kelly. "So we have Ish and Haj *actually* in the story, and Zip in it in virtue of being nothing, and therefore absent. There's not a lot left.

"We have Sarah. She's a complex character, with some highly unpleasant characteristics in my opinion, and a female to boot. So I think that's probably not a good one.

"We have Abraham himself, of course. A tough name to live up to. Also very complex, not necessarily all good. Well-intentioned, perhaps, but maybe also misguided.

"You know the Leonard Cohen song 'Story of Isaac'? He says *A scheme is not a vision*. Abraham didn't necessarily *get* that. We could go with *Abe*, but it's not grabbing me. You?"

We agreed. Anyway, Greg pointed out that *Abe* had the anagram of a real girl's name, *Bea*, which made it a bad choice for a masculine nickname according to him.

"Well, if we don't want to get out into some obscure relatives, we're out of humans. We're pretty much left with either the ewe or the Angel of Jehovah. *Malak Yahweh*. But nothing is jumping out at me? Greg?"

"Well, *Malak Yahweh* has millions of anagrams. *Leaky ham haw. Whale ham yak. Hawk may heal.*"

"*Hawk may heal*! That's good!" said Kelly. "I say we tell him to say *Call me Hawk. Hawk* is a good strong masculine name. As far as I can see it's prime, isn't it, Zip?"

"It is," said Greg.

"Sounds good to me," I said. I liked that we had named him, and I hoped he would like it.

Greg continued from where he had become sidetracked.

"So you know I met Hawk in group, right?"

I didn't say what I was thinking: that as far as I could see, Greg had met everyone he knew in group therapy.

"Yes," I said, because I knew that a response was required.

"He was a washer. All the usual phobias, compulsions, unwanted thoughts, behavior-control issues.

"But he had one thing I had never seen before in group. He had a job that was entirely excellent for someone prone to over-focusing. He built models, for, like, movies and museum exhibits and for whoever would pay him. Some of them were really insanely complex, stuff that no normal person would either want or be able to build. Sometimes the shrinks asked him to bring something he had built into group, you know, to raise his self-esteem and inspire us and pass 15 minutes of the group's time pretty happily, which is something in itself, right, Ish?"

I nodded when he turned to look at me.

"Once he brought in this model of a house he had to build for a movie. It was unbelievably detailed. It had to be, because they wanted to use it as a stand-in for the real house in the movie. I forget why, exactly, except that they had to blow up, or have it carried away in a flood, or somehow destroy it. Apparently it was cheaper for them to hire Hawk than it was to hire the computer animators.

"So he had built this three-story house almost literally brick by brick. He had these tiny little bricks that he held together with some kind of glue. And he had to finish some of the inside too. Not all of it because the way the camera was going to be set up, they would only see inside part of the house. And I remember him saying that they had also written the scene so that most of the curtains could be closed, to make it easier for him to model. So most of the house was just bare. He finished the walls and painted them white, but he didn't put any furniture or anything in those rooms. He basically only had to finish half of the living room, which the camera was going to be able to see. He built this tiny fireplace in there, and instead of just faking the fire somehow, which I think most people would do, he rigged up this tiny pipe that went into a butane bottle or something like that, which they were supposed to bury under the house, so that there could be a real fire in the fireplace.

"And because he had a real fire, he had to make a real fire grate out of metal, instead of just using a plastic model of a grate, so that it wouldn't melt. So he hand-carved molds and then cast his own tiny iron gratings.

"And he had coated the inside of the chimney with some chemical so that it would actually smoke when the fire was on. The chimney had to be made removable, because you had to be able to re-coat the inside every time you wanted it to smoke, so he had built this little latch that depended on you removing two particular tiny bricks from the bottom of the chimney and then pushing down somewhere else on the chimney to open the hidden latch.

"He was diagnosable. There was no doubt about it! He spent hours and hours doing completely unnecessary things. But everyone knew this about him and they hired him anyway. Or maybe they even hired him *because* he would spend hours and hours doing completely unnecessary things. The point is that he was making good money for his obsession, and the rest of us were just losing time for ours.

"Hawk was the main reason I went to university. He's the one who introduced me to Duchamp. 'Cause I do have master's degree in art history, didja know that, Haj?"

"I do know," said Kelly, because I had told her. "You wrote a thesis on Duchamp, right? Good for you!"

"I did it by correspondence, which worked out well for me. I didn't have to go to any classes or anything.

"You can't just turn your obsession with hand-washing or germs or the corners of doors into an obsession with model-building or with Duchamp. It would be so cool if you could though, wouldn't it?! Man, I'd be so rich if you could do that!

"But I gotta say that after I started thinking so much about Duchamp, life felt a lot better. I still washed my hands and stared at spoons just as much as ever, and I still was more or less completely dysfunctional, but at least I was doing something interesting with my life.

"Which you do need to have.

"It was because of Hawk that I got that. So I owe the guy big time, man!"

"Don't you get paid to write about Duchamp now?" said Kelly.

"A little. Sometimes. Not very often. I've written a few articles here and there. But it's not much of a living. So far. I'm trying to turn my master's thesis into a book about Duchamp. But I think maybe eight people in the world might be interested enough to buy it. So that wouldn't even make me 20 bucks. Enough for a few cups of coffee.

"I think Hawk was making pretty good cash back then. He had a nice car! Most of the people in group didn't even have a car. Hawk had some new hot one. I forget what. I don't know cars. But someone told me it was really expensive. Like a BMW or a Mercedes-Benz.

"And he always seemed to have tons of work.

"Another thing I remember him bringing in, which is why I thought of contacting him about Ish's chocolate grinder, was a fake Picasso sculpture. I remember he showed us how he had engraved his name and e-mail address on the bottom, partly just for advertising, partly so no one would mistake it with the real thing or try to sell it as an original. It was meant for some museum that was going to say it was a copy. Because the real sculpture was worth like 20 million bucks or something. So it was just way cheaper to pay a license and get Hawk to make a copy than it would have been to try to buy a real Picasso. Even if they could have gotten that much money together, which I doubt.

"Anyway, it was perfect model. Absolutely perfect. As far as I could tell. Hawk said it was. He said that if you didn't look at the bottom or do some kind of chemical analysis, there was no way you could tell it from the original. Which I believe! Not that I have ever seen the original. I've seen pictures of lots of Picasso sculptures, including the one he copied. It just really looked like a Picasso.

"I touched it with my bare hands and so did a lot of other people in group, I remember. Weird, huh?"

He looked at me. Most people in group wouldn't touch a doorknob or an eating utensil they hadn't washed themselves with their bare hands, so it was a little weird that they had apparently all been willing to touch the same statue, knowing that a lot of other people had just touched it.

"That is weird," I agreed. "I wonder why they touched it?"

"I dunno," said Greg. "I really don't know. It was the same with the house. I remember everyone wanted to have a turn to take out the chimney. And the same thing happened with other stuff he brought in too. Everyone was just electrified by his stuff. Everyone just knew that the amazing things Hawk made couldn't be contaminated.

"I'm pumped we're going to see him! It's so great! He's a really cool guy. He'll love the name. You guys are going to like him."

"Everyone likes to touch what they love," said Kelly. "Don't you guys ever go shopping?!"

::

About six months after she had stopped doing everything, my mother asked me one day if I would kill her. Of course she didn't say it just like that. Almost, though. She just came right out and asked me point-blank if I would help her die. By then she was trying not to even eat, but they had her on a drip and they made her drink liquids that were stuffed with all the nutrients that medical science could stuff it with.

I told her not to talk that way.

I told her not to think that way.

I think I even told her that she was going to be OK.

It was totally ridiculous.

::

By the time we were getting close to the outskirts of Philly, Greg was trying to talk Kelly into becoming a washer. It was an amusing enough topic to keep us all happy.

"Antibiotics! You're kidding yourself, Haj. Do you have any idea what percentage of bacterial infections don't respond to antibiotics?!"

"Ten percent?" hazarded Kelly.

"Ten percent! Ha! I'll tell you, Haj, if only 10 percent of infections failed to respond to any antibiotics, Ish and I would be federal judges or professional soccer players by now! And we wouldn't be riding in this Winnebago together. We'd be dashing over to Philadelphia in our private jet.

"I'd love 10 percent. If it were just 10 percent, I'd be out there rolling in dirt and singing songs from *Hairspray* while I did.

"Wouldn't you love 10 percent, Ish?"

I didn't actually know. My own symptoms had never been grounded in any actual facts.

"I dunno, Zip. I wish I did. I guess I'd have said about the same as Haj, 10 percent or so. Maybe 20 percent?"

"Twenty percent?! You guys live in dreamland. Jeez. I'd love to be you guys. It must be nice to have it so easy. I'd be a dentist or a four-star general by now if I knew that only 20 percent of infections wouldn't respond to antibiotics.

"Try 50 percent, lady and gentleman. Fifty percent. Half.

"Flip a coin if you want to know whether the treatment's gonna work.

"Ten percent? Twenty percent? Man. You guys have it so easy."

We sat in silence for a second before Greg started up again.

"OK, Haj, if you're still not convinced after that that it's better to join us than fight us, let me ask you this: What percent of infections are spread by touching someone else's body? You like that? Touching other people's bodies? Like your boyfriend's. So take a guess what your odds are."

"I dunno, Zip. I'm gonna put my money on 1 percent. A 1 percent infection rate," said Kelly.

"With direct physical contact?" said Greg, just to make sure it was clear.

"Yeah," responded Kelly.

"So you think that just 1 percent of infections are spread by direct physical contact?"

"I really dunno, Zip. I'm sure you are going to tell me that I'm low again. But I did say 1 percent. That was my guess, given that I really had no idea at all."

"What do you think, Ish?" said Greg, turning toward me.

"I dunno either. I really don't. But I agree with Haj, she's probably low or you'd have told us what it was by now. So I'm gonna bet 5 percent."

"Five percent," replied Greg, clearly implying it was the wrong answer.

"Ten percent," I countered.

"Ten percent," said Greg, in the same tone.

"Yes, Greg," I replied, slipping into my well-practiced Greg-debating voice and accidentally calling him by his real name as a result. "I say 10 percent. And that's my final answer. I'm sticking with 10 percent."

"Ok, so Haj went with 1 percent and, Ish, you went 10 times higher."

Silence.

Sigh.

"Yes, Zip. Correct," I affirmed.

"Well, guys, I'm going to go eight times higher than Ish. Not 1 percent. Not 10 percent. But 80 percent. Four out of every five infections are spread by someone touching someone else.

"So, Haj, what do you say? Thinking of coming over to the dark side?"

Kelly drove in silence for a few minutes.

"No, Zip. Sorry. I'd rather touch people and die of an infection than live in a bubble like you guys. It's messed up. Life can definitely suck sometimes, I know. People get sick. People die. Stuff hurts. But is that enough reason to just give up and hide in a safe little bubble from the world? Not for me, guys. Sorry. I'm just saying.

"Tonight I'm going to find a nice place to have a glass of wine and a decent meal, and afterward, I'm going to lay my head down on a soft pillow and wrap myself in the same soft sheets that hundreds of strangers have used before me.

"If you guys wanna warm up some pasteurized organic gloop, wash your hands for three hours, and then put a 10-dollar set of Chinese-made Walmart sheets on your tiny hard mattress, that's fine. Count me out."

::

It had only been 18 hours, and we had arrived. We were officially in Philadelphia. When we passed the sign, we all let out a whoop. Greg reached into the glove compartment and took out a CD he had stored in there for the occasion, reminding us that he had the contractual right to control the music as we drove into the city.

"Lady and gentleman," he said, "welcome to the City of Brotherly Love."

He put the CD in, and Elton John's "Philadelphia Freedom" boomed out from the stereo.

Greg was moving his arms up and down in a spastic parody of dance as he sang the lyrics at the top of his lungs. Kelly and I didn't really know the exact words, but everyone knows the song, and we both mouthed along as best we could.

"Shine a light through the eyes of the ones left behind . . .

Shine a light, shine the light

Shine the light. Won't you shine the light?

Philadelphia freedom! I love you!

Don't you know?

I love you!

Don't you know that?

I love you!

Yes I do!"

The song ended. Greg looked at each of us.

"For 10 points, and today's grand prize, who can tell me what that song has to do with Duchamp?"

THIS TIMID-POWER [. . .] IS USED
FOR THE BLOSSOMING . . .

G reg had of course printed out a map showing the location of
every Walmart in Philadelphia. He had highlighted the one
closest to the Philadelphia Museum of Art, and on the way in, he
listed for us many excellent and convincing reasons that we should
choose it. Kelly pulled the Winnebago into that parking lot and
turned off the vehicle.

"Well, guys," she said. "It's not even one o'clock yet. Still lots
of time to do stuff.

"So, do you guys wanna do anything? Go shopping in Walmart?
Walk around town? Drop in on Hawk right away? Grab a world-
famous Philly cheesesteak sandwich? Go see the Duchamp stuff?
Warm up tasteless organic gloop and wash our hands by ourselves
for a few hours?"

Greg and I looked at each other and said, at almost exactly the
same time: "Go see the Duchamp stuff!"

"Yay!" said Kelly.

::

We did have to eat again first. Greg and I thought we might as well go for our burritos again, since we had them. Kelly refused to join us, on the grounds that she didn't want to "waste Philadelphia." We soon realized that she would need a vehicle if she was going to find anything better to eat than generic Ding Dongs from Walmart. Our own burritos were frozen and would keep, so Greg and I capitulated after a little discussion and agreed that we would go to another restaurant. To be honest, I was looking forward to it. I think Greg was too.

Kelly insisted that if we were going out in Philadelphia, we were going to eat a cheesesteak sandwich.

"And if we are going to eat a cheesesteak, then by God we are going to eat it from *Pat's King of Steaks*."

Greg had not foreseen this necessity. Fortunately, the guidebook in our library soon had us agreeing with a mixture of trepidation and enthusiasm to go. The *Philly steak sandwich* was invented at Pat's, which was reason enough for us both to want to go. Whether Pat's had also invented the *Philly cheesesteak* depended in part on whose story you believed, and in part on exactly what you consider to be cheese.

Greg was also impressed to learn that the restaurant was open 24 hours per day. He believed everything should be open all the time. I had heard his many excellent reasons for this belief many times and was happy when he did not push his explanations too hard that day.

We strapped ourselves back into our seats, and Kelly drove us out of a Walmart parking lot for the third time.

We had come equipped with many maps of Philadelphia, but none of them had seen fit to mention the size of small urban streets. A small street in the suburbs is not just a small street in the suburbs. The former hot-dog stand that is now Mecca for Philly cheesesteak fans is located in South Philadelphia, in an old Italian and Portuguese section of town that has crazy narrow streets and almost no parking. Kelly could guide the Winnebago slowly through the streets, just, but it quickly became clear that there was no possibility of parking it on the street. We circled our destination in a widening spiral, trying to find a legal space large enough for our vehicle. Eventually we ended up pulling into a public parking lot, where the attendant told us we would have to pay double to park the Winnebago. Greg wanted to argue, but since he did not have the facts about average car length at his command, he really had no idea whether this was an unfair request or not. Neither did I, but I was both hungry and on a spree, so I paid the good man double, and Kelly parked.

Of course Greg and I were not so far gone in our diagnosability that we could never venture outside in Medford/Boston. I regularly went to my museums, and Greg went to his local Starbucks almost every day, as long as the barista that knew him was serving. However, we did prefer to stick to more or less routine routes. My transit route could vary occasionally, but only occasionally and only because I was used to the T (as Bostonians call their public transport system) and had a desire to look at art. Greg had not always gone to Starbucks, so even he had varied his routine at least once. But he had not varied it a lot more than that in many years. Neither of us had ever walked about in a strange city.

"How do I look?" said Greg, standing in front of a closet mirror looking at his tie, looking a little too serious. I knew he was feeling scared. "How does that note go again, Ish? 'Good colors and cut right, angled like any tie'?"

I went over to stand beside him, so I could look at my tie too. I pulled it snug up against my neck and smoothed it down over my shirt.

"Resplendent in color," I reminded him, "and provided at all four corners . . ."

I had jogged Greg's memory and we finished together.

". . . with very sharp points (like all neckties)!"

We said the last phrase almost as if it were a team motto, each of us doing the little he could to give needed courage to a good friend.

Kelly led us out of the Winnebago. I squinted in the sun and held up my hands to cover my eyes. Kelly looked at me and then at Greg, who was carefully watching where he put his feet as he stepped down, as if he were stepping on to the moon's surface and wasn't sure yet if it was hard or soft.

"Well, boys," said our girl, "welcome to the real world!"

She held open her arms and rocked a little in the sun, as if to imply that the world was all hers.

::

If you keep your eyes carefully to the ground, you might be less likely to dismiss hand-washers as crazy. The asphalt surface of the parking lot was covered with stains of varying colors and textures. Each one was no doubt a testament to some accident of biology or auto mechanics. Each stain we trod across might be infectious or toxic.

Greg and I glanced at each other. We knew what the other was thinking.

Kelly set off to the front exit of the parking lot, oblivious to where her feet landed with each stride. I watched her walking away from us with a mixture of love and horror.

"Thanks for getting the good shoes, Ish," said Greg. He had requested in our contract that I buy him a particular brand of shoes, apparently popular in the eighties, that had tall soles and large treads. They looked like highly polished army boots that had been cut off to make shoes: elegant on the top but clunky below. They were great shoes; I bought myself a pair too.

"No problem, Zip. Thanks for finding them for us," I said.

"No problem," he said.

And then we each took one step forward.

∷

"You guys have trouble just *walking*?" said Kelly when we arrived by her side on the sidewalk in front of the parking lot, having apparently taken diagnosably long to get there. Greg and I explained about the stains and some other hazards we had noticed. Greg reminded her again that half of bacterial infections didn't respond to antibiotics and also mentioned that there are over 7 million accidental poisonings each year in the United States.

"You know what my advice would be, boys?" she asked, looking at us. We looked at her, waiting.

"Don't lick the pavement."

She smiled and started walking down the sidewalk.

"No cases of airborne poisoning have been reported in South Philadelphia since newspapers were invented," she called back to us before she stopped and turned around.

"OK, I made that one up. But I'm sure it's approximately true. If this place were poisoning people in droves, we'd know about it by now. It'd be all over the Web and CNN. C'mon, boys, let's go explore this town."

Greg and I looked at each other. I turned to him and smoothed down my tie. He smiled and turned to me as he smoothed his down too.

"*Resplendent in color,*" I said.

"*And provided at all four corners . . .*" he said.

"*. . . with very sharp points!*" we pretended to shout, smiling broadly. "*Like all neckties!*"

"After you," he said, pointing down the sidewalk. "Please."

"Thank you, sir," I said, and I walked.

We caught up to Kelly before she reached the end of the block.

::

The area around Pat's King of Steaks was like nothing I had ever seen around Boston. The narrow streets were lined with narrow

row houses, many decorated with flowers, wreaths, Christmas lights, or tile mosaics.

We passed one house, otherwise exactly like all the others, which had a hand-painted plaque in the front window that said DENTIST, with a name listed on the line below, DR. ANTONIO ZADRA. I tried to imagine walking into a tiny row house like that to go to the dentist. When I went to the dentist, which I do faithfully because tooth pain is a leading source of unhappiness, it was to a large, sterilized waiting room inside a large, sterilized skyscraper. My dentist's consulting room had a view of greater Boston from 24 stories up. It was so clean that I took a special deep-cleaning shower before I went to my checkups. I imagined the Philadelphian dentist's chair inside a converted kitchen on the first floor. The picture made me feel both horrified for and jealous of his clients. It seemed almost medieval in some ways, a frightening throwback to the bad old days before antibiotics and fluoridated toothpaste were discovered. But there was something very friendly about it. One could not help feeling that Dr. Zadra had grown up on the same street where he now practiced, and that his clientele included many grateful, much-loved friends and relatives.

Kelly explained to us that some of the decorations were celebrating confirmations, pointing to a gaudy pink display that included a large pink cross with rhinestones on it, hanging from a pink ribbon, and others were celebrating weddings or births, or commemorating a death.

"Death?" said Greg.

"Yes, Zip. Death. I didn't say that nobody ever died of *anything* in South Philly! They do," she said, looking at him, smiling.

"Why? Does the very idea of death bother you?"

"Not at all," replied Greg. "It probably bothers me a lot less than most people."

"His dad was an undertaker," I filled in.

"Was he?" said Kelly.

"He was," said Greg.

"*Zipf and Sons?*" asked Kelly.

"Nah," said Greg. "He didn't have his own business. He worked for other people. For a funeral home. But I did grow up with death around. I know what it really is. It's normalized for me."

"In what way?" she asked. "Like, you went to a lot of funerals?"

"Not really that. I probably did go to *disproportionally* many compared to the average person, for whatever that's worth. I'm probably diagnosable with *funeral exposure disorder* or something like that. We grew up in a fairly small town. My dad buried quite a few people that he knew. I guess he was really tuned in to who had died. Once in a while, I used to go to where my dad worked. We didn't hang out there or anything, but he never had any problem with what he did for a living. He was very down to earth about it. I think it was just that he didn't mind death himself, didn't mind making a living from the dead, didn't seem at all freaked out by being around dead bodies. So I just grew up thinking that people died and being pretty OK with that. It just wasn't a big deal."

"So how come you're so terrified of low-probability odds of dying?" asked Kelly. "If you have such a friendly relationship with death anyway?"

"Good question!" said Greg. "If I knew the answer, I'd probably be proportional, right? Because if I was at all rational about it, I'd be much more terrified of being killed in a car accident on the way here than I would be about contamination in the parking lot, right?"

"*If* more people die in car accidents than they do of contamination," agreed Kelly.

"Right. Which they do, of course. Way more. Riding in a motorized vehicle is just stupidly dangerous compared to the minuscule, probably totally insignificant, risk of contracting a deadly illness by stepping on someone's vomit or baby poo. And I know that perfectly well. That's exactly what makes us diagnosable, right? If what we did was sensible, we'd be in demand as public speakers instead of being sent off to talk about our feelings in a group. Right?"

"Yeah, I guess. Obviously you're right. I just find it weird that you can see that and still be 'diagnosable,' which I don't think is a real word, by the way. I get the part about not having your feelings and your thoughts pulling totally together. That part's normal. We all feel scared of what we know we have to do, or get attracted to someone we know is bad for us, or are overcome by the need to take one more serving of ice cream than we really should. Obviously we can't rule ourselves by rationality alone. But the difference between you and me is that for me, there is kind of an even battle, sometimes leaning toward rationality, sometimes toward compulsion, with neither one getting too much of a big advantage over the other one. For you guys, it's like all compulsion, all the time."

"Not all the time." corrected Greg. "I don't have *every* compulsion."

"Maybe that's the exact thing that makes you diagnosable. It's that your compulsions, your symptoms, have no balance from other compulsions. Like if *I* felt a little freaked out by stains on the pavement—which I don't, by the way, since I can guarantee that they are entirely harmless by any rational measure—that fear might be balanced by a positive *compulsion*, like, say, my *compulsion* to see new places or my *compulsion* to have a Philly cheesesteak from Pat's before I die.

"If desire counts as compulsion.

"Or it would be balanced out by any one of a million other things. So my freaking out would be tempered. I might feel scared, but I would never *just* be scared. So what's up with you guys? What happens with all that other stuff?

"I mean, look at you now! Here you are, outside in a strange city, walking down a strange road, with a strange woman, on a strange quest for a sandwich as part of an even stranger quest for a horrendously expensive chocolate grinder. Why are you doing it? Why aren't you running back to the Winnebago to cower in the bathroom?"

"Because," I said, producing a small package from my suit's breast pocket, "we have Sani-Wipes!"

I pulled out a wet wipe and passed the package over to Greg, who pulled out another.

"You want one, Haj?" offered Greg.

"You know, I don't mind if I do," said Kelly. "My hands do feel a little sticky after that drive. Thanks!"

She handed the package back to me. Evaporation from the wet wipes had chilled my hands so that I could feel that the package was warm where Kelly had just held on to it. I closed my fingers around the package. I was almost overcome by my longing to put it away and throw my arms around Kelly. I knew that was outside of the range of normal and would not be right. I sighed and stuck the package back into my pocket.

"I know that doesn't really explain it," I said. "Sani-Wipes only kill 99.9 percent of germs, and they can't do anything against airborne contaminants anyway."

••

Pat's is kitty-corner from its upstart rival, Geno's Steaks, which was founded 26 years after Pat's, in 1966. Geno's is bright with flashing colored neon signs. Pat's has a more down-to-earth style, looking like what it is: a glorified hot-dog stand. A sign at the front of the place explains how you are supposed to order and claims you will be sent to the back of the line if you do it the wrong way.

After a brief vote, it was unanimously agreed that Kelly would order for all three of us.

Greg and I both ordered exactly what she did, one Philly cheesesteak with fries and a birch beer. We did not know what a birch beer was, but Kelly was having one. That was good enough for me. What was good enough for me was good enough for Greg. Birch beers all around.

We washed our hands with another Sani-Wipe while we waited on the curb for Kelly to come back with our food. Greg and I had persuaded Kelly we should eat standing up. Pat's only has outdoor seating, and we were not ready to tackle their picnic tables, several of which were still littered with the garbage from previous customers.

"This is fun, man," said Greg, jiggling a little nervously up and down. Which I could understand.

I smiled.

"It's great that Kelly came with us, huh?" I said. "Can you imagine us coming to this place by ourselves?"

We both burst into laughter at the idea, then smoothed down our ties simultaneously.

Kelly brought back the food in three separate bags containing extra napkins, as requested.

"Thanks. Could you see the kitchen at all?" asked Greg, taking the bag from Kelly and opening it up as if he feared it might contain a live animal.

"Yup, got a bit of a look through the window," said Kelly in a matter-of-fact tone of voice. "Looked good. Very sterile. Lots of employees cleaning up. No visible mold, cockroaches, rodents, or dangerous-looking people. Sizzling, germ-killing heat on the stove and in the fryers.

"I estimate the probability of food-borne contamination today as vanishingly small."

I was really hungry, and there are few things better than a Philly cheesesteak sandwich and fries when you are really hungry. What is there not to like about fried protein and fat over a carbohydrate filler?

Pat's sandwich had been invented specifically to satisfy hungry workers.

It was fantastic.

::

Kelly insisted that she could find the way back to the Winnebago even if we took a different route than we had come.

Greg and I said that we might be better off retracing our steps, just to be on the safe side.

Kelly said the safe side was no longer an option. If we wanted to stay on the safe side, we should be washing our hands in our own bathrooms in Medford.

She set off down a street we had not come in on.

Greg and I walked along with her.

::

Many people in group had a phobia of bridges. I always thought this was a very understandable fear. Bridges are very scary places. The fact that they have a very low probability of falling apart explains why it is not normal to have a debilitating fear of bridges. But it is also true that the idea of dying in the middle of a bridge is a very scary one. When you decide to cross a bridge, you commit yourself. You cannot just get off. You can only go on.

A woman named Anne Bartlett was in our group once. She is a very nice lady, but only a fair Scrabble player. Greg and I still get together with her sometimes to play Scrabble with her, and Greg always beats her, same as he beats me. Anne's main fear at the time she first came to group was a fear of bridges.

When Greg and I were talking about this after Anne's first meeting, we decided that we would show her that this was a silly fear by pointing out that she was less fearful of many far more dangerous things than bridges. Greg insisted that driving to group and riding in the elevator after she had arrived were both far more dangerous than crossing a bridge. And Anne was doing these two things without a problem. Greg and I both knew perfectly well that symptoms don't respond to reason. Things that respond to reason are not symptoms. We felt compelled to reason with Anne anyway.

At the next group, Greg raised his hand to speak and told the group leader that he couldn't understand why Anne wasn't afraid of elevators or driving, both of which were far more likely to kill you than bridges.

After that, Anne asked a few clarification questions, which Greg answered in great detail. When he was finished, she replied: "OK, I'm convinced."

Greg and I became pretty good friends with Anne because after that meeting, she didn't come for two months. When she did, she had to come as an inpatient because she was so terrified of the elevator and car ride that would be required if she was not.

Her response to Greg's argument proved to us that she was one of us. Crazy, yes, but in ways that verged on being totally logical.

::

Kelly's route back took us past an Italian bakery that made absolutely amazing pastries. You had to point to the ones you wanted from a long display that ran down the middle of the store, so we all went in and got one. Mine was something a bit like a croissant with some kind of hazelnut whipped cream inside and dark chocolate sprinkles on the outside.

It was *schlooby* fabulous.

::

"OK, boys," said Kelly when we were back in the Winnebago. "That was pretty fun! You have to admit it! You liked the little excursion into the dirty, disgusting, diseased real world! Right?"

Of course it had been fun.

It had been more that that. It had been *wonderful*.

"That was great," I said.

"It was," agreed Greg.

"Thanks, Haj."

"No problem, Ish.

"So, you guys are both OK? Don't need to wash your hands for a while or anything?"

Greg and I looked at each other.

"No," we said.

"OK!" she said. "So now it's the moment we've all been waiting for, then! Right? We go to the Duchamp museum?"

Greg explained that there was no Duchamp *museum*, only a Duchamp *room* in the Philadelphia Museum of Art. I could tell he wanted to go through its whole history before he told Kelly how to get there. Luckily, Kelly could also tell, so she cut him off and asked him just to tell her where it was.

Greg reluctantly produced a small stapled set of maps of increasingly fine-grained resolution that showed where the Philadelphia Museum of Art was in relation to any street in Philadelphia, as well, on the first page, as where it was in relation to several of the closest major cities in the American Northeast, just in case. Kelly studied it for a few seconds, settled on page four, a map of greater downtown Philadelphia, declined her well-deserved chocolate on the grounds that she had just eaten a pastry, and took the Winnebago out of Little Italy.

::

Philadelphia is a great city. You might be surprised if you have never visited it. There is an excellent collection of public art. You come across art everywhere you go. The drive was more interesting than I was expecting.

The road that leads both to the great Philadelphia Museum of Art and to the Rodin Museum is lined with the flags of many nations. I felt vaguely heroic as we drove along it. At the end is the famous statue of Sylvester Stallone as Rocky that I knew about, like everyone in the art world. I think Duchamp would have enjoyed it very much because at first, no one could agree on whether or not it was actually art. It had been moved around several times to placate those who found something distasteful about having a statue of a lowbrow movie character on the same level as works by Picasso, Pissaro, Monet, Van Gogh, and Gauguin, not to mention Duchamp. Now Rocky is tucked away a little, on the ground at the bottom of the stairs leading in to the museum. I think of the statue as a secret monument to Duchamp. Of course it's art.

Duchamp himself does get to be on the same level as Picasso, but his most important international collection is also a bit tucked away, in a far corner on the second floor. It is protected from many visitors by a room nearby, on the path from the main wing, that contains huge oil and pencil works by the wonderfully named Cy Twombly, his *Fifty Days at Iliam: Heroes of the Achaeans*. The pieces look as though they are the crayon scrawls of a floridly schizophrenic six-year-old. They are important, if one cares to take the time to consider them in context, but I think many visitors do not care to do that. They turn back at the Twombly room, to revisit *European Art From 1850 to 1930* or to take a look at the museum's (excellent) collection of 137 Chinese snuff bottles.

You miss Brancusi too if you are defeated by Twombly. Constantin Brancusi was an excellent artist, another person whose works were collected by the Arensbergs, and a friend of Duchamp's.

There is a famous story about the two of them. Around 1932, Duchamp went to an aviation exhibition with Brancusi. Pointing to a propeller for one of the planes, Duchamp famously asked his sculptor friend: "Painting is washed up. Who will ever do anything better than that propeller? Tell me, can you do that?"

Greg and I loved that story. The real world was better than anything art could offer. We had written a ritual inspired by this story into our travel contract.

∷

"So, boys," said Kelly, pulling out her copy of our agreement from her purse after she had parked at the museum. "Let's go over the deal here. Do you remember?"

Greg and I got out our copies of the agreement, and we all turned to the section about the Philadelphia Museum of Art. What it specified was actually problematic for us. Greg and I had signed our names in agreement to spending a full day at the Duchamp collection teaching Kelly what we loved so much about him. A full day seemed like a very short time to me, as you can imagine, since I regularly spent weeks and months with a single piece of art. Even Greg thought we would need more than just one day if we were to do our topic any justice. For example, he told us that he would need at least an hour to explain even a fairly obscure work, the assisted ready-made *Apolinère Enameled,* Duchamp's altered advertisement for enamel radiator paint manufactured by a company called Sapolin that was signed "From Marcel Duchamp," as if his own involvement was hardly worth mentioning because he was just passing the object along.

What Greg told Kelly is true; you can't possibly understand *Apolinère Enameled* without reading Guillaume Apollinaire's poetry and knowing something about the prehistory and history of the ready-made.

It's not like you can just waltz in to a Duchamp collection and *look* at things.

But it was already almost 3:30 PM.

If the museum was only open until 5 PM, it just didn't seem doable. We had less than an hour and a half, and that included the time it would take to weave our way through *European Art From 1850 to 1930.* Which certainly did not deserve to simply be ignored, as I argued. I had also been hoping to spend some time with the Chinese snuff bottles.

We agreed that we would at least go up and see how long they were open before we reached any decision. Greg and I went over what we had written in the section about our Brancusi ritual one more time. We were both looking forward to it.

With our ties straightened and flattened, Greg and I walked beside Kelly up the grand stairway that led to the West Entrance. We walked in together to the teller. I looked at Kelly, hoping she would negotiate for the tickets. She looked back at me and raised an eyebrow to let me know that I had to do it. I guess because I had to pay anyway.

I turned to the teller window.

"Umm, what time are you open until today, please?" I asked.

"We close at 5 PM, sir," answered the beautiful black lady behind the glass.

"Three adults, please," I said immediately, and I handed over the cash to pay for it.

I couldn't tell Kelly or Greg after that why I had so quickly paid for us to go to the Duchamp room for just about an hour. We were at the till already, I was slightly unnerved by the beauty of the woman selling the tickets, and I just decided that it really didn't matter how long we went for. I really wanted to at least get to do the Brancusi ritual with Greg.

And money was no object because I was a fact millionaire *on a spree.*

::

They don't let you take any big bags or jackets in to the museum, so we had to go back to check in Kelly's bag and our jackets just when everyone else was checking out their stuff, so our time was even shorter. We hadn't made any contingency plan in the Winnebago of what to do in the event that I accidentally decided we should go in even if they did close at five, so no one knew exactly what the contractual status of our visit was. Would we persuade Kelly to accept a single hour as a day? Or was this just a *practice* visit prior to our real visit for much longer sometime after tomorrow, when we were going to visit Greg's skilled friend? I didn't know and no one brought it up, so I didn't either. We were all just going along to see what happened.

European Art From 1850 to 1930 is pretty amazing. It's an excellent collection. We didn't stop or even slow down, but we did zip by some excellent art.

Cy Twombly's room is one of the best places to go for an education in popular art appreciation. Almost everyone who comes into the room has something critical to say. Many announce in a loud voice that either their kid or their dog could do as well.

For Duchampians, the Twombly room is a great place to hang out. For us, it isn't just dogs and children: *Anyone* can do as well. Duchamp's ready-made shovel or wine rack or urinal or propeller is no more momentous than anyone else's experience of exactly the same object. If his *pissoir* is art, then so is yours.

Greg explained persuasively as we moved through the halls that Twombly and Brancusi were "excellent appetizers for the feast that is the Duchamp collection." We stayed to listen to a few tourists explaining the works to their wives by comparing them to the works of infants and animals.

We stopped at Brancusi's glimmering bronze 1924 sculpture, *Bird in Space*. This four-foot-tall highly polished abstract looks only a little like a bird, but very much like a propeller or a rocket. It certainly suggests flight, graceful motion upward. Greg and I both think it is a great piece of art.

We stood in front of it, ready for our performance piece. Kelly got her camera out and stood back a little.

You are allowed to take pictures at the Philadelphia Museum of Art as long as you don't use a flash.

Greg and I stared solemnly on each side of the piece together, hands behind our backs, almost as if standing at attention. We waited for a small straggle of tourists from Kansas to leave so that Kelly would be able to get us both in the picture, with the Brancusi between us.

We looked at each other, and Greg nodded almost imperceptibly. On his cue, we both spoke at once, in clear, loud, and distinct, slightly robotic tones so that no one within earshot would have any doubt about what we were saying.

"Painting is washed up. Who will ever do anything better than that propeller?"

We turned toward each other and smiled. At that cue, we both pointed to the piece at once, in perfect synchrony like a dance, and spat out the last line of the ritual as if taunting each other, in exaggerated, demanding, excited voices:

"Tell me, can *you* do that?"

We smiled at each other, and I held up my hand for a high five. Greg hit me and walked up to Kelly with his hand in the air.

She high-fived him.

Then she high-fived me.

We only had 50 minutes left for the Duchamp room. We walked up the hall filled with folk portraits. We turned to the left and strode forward.

And there it was, looming in front of us, in all its nine feet of glory, on the very spot where it had been installed in 1954 by Marcel Duchamp himself.

The Bride Stripped Bare by Her Bachelors, Even.

::

The Bride Stripped Bare by Her Bachelors, Even has only been exhibited outside of the Duchamp room once, in Brooklyn in 1927, decades before it was permanently installed in Philadelphia. It was when they were taking it to that show that it shattered. Ten years later, Duchamp glued it back together and declared the piece to be definitively unfinished.

You really have to look at the shattering in real life. In reproductions, the cracks may look consistent, as if they fit in well or belong together with the piece. In real life, it is clear that this really is a piece of art that has been smashed to pieces. The cracks do not look like *part of* the piece. They look like *what happened to* the piece.

But according to Duchamp, the cracks brought it to its final definitively unfinished state.

It was art because of its history. You or I would not be able sell it to the Philadelphia Museum of Art if we made it today.

But it was history because it was art.

I was filled with strange and fantastic feelings, as if the piece were irradiating me.

Greg stood beside me, breathing deeply. Neither of us had seen the piece in real life before. Both of us had spent years of our lives thinking about it. I saw Greg look over at Kelly, who was standing behind us, her camera out again, taking pictures of us.

It was hard to know where we could possibly begin in telling Kelly about the piece and explaining the effect that it had on us. She walked over to our side, looking at the piece.

"Boys," she said, "that is one hell of an Ishta-deva."

We were silent, thinking.

I was thinking: She is right.

Since neither of us was speaking, Kelly tried again to engage us.

"So this is where the black ball Ishta-deva comes from too, right?" she asked.

We assured it her it was.

"However, if I understood what you were talking about in the Winnebago, there actually is no black ball in the piece?"

So we explained about how the black ball was like the Holy Trinity, and how it was alluded to by its absence.

To explain that, we had to explain about the Bride, her blossoming, and her blossoming barometer.

And to get into *that* we had to explain why Duchamp had abandoned painting.

After Greg had talked about all this, with a few interjections from me, we only had five minutes left until the museum closed. We had not yet moved from our places in front of *The Bride Stripped Bare by Her Bachelors, Even*, except to let a tourist take a picture of his children and wife through it with much hilarity.

When I pointed out that we were running late because we had spent so much time in front of this one piece, Greg started to explain to Kelly about Duchamp's idea that works of art were actually intended to be "delays." I had to interrupt him.

"Zip, we're going to have to go over this later. We can come back another day maybe, or we can talk about it somewhere else. We have to go and look at *Given: 1. The Waterfall, 2. The Illuminating Gas* before we leave!"

Much to my amazement, Greg did stop talking, and he nodded. He pointed to a doorway to our left. We were both intimately familiar with the layout of the gallery and knew Duchamp's final piece had been installed in a small room off the gallery, at the very farthest corner of the museum from the main wing.

"Let's go!" he said.

As we walked the few steps from the broken piece to the final piece, we passed a thin pale girl, about seven years old, in her Brownie uniform.

"Why would anyone want to stare at someone else's private parts?" she asked her parents in bewilderment as they shepherded her back through the main gallery. "I don't want to look at someone else's private parts! That's gross! Do you?"

Her mother assured her that she did not want to. Her father just laughed a little to himself at his daughter's question. He probably did want to look at girls' privates. According to Jannie's statistics, most men do.

::

No one else was in the room when the three of us entered, all dressed up for going to a holy shrine, as I had always pictured we would.

At first sight, *Given: 1. The Waterfall, 2. The Illuminating Gas* is just a plain old door, weather-beaten and framed in brick, looking like something out of a fairy tale. In the door are two small peepholes that you have to look through to see the real work. If you peep through that hole, you will see a naked lady sprawled on a bed of grass and twigs, legs spread wide to show you her clean-shaven privates. You can also see her left boob. You cannot see her face. You know nothing about her, except what you can see in the dim flickering light.

In her hand the lovely lady holds a gas lamp. She is holding it high enough that you know she cannot be dead or unconscious, high enough so you know that she must be willing to hold it. High enough so it will light her sex.

There is a cheesy fake waterfall in the distance.

A lot of people who made it through Twombly think this piece is meaningless crap, signifying nothing at all.

Even if it were only that, we'd have to ask why.

Why would a very intelligent man like Marcel Duchamp decide that it was worth working for 20 years to make a piece of crap that signified nothing at all?

::

We each took turns peeking through the two holes that had been drilled in the door for that purpose.

When Kelly came back from her turn, I told her: "He took 20 years to make that."

"Twenty years!" exclaimed Kelly.

"Twenty years," affirmed Greg, standing beside me. "Give or take. Mid-1940 or so to mid-1960 or so."

"It makes me think of Lorenzo Ghiberti's *Gates of Paradise* in Florence. It took Ghiberti 20 years to make just one door," replied Kelly.

"*The Gates of Paradise*," said Greg, deadpan. "I guess Duchamp could have named it the same."

We smiled. I thought of Gustave Courbet's 1866 painting *The Origin of the World*, now installed in the Musée d'Orsay in Paris. It is a more realistic view even than Duchamp's of a naked woman with her legs spread open, her face also obscured out of frame, often considered to be an inspiration for Duchamp's piece.

The gates of paradise.

You can glimpse, but you cannot enter.

::

A voice announced that the museum was closing in five minutes.

After checking to make sure we were still alone, Greg reached into his pocket and took out a spoon, which he placed reverently on the ground in front of Duchamp's door.

The three of us walked quickly out of the side room. As we passed in between *With Hidden Noise* and *The Bride Stripped Bare by Her Bachelors, Even*, I glanced at my feet. Not far in front of *The Bride Stripped Bare by Her Bachelors, Even*, a polished brass fixture was set in the floor. I did not know what it was for.

To plug in a vacuum cleaner hose, maybe, or provide water in case of fire, or to hide an electrical outlet.

I stopped above it.

"Haj," I said. "You really wanna know why I love Duchamp so much?"

"I do," she said, stopping to look at me.

"Because," I said, "he made me realize that that brass outlet there is one heck of an Ishta-deva, girl."

Kelly gazed at me, smiling.

I wanted to hug her.

But how could I?

10

THE SECOND FOCUS OF SPARKS
OF THE DESIRE-MAGNETO BLOSSOMING

Kelly left Greg and me in the Winnebago, parked facing north at the usual distance from Walmart, telling us she would walk to find a cab. I looked over at Greg when she was gone.

"So, Zip, you have a Duchamp piece for tomorrow?" I asked.

He looked at me for longer than usual before he answered.

"I got a couple of ideas. Why? You have one you wanna do?"

"Yeah." I smiled. "I have an idea. If you wanna do it."

"For sure," he said. "I wanna do whatever you wanna do."

I told him what I wanted to do.

::

Going into a foreign Walmart was not something completely outside our range. Every Walmart is the same.

You're always at home in Walmart.

::

"So," I said when we were inside, smoothing down our ties and bouncing a little on our heels. "Where do you wanna start?"

"Women's underwear," he said.

::

Woman have a lot of kinds of underwear.

Men have to choose between boxers and jockeys.

But women. Jeez. A lot of the stuff I couldn't even recognize. There were pieces that could have been a bra for a very tiny woman or a G-string for a very large one. There was stuff with so many straps that I couldn't think of enough things on a woman's body that might need strapping up. There was tummy-flattening underwear that seemed insanely long for its tiny waist size and sexy underwear that looked dangerously short for its huge waist size. There was underwear with extraordinary elaborate flower decorations sewed on it. I could not understand who was supposed to look at them. There was underwear so drab, so brown, so boring that I felt sad that Walmart found it worth selling. Greg and I wandered around as if in a daze.

"We really need underwear?" I said to Greg, holding up a small purple bra.

"Of course we do," said Greg. "Don't you think? I mean, if you think it's worth it. 'Cause you have to pay."

"So it's all girl, all the way?"

"All girl, all the way," repeated Greg.

"OK," I said, putting down the purple to look over the reds.

::

Finally this girl Angela helped us. She was a Goth or something, a little overweight, with lots of black makeup, red lipstick, masses of unruly black hair, and black clothes. But she really knew her underwear.

"So," she asked us, after we had explained our needs to her. "You guys wanna buy these clothes for yourselves, right?"

Greg and I looked at each other and nodded almost imperceptibly at the same time.

"Yes," I said, looking at her nametag to read it. "Angela. We do. My friend here is known as Zip. Call me Ish. We need to dress up like a woman tomorrow. Like two women. In the name of art."

Angela was silent for a few seconds, as if she had never heard of art before and needed some time to digest the concept.

"So your names are Zip and '-*Ish*'?" she finally replied, pronouncing my own name with particular delicacy.

"Yes," I said. "And your name is Angela."

Like an angel, I thought.

She was silent again.

"OK," she said. "I'm cool with this. What color bras do you guys wanna wear?"

::

Greg and I wanted to go with differently colored bras and panties so we could have a bit of hidden color, but Angela told us that matching was better, so we didn't. I ended up going with all pink just because that was what Angela told us she always wore. Greg was going to go for black, but Angela and I talked him into red, which we both thought would be way cooler.

Angela called over her friend Lisa to ask what was the best way to do the boobs. Angela had these really massive boobs, but Lisa was like a preadolescent boy, except she was really beautiful and smelled of cinnamon and roses. In the end, Angela and Lisa decided that it would look better if we stuffed than it would if we tried to buy bras for girls who didn't really have breasts, who apparently still wore bras. Lisa pulled her T-shirt sleeve aside a little so we could see hers. It was white and lacy.

So we went with a B cup, which seemed female without being outrageous.

For the panties, we all thought it was best to wear these female boxers they have. Angela and Lisa, and their friend Kim who worked in female outerwear, all agreed that tight panties were probably more usual (they were all wearing them), but all of them thought it might be more comfortable for men to wear the boxers. It wasn't so easy to find ones that fit. If they were good at the waist, they bloomed absurdly on the legs. If they were as tight to the legs as male boxers are, we could not even pull them over our waists. Finally we settled on big loose ones.

Angela complained about how much it sucked being a large woman while Lisa folded up our underwear.

The five of us walked over to ladies' clothing.

"So, what are you guys thinking?" said Kim. "You wanna wear pants? A dress? Skirt and blouse? Casual? Dressed-up? Alt? What look are you going for?"

Greg and I looked at each other.

"Sexy," I said.

"Sexy!" said Greg.

::

Lisa thinks that if your skirt is too short, you don't look sexy, you just look slutty.

Angela thinks that sexy is all in your mind, and it is better to just dress interesting.

Kim thinks you can be sexy in many different ways.

Apparently there aren't really any hard rules about how to dress as a woman. Sexy is anything you can get away with.

Greg went with a one-piece dress, if that is what they call it. Everyone agreed it was the kind of thing a girl could wear to a prom. It was blue, came down a little below the knees, and had a lot of different embroidery up on the top.

I went with a striped blue skirt and white blouse with a scarf that had a green vine motif, mainly because Angela liked that outfit and I felt she was the leader of the group. Lisa said I looked liked a private-school girl in it, but Kim said she knew lots of women who would wear it to work.

Greg said it looked really cool.

::

I thought it was excellent that the makeup artist that they had that day was named Sarah. She is an extremely beautiful lady, with brown eyes and long, shiny, curly brown hair. She was wearing a dark low-cut sweater, and the sight made me of think of my buxom angel. I told her she was my mother, but Angela made some signal to let Sarah know I was just a little crazy, so she didn't reply. So I didn't get to get to explain why it actually made perfectly good sense for me to say that.

We didn't get any makeup put on at night because everyone said that it would all get rubbed off on our pillows. It turned out that everyone was willing to come over to the Winnebago at 7 AM for just a hundred bucks. Sarah was going to get all the money because she was the one who originally said she would do it for that, but first Angela and then all the others said they didn't mind coming for free. Greg and I both thought it was a pretty good price considering that we had no idea what we would do without some help, so we bought a whole bunch of makeup. I didn't really know what any of it is was, but, jeez, it sure cost a lot. It was part of the spree, so I didn't mind, but I have to remember to get Mr. Salandhi to look into investing my money in makeup companies.

::

I was all ready to get out of there, but Greg pointed out that we didn't have wigs. He didn't even mention shoes.

Stephanie works in wigs. She's black, and apparently half of the black women you meet are wearing wigs or fake hair of some kind. You know those super-regular thin braids you see black ladies with all the time? Wigs! You know how some black women seem to have really straight hair? Wigs! No black woman has straight hair. You know those hairdos you sometimes see that are all crazy colors, like red and white and blue? It's all fake hair. They just weave it into their real hair.

I didn't know any of this.

Stephanie thought we should wear culturally relevant hair, which basically meant we had to wear blond wigs.

Angela thought that this was a bigoted view of the world. She said we should wear these huge black Afro wigs to protest the "new hedge-a-monic imperative." I don't know what she meant by "hedge-a-monic," but I thought maybe it was supposed to be an insult. I thought maybe the Hedge-a-monic Company actually makes hedge-trimmers or something like that. Now I know she actually meant "hegemonic."

Kim said that real women didn't define themselves by their hair.

Sarah said that a person can be sexy in a lot of different ways.

I was with Sarah on that, so she and I left the others to argue over Greg, and together we settled on a fairly cool blond wig that had a lot of braids. After the underwear regulation, I wanted to have hair that was different colors, so Sarah said she would take it home for me and dye a few braids other colors and bring it back in the morning. I offered to give her 50 bucks to do it, but she said I didn't have to. She said she would be happy to do it for free and she already had hair dye at home anyway. Which I thought was really nice of her.

Greg went with this super-cool wig that didn't even look real. It was really pink and really straight. They called it a pageboy cut. I thought it looked cool.

⁘

You'd think that after all that, the shoes would be the least of our problems. But Kim left us in tears, and Stephanie and Sarah got really mad at each other before we finally decided which shoes we were going to wear. Apparently shoes are always the hard part for women. It's even harder for guys to buy women's shoes because most of them are way too small. There were only about four pairs of shoes that either of us could have worn. Stephanie said we shouldn't try high heels (which I think is one reason Kim ended up leaving in tears), so there were only two pairs that fit, these strappy white things that had something like cork in the sole, which I ended up buying, and these really flat black things that looked like you were supposed to wear them on a beach, which I ended up buying for Greg.

⁘

Man. That was a super-fun night.

⁘

It was later than I thought when we got back to the Winnebago with our purchases. Greg and I took all the stuff out of the bags and laid it out on the table like a museum display: make-up, bras, panties, dresses, shoes, all in a row. When I saw all of the stuff laid out, I felt for the first time that we were doing something outside of normal bounds, possibly diagnosable.

"Do you think this proves that we're diagnosable?" I asked Greg.

"Diagnosable?! We're not doing this because we're *diagnosable*! We're *artists*, man! This is going to be a great performance piece!"

I think he was really pumped by how the Brancusi piece had gone. We both felt it had been a big success.

I felt a welling up in my heart. I felt grateful for a life that had brought me there to that Winnebago, with that friend, in that Philadelphia Walmart parking lot.

That was a great feeling.

Thanks, man. You *schlooby* rock.

∷

By the time she decided to ask for my help, my mother had definitely decided what she was going to do. She would not talk about anything else. She didn't have anything else happening anymore. Her entire life was about getting to her death.

After the first week, I started going out to museums for most of the day just to avoid having the conversation all the time.

Greg tried to tell me later that maybe this meant that my mother and I were compatibly disproportional: My obsessions made me want to stay inside the house all the time, and hers made me want to leave the house all the time. He says she cured me of one case of my extreme disproportion, and he cured me of the other.

I guess he's right.

::

We warmed up a couple of frozen burritos and ate them while we silently read books on Duchamp. Greg spent about 18 minutes in the bathroom. I spent much less time.

When we were lying in bed with the lights out, I asked him.

"Hey, Greg. I mean, Zip."

"Yeah."

"Do you think we'll always be diagnosable? I mean, does it end? Is this it? Do we go into our graves with OCD?"

Greg didn't say anything for several seconds.

"How long did you wash your hands for today?" he finally asked.

"I dunno. But not very long. I'd say not more than 90 seconds per time. Maybe 10 or 12 times? Something like that."

He didn't reply, so I continued.

"Which is within the normal range. I think."

We lay in silence for almost a minute before Greg finally spoke.

"Do you want to stop being diagnosable?"

I had to think about it, but not for so long.

"Yeah," I said. "I do."

"If you really do, then you will," he said. "You just gotta figure out what you want to do more. Like Joseph . . . what's his name, remember? The guy who practically cured himself just so he could play junior high football?"

::

We didn't speak again after that. I thought about Joseph C. Some Polish last name, I think. I didn't know him well because I never got to talk to him myself, but I did remember him. He was a young guy, around 13, who was forced to go to group because he wasn't doing well in school. He had mild OCD by our standards, but it was starting to get hard for him to go to school, which was interfering with his grades. It's not good if your symptoms interfere with your real life. That's what makes you diagnosable.

One day in the summer he came in and said that his parents had agreed to let him try out for the football team, which was his most ardent desire and something they faced with fear, I guess because they had their own phobias. The odds of death or life-changing injury due to playing football in junior high school are very low, according to Greg's calculations, which were presented in group the following week. But a lot of Joseph's obsessions made it seem like he wouldn't be able to play football.

Even though they knew Greg's calculations, most in group admitted that they themselves would not risk contamination by playing football. The therapist was annoyed at us for normalizing symptoms, but it was 15 to 1, so we all felt like we won, same as we did every week.

The week after, Greg came in, held up his hand, and asked if he could ask Joseph if he wanted to play football and keep his symptoms too—the "all gain, no pain" solution, as he put it. The therapist said it was OK for him to ask because the whole idea of group was to get people talking, so Greg asked Joseph his question. Joseph, being 13, muttered something that could be interpreted as either agreement or mocking defiance. Greg didn't really care what the answer was. He just wanted to tell everyone his idea. He suggested that we give up on trying to "cure" Joseph in just a month or two (seeing as many of us were uncured after many years of group), and instead focus on figuring out how someone who *did* have OCD could play football. He said we just had to view the problem as *a scheduling problem*, figuring out how to get enough time to play football and have OCD too.

So the whole group spent weeks trying to get Joseph's disproportionate behavior on a schedule. Our therapist thought it was a charming outbreak of behavior therapy and helped us set up the measures and all that. Basically, what we did is "edit" Joseph's symptoms. Like, say he thought he really had to wash his hands for four minutes. We said: "OK, four minutes would be *great*! More would be even better! But you can't have that long if you want to play football. So how much can you accept as if it really were good enough to stand in for the full four minutes?" We started out at around three minutes and 30 seconds, I think. Joseph whittled it down every day with the unwavering will of a *schlooby* warrior.

He eventually got to just 10 seconds.

That's within the normal range.

Joseph told us that one thing that helped is that he used to close his eyes in front of the sink and pretend he was doing the ritual in real life, until he felt satisfied, and he found he always did it shorter when he imagined it than when he actually did it. We had him reduce some counting rituals he was developing into saying just the single number 14 to himself. We got a whole list of his obsessions about cleaning whittled down to a mnemonic mantra he could only say to himself for five minutes before he got out of bed, like an early-morning prayer.

It worked perfectly. He did go play football. He wasn't actually cured, but it was close enough. It didn't make any difference to anyone else's symptoms in group, but it worked for Joseph. He got better just because he loved the idea of playing football more than he loved the idea of listening to his symptoms.

::

Soon I heard Greg snoring. I must have fallen asleep myself. I was dreaming. I was up in the sky looking down. I could see myself, as a child, huddled in a sand pile in the desert. Sarah, the beautiful makeup artist, was kneeling in the sand not far away, praying out loud. She was wearing the same skirt, blouse, and scarf that I had bought for myself.

"*Call me Ishmael,*" I said, as if I were reading the lines for the first time from a script.

They seemed to hear me.

I glanced up, startled, from the sand. The young woman stopped praying and looked with worry into the sky.

"*Call me Ishmael*!" I demanded, a little more loudly to see what would happen if I did.

Sarah stood up, gazing up into the sky. She turned her head back to look at young me lying in the sand and saw that I was turning myself over to stand up.

She spoke up uncertainly.

"Your name . . . is . . . oh, Lord . . . your name. Is it Ishmael? The same as . . . as my son's name? Is this what you . . . are telling . . . me . . . oh, Lord?"

"Ish," I admitted, perhaps not loudly or clearly enough for her to be able to hear. I could feel a smile spreading across my face.

The child that was me stood up, and the makeup artist turned her face toward him, too bewildered to move, rooted to the spot.

"Oh . . . Ish . . ." she began, uncertainly and rather hopelessly, as if the very fact of saying my name aloud was her defeat.

I couldn't help but snort out loud because any prayer that starts "Oh . . . ish" is self-defeating from the get-go.

It was like seeing someone hit their thumb with a hammer and say, "Ouch-ish."

Beautiful Sarah heard me laugh.

She stopped speaking and stood mute, her lips now shining with glossy red lipstick thickly applied. She was wearing only complicated purple underwear, staring at her son still marching toward her. Purple straps dangled ineffectually from her limbs and crisscrossed her body crazily.

The young Ish strode across the sand, smiling, toward his mother, this beautiful young woman looking ever-more bewildered by his total unconcern.

When I finally reached Sarah, I put out my hand and held it to her leg, smiling.

"Don't call him Ishmael, Mommy! That isn't *Ishmael*! *I'm* Ishmael. That guy's *Isaac*. Didn't you even *recognize his voice*? That's why he's laughing!

"Call *me* Ishmael! Call *him* Isaac!"

Sarah looked into the child's eyes and burst out in a smile. Everyone started laughing, the child, the bewildered mother, the sexy makeup artist, and me. I laughed myself awake and lay in bed, smiling now in real life.

That is exactly what a millionaire's spree should be.

Even my dreams were fun.

::

Greg and I were awoken early in the morning by a delicate tap on the door that soon grew into the sound of many hands pounding. Sarah, Angela, Stephanie, Kim, and another woman were standing outside, carrying bags and boxes and coffee cups and pastries. They poured into the Winnebago and soon pulled Greg out of his bed and onto the seat behind the front passenger seat, and me beside him on the seat behind the driver's place. Greg was dressed in a pair of white jockeys and his Puerto Rican car repair shop T-shirt. I was wearing the same daily jockeys but had managed to get into my black silk dressing gown before I opened the door. Angela was wearing black sweatpants, a black *The Cure* T-shirt, black boots that she left on when she came in, a lot of black mascara, pink lipstick, and a small amount of pink blush. Lisa was dressed in a pink sweatsuit with a white T-shirt in support of some good cause that I can't remember now even though I ended up giving her 80 bucks for it later that morning. She had sparkly purple makeup on her eyelids. Sarah was dressed all in black: pants, tight black low-cut sweater, short socks, low shoes, and a long smock embroidered in gold thread with the name of a makeup company. She had pink lipstick on. She showed me the wig she had dyed for me, which looked great: It had one blue and one red braid, and the rest were still a light blond. Kim was wearing exactly the same skirt I had bought ("To let you see what it is supposed to look like," she said) with a dark blue blouse. She also wore a round button that said THAT'S DOCTOR BITCH TO YOU above a picture of a beautifully coiffed woman from the 1950s.

She just gave it to me when I asked her if I could buy one like that in Walmart. The people they hire at Walmart are really nice.

The last woman was Sarah's older sister, a very pretty black-haired blue-eyed woman in her late 20s, with a thin nose, a long mouth, and amazingly white teeth, named Kyla. She was dressed up the same as Sarah, all in black, so I guessed she was a makeup artist too. When she came in, she held out her hand to introduce herself, and I shook it before I had time to think about it. It was warm and dry and tiny, and it felt good to hold it in my own hand. I didn't feel contaminated by it at all.

∷

"OK," said Sarah. "So. You guys wanna look like sexy babes, right?"

Greg and I nodded.

"What's the occasion? If you don't mind me asking. I mean, what exactly are we trying to achieve here? I take it you guys aren't trannies?" She said the word "trannies" a bit more deliberately than the other words.

I tried a different tack.

"Do you guys know who Marcel Duchamp is?"

None of them did, so we had to explain from the beginning.

"OK," I said. "I think it's kind of important that you guys understand Duchamp so you will know where we are coming from."

They all agreed with delighted feminine chirping sounds.

"OK. So. Well. Marcel Duchamp is an artist, OK? A lot of people think that he was the greatest artist who ever lived."

I paused. I really had no idea what else I should say to make my point because I was not quite sure what my point was going to be, so I switched tacks again.

"Do you guys want any champagne? Because we have a whole case here, except for one bottle. That I already drank. Myself. It's Spanish. So it's really cava, not champagne. If you want to be exact. I call it *sham*-pagne. S, H, A, M. That's supposed to be a joke, by the way. But it tastes exactly like real champagne. It's very good. Champagne for breakfast! Right?! It's good for you! Don't they serve it with brunch in fancy hotels?"

Several of the women assured us that they did, and they shared their most recent brunch experiences. There was general enthusiasm for the idea of opening a bottle, but Angela wanted her sparkling wine with orange juice, so I gave her 20 bucks and sent her over to Walmart to get a couple of containers of juice and some plastic disposable glasses.

When she was gone, I tried again.

"Look, um, girls. Welcome. You are very welcome here in this home. This Winnebago that we . . . that Zip and I . . . call, um, *home*."

"*Home sweet home*," affirmed Greg.

"Our temporary home," I continued.

"But . . . um."

Greg was still sitting, rather regally I thought, on his chair in his underwear and T-shirt.

He spoke up on our behalf.

"Ladies . . . *Sarah* . . . *Kim* . . . *Stephanie* . . . and . . . uh . . . *Kyla*. It's great that you came, like you said you would. As you have probably guessed, my friend . . . I call him *Ish*, and you should too, because that is the name he goes by around these parts . . . my friend Ish and I have mental disorders. We are what is lovingly known in the medical world as obsessive-compulsives. Do you know what that means?"

Kyla said she did, that it meant we felt like we had to do things or think certain things all the time. It turns out she was a medical student.

"Exactly!" said Greg. "Exactly! We don't bite. We're not contagious. We just have to do certain things and think certain things. Certain totally harmless things."

"You have to understand that it's, like, totally out of their control," clarified Kyla, helpfully.

It didn't seem like the others needed any more information though. They were all totally cool with it.

"OK," said Kim.

"Man, I have that all the time," said Sarah, turning to her friends. "You know? Like how some song gets stuck in your head and it plays and plays all day long?"

The other girls nodded and chattered a bit more.

"So you guys are dressing up as women because . . . you have some mental compulsion to?" said Kyla.

Greg said, "No. We are not *just* compulsives. We are also *artists*. It's *complicated*."

"You guys have to know who Marcel Duchamp is," I said.

Then I went to the bathroom to wash my hands.

⠿

When I got back, Angela had returned with the orange juice and glasses and was pouring champagne diluted with a little juice into everyone's glass.

As soon as I sat down, Greg had to go wash his hands, so everyone just figured out that we were hand-washers. They all seemed pretty interested in that, so we talked about it for a while. Then it turned out they all had their little obsession stories to tell, so we all listened to those, which were interesting. Sarah's thing was that she said the same words whenever she sat down to pee, a child's prayer, before any pee could come out, and she had been like that for as long as she could remember, ever since she had known the prayer. Kyla had a ritual where she had to doodle a certain way when she was talking on the phone to a guy she was dating or going to date or whatever and then some other necklace-touching thing she had to do when she was actually on the date. Everyone had stories about pop music getting stuck in their head.

After we had all those stories, we told them about Kelly, and the chocolate grinder I had ordered, and how I was a fact millionaire, which they all thought was very cool because I was the first millionaire of any kind that they'd ever known. Greg tried to explain why we had gone to Cranston, Connecticut, but they didn't seem as enthused about that as Greg and I were. When they wanted to know more about the chocolate grinder, Greg got up out of his chair and took some books out of his library and showed them the original chocolate grinder paintings, and Duchamp's chocolate grinder, and then the chocolate grinder built into *The Bride Stripped Bare by Her Bachelors, Even.*

We opened another bottle and talked for a while about Duchamp and why we liked him so much and what we thought was art and why we cared. Then the conversation wandered to the suits we had been wearing. After we told them about how we changed clothes every day but always wore the same thing, everyone wanted to see what we wore again, even though they had already seen it the day before in Walmart, so Greg and I had to go into the bathroom and put on our suits and ties. We explained that Greg was not contractually obligated to wear his tie, but chose to wear it of his own free will.

Greg and I taught them to stand up and chant more and more loudly with us as if we were all on the same sports team:

"*Description of the necktie:*

1. resplendent in color

2. provided at the 4 corners with very sharp points (like all neckties)."

They really enjoyed learning that. They even all pretended to smooth down their imaginary ties after they said it. We decided that should be the symbol of the trip: the right hand sliding down the chest as if to smooth a necktie.

We opened another bottle.

"OK," I said. "Ladies. We gotta get to work. To make the long story short, Duchamp dressed up as a woman named Rrose Sélavy, whose name makes a couple of risqué puns in French, and every day Zip and I . . . well, usually Zip . . . always Zip until now . . . he dedicates the day to a piece created by Duchamp. We call it a *ReMade* . . . because . . . well, forget about why, we just do call it that. Today we are doing *Rrose Sélavy*. As our *ReMade*. Which is *a piece of art*. So that's why we have to dress up as women. OK? So let's do it."

::

Under the circumstances, and given the rather malic appearance of Duchamp's Rrose Sélavy, we all felt that it was right that we should keep our suits on while we were made up by Sarah and change into our dresses afterward. Sarah made us go and shave three times before she let us sit in our chairs again.

"So what do you guys want?" said Sarah. "What's the look?"

"Sexy," I said.

"Sexy!" said Greg.

"Well, OK, sexy. Of course. Sexy's all I do. But what kind of 'sexy'? I mean, you want something raunchy? Something delicate? Something innocent? I mean, Marilyn Monroe sexy or Manga girl sexy . . ."

Before she could finish, the door to the Winnebago opened and Kelly called in.

"Hello, boys."

Her eyes widened when she saw the crowd.

"Hello . . . uh, everyone. Hello! I'm Kelly. Kelly Baxter."

Everyone got up and started talking and introducing themselves and each other and explaining to Kelly about how they totally understood that Greg and I had OCD and how cool it was that I was a real millionaire (even though I had explained that *fact* millionaires were not necessarily *real* millionaires) and explaining that we were doing Rrose Sélavy today and telling Kelly how we had all met up and how clueless Greg and I were about women's underwear. Someone was pouring Kelly some champagne and OJ while she hung her jacket up and joined the party.

Kelly was wearing dark blue pants that were embroidered almost imperceptibly at the top with a flower motif in thread just a little bit darker than the pants. She had on a matching blue jacket with short sleeves over a bright red silk shirt slashed diagonally with a white streak. Her hair was down, with one thin braid on the right side that had a clear blue glass bead on the end. She was wearing a long silver chain around her neck.

I turned to look into Sarah's soft brown eyes. I gestured for her to come a little closer so I could talk to her privately.

I put my lips close to Sarah's perfect little ear.

"Make me sexy like she is," I whispered.

11

THE LIBERTY OF INDIFFERENCE

Greg said he didn't mind if I was made up first, so I was. Sarah was really great, very gentle and careful about touching me. I told her I didn't mind at all if she touched me, and it was true. I didn't feel like she would contaminate me, but the opposite: I felt that each touch from her was actually making that part of me cleaner. Beautiful Sarah was anti-contaminating. As she worked on me, I could feel my purified face glowing with healthful vigor.

Kyla talked to her sister and me while Sarah was making me up, and she kept our glasses full for us. She went to school across the river in New Jersey, but she said she came into Philadelphia pretty often to see her sister and just hang out. She said she hoped we didn't mind that she had come along. I didn't ask Greg what he thought because I'm sure he didn't mind, but I told her that I was really happy she had come and it didn't seem too cramped in the Winnebago to me. Kelly talked with the other girls a little, and every so often they came over and looked at my face and said things like "Oh! Sarah! You are *good*, girl!" and "Oh, you are gonna love this look, Ish" and stuff like that. I wanted to ask her if she was OK with us having a makeup party, but I didn't really see how I could do that in front of all of the Walmart girls, in case it wasn't OK, so I didn't ask. I noticed she didn't drink much champagne, which I thought was good since she had to drive us over to get the chocolate grinder. Sarah admired Kelly's bone structure and told her she was going to try to make me as beautiful as her, like it was just some notion she had, but she didn't say anything to Kelly about what I had whispered to her.

It took a lot longer than I was expecting to put on all the makeup. I thought maybe we'd be in the chairs for five or 10 minutes, but it must have taken at least an hour. It was pretty relaxing, though, especially with the cava.

When Sarah said she was finished with the makeup, she put my wig on for me. I got up and looked at myself in the long mirror that hung in a cupboard. The juxtaposition of the strangely familiar yet uncannily odd female face with the very familiar suited body took me by surprise. The face was odd in part because it was doubly familiar, both as me and as Kelly. I had really thought that makeup would not make much difference, even after an hour of it being applied.

Duchamp's Rrose Sélavy looked like a man playing dress-up. My Rrose Sélavy looked like a woman.

I stared in stunned silence.

There really was no simple resemblance to Kelly. No one could have looked at me and at her and thought: *Hey! He's been made up to look like her.* But Sarah had left me some small clues if you knew where to look. The eyes were definitely not Japanese, but they were more slender and long than my real eyes. They had definitely morphed in the direction of Kelly's eyes. It was the same with the other features. The lips, a deep strong red, looked more luscious than my real lips and reminded me of Kelly's strong lipstick. They were lips that a man could not help but feel a pang of gratitude at seeing. The cheeks were higher and flatter than my real cheeks, moving in the direction of Kelly's on both dimensions.

It was as if my body had been grafted beneath a woman's head.

"Holy *schlooby*!" I said, having spent too much time in my life with Greg. "I can't believe that! I mean, wow, I look totally like a woman! How can that be?! It's crazy! Man, Sarah, you do have the touch. I am totally gorgeous. Thanks!"

She came over smiling, and for a second I thought she might be expecting me to hug her, so I whipped up my hand and we did a high five instead. I liked her, but I didn't want to hug her. Before she made up Greg, she went over and had a whispered conversation with him, so I didn't know who he said he wanted to look like until he told me later. He wanted to look like Judy Garland playing Dorothy in *The Wizard of Oz* in 1939. It was a very good choice because he looked totally excellent, like I did, and he did move in the direction of a young Judy Garland.

Greg was as amazed at his own transformation as I had been at mine. I don't know anything about makeup artists, but it seemed like we had lucked onto an excellent one. I gave Sarah her hundred bucks and offered her more if she thought she deserved it, but she just laughed, told me she hated to take advantage of millionaires, and insisted on giving me back $40 as the girls' contribution to the champagne.

::

By this time, we had all agreed that the girls would all come with us to get the chocolate grinder, partly because they all really wanted to see it, and partly because we thought it might be good to have people to help carry it in case it was heavy.

We were going to give them each a travel name, but Greg suggested that instead we name them as a group: the Ready Maids. They all thought that was a great idea when we told them what a ready-made was and even more so after Greg told them that the anagram of "Ready Maids" was the good omen "Is dream day." So that's what they became. We asked Kelly if she wanted to be part of the Ready Maids or stay in her own Haj category, and she said she definitely wanted to be one of the Ready Maids, so she got to be one too.

Greg and I of course got to be the Re-Maids, which Greg pointed out has "misread" as an anagram.

::

Getting dressed was a blast. Greg and I wanted to be decent, but we were worried that we wouldn't get all the bras and stockings and dresses right, so we just changed into the panties in the bathrooms and came tiptoeing out like that, to be met by much hooting and cheering from the ladies and each other, so that we could get dressed. Everyone helped, mainly by shouting advice.

Unlike getting made up, getting dressed didn't take as long as I expected. I had in my mind that there was going to be lot of mysterious snapping of straps and threading of elastic or something like that, which is why I wanted help. But getting dressed when you are a woman is almost the same as getting dressed when you are a man: You just put the stuff on your body. Greg and I stuffed our own bras with cotton padding that we had bought the day before, and Sarah snapped them shut behind our backs for us, so I never got to see how those worked that day. The shoes really were less than ideal—they were one thing that made us look more like men dressed up than like real woman—but they were OK. The girls had insisted we had to buy scarves the day before so we could cover our Adam's apples, so the scarves were arranged in an artful way to cover those and were somehow fastened in place.

We both looked totally amazing. Of course you could tell that we were really men, but you'd definitely have had a second of confusion first. We are both pretty small guys.

With the dressing done, we realized that no one except Kelly had had any decent breakfast yet. Kyla knew a pizzeria that delivered 24 hours a day, even on Sunday morning, so we called them up and got a bunch of pizzas. I tried to pay for them all, but the girls all chipped in their fair share, claiming that they were millionaires from working at Walmart, which made us all laugh.

Those pizzas were yummy.

::

I expected that getting in to see Hawk, as we had previously decided to call Greg's friend, was going to be a little complex, seeing as he seemed to have odd ideas of his own, like the one about not using telephones even though the risk that they would harm a user was almost immeasurably low. The way it was set up was that Greg had to go and ring Hawk's buzzer and arrange a time for us to come in, which might be right away or might be later. Now, of course, he also had to take the time to tell Hawk that his name was Hawk and why, and to let him know that we would be coming in drag, and that we would be bringing the Ready Maids with us when we came made up as Re-Maids to pick up our remade readymade.

Greg was pretty sure that Hawk would appreciate the pun on the Ready Maids, and he said Hawk was a nice guy who seemed to like people well enough, so he didn't see the girls as a problem. He didn't really know what he would think about the Rrose Sélavy outfits. But we all found seats in the Winnebago, I gave Kelly a chocolate to officially start her workday, and we glided out of another Walmart parking lot.

::

The main pun in "Rrose Sélavy," in case you don't speak French, is that it sounds like "Eros is life." Some say there are other puns too, but they're more of a stretch. Most people assume that "Eros is life" means that sex is all there is to life. But most people are not as well educated as Duchamp was, or as Greg is, anyway. Greg told me that Eros is the Greek god of love and sex, the counterpart to the Romans' Cupid, who now hogs all the limelight on Saint Valentine's Day. But he is not just the god of love and sex.

He is also the source of creativity, the fount from which all new ideas spring forth.

So "Rrose Sélavy" really means: *New ideas* are what life is all about. New ways of seeing things.

::

Greg had again provided Kelly and me with a bound series of maps that showed where Hawk's place was at various map scales. Kelly turned to page four and followed the directions. We ended up in what seemed an old industrial part of town, full of dark, dilapidated buildings. We turned where Google told us to turn. There was a single low building at the address.

"This looks like it," said Kelly, pulling in to park by the side of the street because there was no driveway. "Right?" she asked, looking at Greg.

Greg compared the number on the paper in his hands to the number on the building.

"Right," said Greg. He put down the paper.

"I'll go over and see what's happening."

Greg stepped out, then bounced right back up, sat back down in the passenger seat, and closed the door he had just opened.

"Uh, guys, I think we forgot something," said Greg, smoothing his right hand down his chest where his tie was alluded to by its absence.

I looked at Sarah, who looked at her sister, who turned with the two of us to signal the other Ready Maids. I nodded almost

imperceptibly and we chanted as one. As soon as we got to yelling
"like all neckties!" with the coordinated enthusiasm of a Gospel
choir, Greg stepped out, closed the door, and was gone.

::

Duchamp wasn't just doing what your child or dog could do.

::

Greg was gone a bit longer than I hoped, but after a few minutes,
we heard the door open and he bounced into his seat and closed
the door.

"OK," he said. "I talked to Hawk.

"Number one, we do get to call him that. He says we can call
him whatever we want so long as we pay. We could even call him
insulting names if we wanted to. I asked. He doesn't care.

"Number two, no problem about bringing everyone in. The
more Ready Maids the merrier, he said."

Greg stopped as Kyla interrupted.

"Or maybe what he actually said was: The more ready maids . . .
the merrier," she said, looking around at her friends as they laughed.

Greg just continued.

"Number three, the piece is finished and waiting for us.

"Number four is—I kind of already said it—is that we do have
to come with that final check made out for the full remaining fee
in hand, *Ish*.

"Number five is that I have advised him that two of us are males remade interpreting Rrose Sélavy.

"Which he thinks is very cool," he continued, looking over at me with a smile.

"Number six is that we can go in right away."

::

I can understand why women like to wear dresses. It feels good.

My mother would be horrified to see that her son had written that sentence.

::

A few months after I had begun my museum vigils, I came back from visiting the Isabella Stewart Gardner Museum and found my mother, not surprisingly, in the same place as ever, lying in her bed. Her nurse was in the kitchen, eating a sandwich for supper and watching the TV.

"I've got it," she said, her voice so low by then that it was little more than whisper.

"Got what, mother?" I asked.

"I have what you *need*."

"Need?"

"You know. To help me *do it*. Move on from here. Kick the bucket. Leave for better pastures. Die."

"Mother. I already told you . . ."

"You can't inject it directly in."

"Mother . . ."

"They can find that. You just have to add it to the IV. But not too early."

"Mother, please. I'm sorry."

"Isaac, my love, there's no one else."

"Mother. Let's talk about something else today."

I thought about the empty spaces where the paintings had been at the Isabella Stewart Gardner Museum. I had never told her about that. I wanted to talk about that.

"There's nothing else. Wait until the bag is almost empty. It has to be only a twentieth full, or it won't work."

"Did I ever tell you about the *Isabella Stewart Gardner Museum*? Mother? Because that is where I went today."

"I had to hide them in the photo album. It was the only place."

"Hide what?"

"I hid pills."

"You've been hiding your pills?"

"Not all of them. Enough. I've done the math. I have exactly enough."

"Enough?"

"Isaac. Listen to what you need to do. You need to use just enough water to fill one syringe. They keep all the syringes in the bathroom; they're not locked up. You need to inject it into the red valve over there."

She tried to gesture to her IV line.

"At night."

"Mother. Stop talking. This is crazy. Your IV will never be a twentieth full at night."

"Don't worry about that," she said. "I'll take care of that. I found a perfect way to fake a leak. It's not a problem."

I got up and walked over to her bedside drawer, where she kept a large photo album. I flipped it open to the earliest photos, of her wedding. The next big event was my birth and first year of life. The last photo was a picture of me resplendent in my suit, taken only a few months earlier.

"They're in an envelope at the back," she said. "The small envelope."

I flipped to the back cover. There was a recycled brown paper envelope taped to the back cover, filled with an assortment of loose photos and envelopes containing loose photos. I slid them out and riffled through the small stack. There was one very small envelope, from a passport photographer. I tipped it over and about a dozen small white pills slid onto the palm of my hand.

"Can you do it tonight?"

"Mother," I said. "No. Wow. What are you even *talking about*? I can't do this. Not tonight. Not any night."

I thought about taking the pills away, maybe reporting my mother to her nurse or to Mr. Salandhi. But I didn't. I poured the pills back into the little envelope, put it back into the middle of the pile of paper, and slid it all into the larger envelope.

"Try and get some rest, mother," I said.

"That is exactly what I am trying to do," she croaked, disappointed.

∷

The gang of us followed Greg's lead to the entranceway. When we got there, Greg hit the only button there was and spoke into the intercom as if he were answering the radio in a battlefield: "OK, uh, Hawk. The Re-Maids and the Ready Maids are outside the door and ready to enter."

The lock clicked, and Greg pushed the door open and entered in front of everyone.

I stopped in my tracks.

The entranceway was blocked from the main space by *The Bride Stripped Bare by Her Bachelors, Even*, complete with the cracks. I exclaimed:

"*The Bride Stripped Bare by Her Bachelors, Even!*"

Hawk was a very tall lanky man. He was wearing faded black jeans and a T-shirt underneath an elaborately filled tool apron.

"Indeed," he said. "It's for sale if you want it. But I warn you that I'm very attached to it (and it is very attached to my floor), so it isn't for sale cheap."

He held out his hand in a strangely unspecific way toward the group, assuming, I suppose, that at least one of us might want to shake hands but having no idea who it would be. It seemed like the Ready Maids all shook his hand while I walked the other way around *The Bride Stripped Bare by Her Bachelors, Even* with Greg. A minute later, Hawk was standing beside us. Looking at me without offering his hand, he said: "So you're my man Isaac, but I call you Ish?"

"That's right," I said, immediately handing over the check, which he stuck into a pocket on his apron after thanking me and glancing down briefly at it.

"Call me Hawk," he said, as Greg had no doubt instructed him that he must.

"Did you really make this?" I went on, pointing to the huge ReMade. He nodded.

I bent down to take a closer look at it, standing far enough back to make clear that I was just looking, the way I was used to doing in museums.

"You can touch it if you want to," he said. "It's not at all fragile."

I looked at him, then back at the piece.

"That's OK," I said. "I don't think I need to touch it, thanks."

Greg ran his finger along the glass strip between two of the long cracks that ran across it.

"It feels just like any glass," he said.

::

Hawk's workshop was in a long building that I learned later was a converted train barn. There was a bright row of ceiling lights at the front of the building over a smooth cement floor that marked the space of a combination showroom and living room. Off on the right wall behind it there was a long kitchen, terminated with a wall cutting the sleeping and bathroom quarters from the back section of the room. The rest of the space was taken up with a large, extremely organized, and extremely well-equipped workshop, lathes and saws and drilling tables aligned in a neat row on one side, with a huge wall of hand tools on the other.

In the show room I immediately recognized the Rodin sculpture *La Danaïde*, a naked woman recumbent on a rough stone. Beside it stood a life-size metal sculpture of R2D2 from *Star Wars*. On the other side of the couch the statue stood by was a ReMade abstract sitting figure by Henry Moore. Above a white leather couch hung a copy of one of Van Gogh's many *Sunflowers*.

In front of the couch, in the center of the room, was my chocolate grinder.

"Did you make all this too?" I asked, holding out my beautifully manicured hands.

"These days, I outsource the painting to China. They have amazing cheap painters there. Better painters than me. I do all the three-dimensional stuff myself. I like to work with solid materials."

He kicked the Henry Moore sculpture. It moved. It was a hollow wood frame with artfully painted plaster on top.

"Well, sort of solid. Most of this is just for fun."

He pointed to the obvious.

"That's the real thing, though. No corners cut. An authentic copy all the way down."

I walked over and leaned in to look at it.

A sculpture of the *Chocolate Grinder* is an odd object. Duchamp didn't ever make a fully three-dimensional version; he just painted it and collaged it into *The Bride Stripped Bare by Her Bachelors, Even*.

It looked exactly as I had imagined it from Duchamp's paintings.

"You can definitely touch that one," he said. "It's a real working grinder. Just like you asked for. And it's all yours."

The girls were milling around me. I knew that if I didn't touch it myself, one of them was going to be the first one.

So I reached out and touched it.

It felt as great as it looked.

I smiled.

::

Greg thinks that it is important that "Rrose Sélavy" has "Or sly as ever" as an anagram, which consists entirely of abstract words. He says the lost accent just makes the anagram even slyer.

But you know Greg.

::

One of the Ready Maids suggested that we should do the tie chant around the chocolate grinder, to general enthusiasm. They loved that chant. They tried to get Hawk to join in too, but he wouldn't.

The girls circled around the piece, looking first at it, then up at me. Stephanie took Kim's hand, and they held out theirs from their sides to get us all to join hands.

So we did.

I nodded slightly.

"Resplendent in color!" we yelled.

Stephanie smiled at me.

". . . and provided at all four corners!"

The hands I held were not contaminating. They felt warm, and soft, and purifying.

". . . with very sharp points!"

I didn't know whose hands I held.

". . . like all neckties!!"

::

It was not hard to get the piece into the Winnebago. Hawk knew how to do it, so we just did what he told us to do. Some of what he told us came in useful when we unloaded it the next day. There was enough space for it in the front part of the Winnebago, but we had to fold the table down to get it in.

I shook Hawk's hand when we left.

::

It had taken us only 20 minutes to get my chocolate grinder. The day stretched out before us. It did not take us long to decide where to go. We turned to page four of Greg's map and Kelly drove us back to the Philadelphia Museum of Modern Art.

::

The same beautiful black lady as before was selling tickets again.

She did a slight double take when I peered in and then looked at me carefully, probably not just to admire my makeup.

I could see she maybe wanted to laugh a little, but she didn't.

"How can I help you today?" she asked.

"OK, so how many are we?" I said. "Let's see, Sarah, Kim, Stephanie, Kyla, Angela, Haj, Zip, and me. So that's eight. I'd like eight adult tickets please."

"Eight adult tickets," she repeated, clicking on her keyboard.

I was glad that Sarah have given me back that $40, or I wouldn't have had enough money on me. As it was, I handed over a wad of cash that would cover it.

"How do I look?" I asked her when I saw that the beautiful lady was looking at me again.

"You look really good," she said, handing back my change, smiling.

I took the change.

"Thanks," I said, peering in to read her nametag, "Abeni."

I had never heard that name before.

∷

This time we got to see *European Art From 1850 to 1930*. It's a pretty good collection. They have one of Van Gogh's *Sunflowers*.

It's a total blast to go to a museum dressed up as a woman, with the Ready Maids along. They told a lot of lies. In one room, they told everyone that Greg and I were dressed up for a movie. In another, they pretended they didn't even know us but they talked among themselves about us so that others could hear. In another room, Stephanie and Kyla pretended that they were men and treated Zip and me as their wives.

I love thinking about those girls.

We took over the Duchamp room. The Ready Maids didn't believe me when I pointed to *With Hidden Noise*, Duchamp's ball of twine, and told them that I would buy it myself if it ever came on the market for only a million dollars. We had a discussion about that. I still don't think they believed me. Kelly took everyone's picture standing behind *The Bride Stripped Bare by Her Bachelors, Even*, first by ourselves and then in a bunch of random groups. Kyla and Kim asked if they could each put an arm around me when they were being photographed, so I held up my arms and let them in.

At one point, I asked Greg if he was doing OK, and he smiled, nodding his head almost imperceptibly.

The Ready Maids had mixed reactions to *Given: 1. The Waterfall, 2. The Illuminating Gas.*

∷

By about 3 PM, we were getting pretty hungry, and Stephanie asked if there was any more champagne because she either had to drink some more or go home and have a nap. We still had quite a few bottles in the Winnebago, so it was decided after a brief group poll that we would head back to the Winnebago for some champagne and frozen burritos, and then take one more run around the museum, maybe to look at the 137 Chinese snuff bottles.

At the front, I stopped and leaned into Abeni's window.

"Abeni," I said.

"Yes!" she said, obviously a little startled to be addressed by her own name. It was easy for me to remember it because it was so unusual.

"Abeni. My friends and I are going to go and drink more champagne. So if we come back later, we will still be able to get in?"

"Sure, just show your stamp at the door," she said. "We close at 5 PM."

::

My opinion of frozen burritos did change a little during lunch. Most of the Ready Maids shared Kyla's opinion that they tasted like old newspapers with mud inside. I told them I'd take them all out for a decent dinner to make up for it if they had any time that evening. Not everyone could make it, but three of them did.

The champagne went over way better than the burritos.

::

Sarah did a little repair work on Greg's and my makeup, and then we were all ready for one final visit to the art museum.

"Abeni."

I was really enjoying saying her name.

She looked up once again, smiling.

"Can I help you again?"

"Abeni," I repeated, under the influence of several glasses of cava. "We are back. As you can see."

She continued to smile.

"We have all had our wrists stamped."

"Good!" she said. "In that case, you can just go right on back . . ."

"Abeni," I said yet again.

"Yes," she said.

"Can I say one thing to you?"

Abeni continued to smile behind the counter.

No one said anything until Abeni realized that a response was required.

"Yes. Please. Do go ahead."

"We are enjoying our visit to this museum very much. We really love it. You have an amazing museum."

Abeni smiled, revealing a row of perfect white teeth.

"Thank you very much. Enjoy the rest of your visit."

::

We did go and see the snuff bottles.

After that, we wandered around a little more and saw a few other things. Greg and I convinced the Ready Maids to go to the Brancusi, and Greg and I did our ritual again for them. They all clapped. We took one more look around the Duchamp room. Greg showed us all where he had left the spoon. Of course it was gone. Kelly and Greg and I talked a little more about some of the pieces.

The last thing we went to see was *Costumes and Textiles*, which I think I appreciated more than I would have any day previously.

::

On the way out, I stopped at the ticket booth again.

"Abeni," I said.

She looked up at me expectantly, waited a bit, and then answered.

"Yes, can I help you?"

I paused. I did not know what I intended to say to her.

"We are leaving now," I said.

She continued to look at me expectantly. I continued to look at her. She truly was gorgeous.

"OK," she finally said. "I hope you enjoyed your visit."

"We may be back tomorrow," I said, even though there were no plans for us to come back.

"It would be great to have you visit again. Tomorrow we are open from 10 AM until 5 PM."

::

It is not always easy to recognize the points at which a life turns. I had only exchanged a few words with this beautiful stranger. I had left her with no notion that I would ever see her again.

But I would.

Reader, I married her.

12

FLAIR, OR THE SENSE THAT RECEIVES THE WAVES OF IMBALANCE

After we had dropped the last of the Ready Maids at their houses after dinner that night, Kelly drove us back to exactly the same spot we had been before, in front of the Walmart. She turned off the engines.

"Boys," she said. "That was a fun day. Are you happy with the grinder, Ish?"

"I love it," I said. "Totally worth everything. Thanks a lot for driving us, Kelly . . . I mean, Haj. That really was probably the best day of my life. I mean, wow. We got the chocolate grinder, we got to hang at the Duchamp exhibit and see the 137 snuff bottles too, we got to do Rrose Sélavy and the Brancusi piece again, and we met all those great people. Did you like them too, Kelly?"

"Sure," she said. "They were a lot of fun."

We looked at each other for a second.

"Do you want one more glass of cava?" I asked. "You had to drive all day, so you didn't really get your fair share."

"Sure," she said. "Thanks."

We drank some wine, and Kelly told us a little more about her boyfriend and that she thought they were probably going to get married and have some kids.

We talked about the next day. We had done everything we had set out to do. Kelly wanted some time to go look in the shops and the market. We agreed that we would meet her in the Winnebago at noon, and go home.

Then she helped Greg and me take off our makeup, which was not as pleasant as putting it on had been.

::

After Kelly was gone, while Greg was snoring, I lay in bed reliving the day and thinking about what Greg had said to me about getting rid of my OCD. The day had been full of excitement and interest. I not only had not been a slave to my symptoms; I had hardly even noticed them. I was not the first person with OCD to notice that many of the symptoms disappeared if you were concentrating hard on something. I had, for once, concentrated hard on what was all around me, on real life. I had been almost normal, and I had loved it.

I wanted this.

I wanted more.

I thought about Kelly, still with a pang, but also with new distance. The gulf between Kelly and other women had been narrowed. Kelly was great, fantastic, incredible, lovely. But the Ready Maids were also very fun and funny and pretty and such a pleasure when they laughed.

I allowed my mind to drift over all the Ready Maids, trying to picture each of them and relive some part of my day with them. Every one of them had brought me pleasure, with a smile, or a joke, or by handholding, or by laughing with me.

I thought about how easily they had accepted that I was diagnosable. They were just normalizing symptoms, my therapist would say to them.

But why not? Why not normalize symptoms?

Joseph C. had literally normalized his symptoms. He hadn't made them disappear. He hadn't denied them. He hadn't defeated them. He had simply made peace with them, given them a place in his life so they could allow him a place.

I thought of Abeni and laughed at myself. I thought of her, of how I had acted when I was talking to her.

I wondered what it was that had made me keep going back to her every time I entered or left the museum.

I wondered why I kept saying her name.

I wondered if she knew anything about art.

I wondered where she lived.

I wondered what she must have thought of me, dressed up and made up, half-drunk.

I wondered if she knew how beautiful she was.

I vowed that tomorrow would be different.

I needed to move.

I needed to make plans.

I needed to live.

Why not?

::

That first day my mother asked me to use the pills was more than six months before Kelly ever told me her version of the story of Isaac and Abraham.

When my mother brought up the topic of the envelope again, I asked her: "Mother, would you do it for me?"

She looked at me for a long time.

"Isaac," she said, "I love you. And so I would. If you were sick like me."

I looked at her almost as long as she had looked at me without speaking. I did love her. I did not want her to die.

I also believed her.

"I'll do it the day after your birthday," I said at last, probably as much to my own surprise as to hers, frowning a little in defeat.

"What day it is today?" she asked.

I told her.

"Three months?"

"Yes. In three more months."

She was silent for over a minute, and I thought she had fallen asleep.

"You wouldn't do it on your birthday?" she asked. Mine was only a week away.

"The day after your birthday, Mother."

She was silent half as long again.

"OK," she said. "You promise?"

"I do."

"Take the pills," she said. "I don't want anyone to find them. Hide them somewhere else."

I walked over to the dresser, flipped open the photo album, and fished out the smallest envelope. I folded it in half vertically and put it into my pocket.

"I love you," she said.

"I love you too, Mother," I said.

"Thank you, Isaac," she said.

∷

The morning after we bought the grinder, I woke up early. It was sunny outside, a beautiful day. Greg turned toward me when he heard me move, and I told him I was going to go out.

"Out?" he said. "Out there?!"

"Yup," I said. "I'm going for a walk in the real world. Tell Kelly I'll be back by noon, OK?"

"A walk?" said Greg.

"Yes, Greg," I said. "A walk. Are you OK by yourself?"

"Sure. Sure. Can I check out your chocolate grinder?"

I smiled.

"Sure."

∷

I set out without any real plan, not even glancing down at the stains on the pavement. The air was brisk, and it felt good to walk. It felt good to walk, by myself, in a city I did not know, along streets leading to places I did not know. The world was pregnant with a possibility that was lost in my narrow, familiar paths in Medford.

::

I had to stop to eat, so I walked into a bakery and ordered a latte and a huge cinnamon roll. I went to a park across the street and sat down on a bench to eat breakfast. The cinnamon roll was hot from the oven, sticky and steaming. I unrolled it and started eating it like a snake. I had not eaten a hot cinnamon roll since I was a child. It was a mistake to have waited so long. It tasted so good that it made me a little sad to think how many years had gone by without my eating one.

After I was finished, I walked on and came to the famous colorful sculpture of the word "love" that had become such an icon of the sixties. It was raised up on a metal pedestal, like a high table, in the middle of a fountain. Through the legs I could see the Museum of Art off in the distance.

Staring at the word, I thought about Kelly's perfume. I thought about the beautiful Sarah, and how I had whispered into her perfect ear. I thought again about smiling Abeni, the beautiful ticket seller.

What I had learned from Kelly, I thought, is this: The Bride is an Ishta-deva. She is a pointer to something fabulous, incredible, that cannot be portrayed by any artist.

Just like this great big word, "love."

::

Shortly after I walked out of the square, I passed a man painting an iron railing. I walked over and watched him. The rococo railing looked beautiful to me. It was pure black.

There was a FOR RENT sign in the first-floor window.

I walked closer and stood in front of it, as if I were basking in it. Impulsively, I reached out and touched the rail, which looked like it was dry. It felt like any other painted metal did. I looked at my fingers where I had touched it. They looked the same as ever, with no black smudge on them.

The painter, a balding middle-aged man, turned to me.

"Hi!" he said.

"Hello," I said.

"Are you looking for a place to rent?" he asked.

I hadn't known I was, but I didn't need to think about it.

"Yes," I said. "I am."

"Would you like to take a look at it?" he said.

"Yes," I answered. "I would."

"OK. Just let me get myself organized here."

He carefully placed his can of black paint on the ground, nestled close to the side of the stairs. Just as carefully, he placed his brush over the edge of the can that lay against that wall.

He studied his hands carefully, front and back, for any flecks of black paint.

Finding none, he held out his hand.

"I'm Gary," he said. "This is my place. Come on in."

I shook his hand.

::

The place for rent was the entire third floor. Gary opened the door and let me go in first. It seemed very cool to me. It had a big front window, high ceilings, and only two real rooms: a bathroom and everything else. The kitchen was tucked along one wall.

"What are you looking for?" he asked.

"This is what I have been looking for," I said. "How much is it?"

I didn't have the slightest idea about rents in Philadelphia, so instead of asking myself if it was a good price for Philadelphia or not, I just asked myself: "Would I pay that much to have *this*?"

"Do you take checks?" I asked.

Gary and I discussed it for a while. I didn't have a lot of the things he wanted from me, like references and all that. I told him I had no references because I had never rented a place, I just owned. Eventually we agreed that I would give him half a month's rent in cash, and a cashable check for the next month and a half. If the check bounced, he got to keep the cash deposit and anything left in the apartment. If it didn't bounce, I got the apartment for a year, as long as I kept up the rent payments.

I still laugh to myself about that.

I didn't even tell him I was a fact millionaire.

I asked him if I could store some stuff in the apartment right away, and he said I could.

I had my checkbook in my jacket pocket, so I wrote him a check there and signed a one-year lease. We shook hands on the deal.

I went to find an ATM to get the first half month's rent.

::

I had to take a cab back to Walmart, as I really didn't have any idea where I was and I had no map. I didn't even know which Walmart we were parked at. We had to go to three.

::

My cab driver, Tom, and I finally saw the Winnebago. I was pretty happy about that. Maybe he was too. But we were having a good time driving around.

Kelly and Greg were both inside when I stepped in.

"Lady and gentleman," I said, "I salute you."

Kelly gave me her salute, and even Greg raised an arm.

Greg said that the grinder seemed totally excellent, which is what he had expected. He hadn't actually ground any chocolate or anything, which I thought was pretty decent of him because he knew where the chocolate beans were. But he had turned the handle on top, and the table had spun, and the wheels had ground against the base. He definitely thought it would grind.

Kelly was eating a warmed-over frozen burrito, which she waved at me when I smiled at her.

"They *do* taste like cardboard," she said, "but they're loaded with complete proteins! And only 180 calories!"

∷

I had a little trouble convincing Greg and Kelly that I wasn't kidding that we would be dropping off the chocolate grinder in Philadelphia instead of taking it back to Medford. I don't think they believed me even when we pulled in beside my new place. After Gary repeated his ritual with putting down the paintbrush and said hello to me, they began to believe.

I showed Gary my grinder and told him enough about it so that he could tell there was no way I was going to abandon it to him by defaulting on my rent. He helped carry it up, as he had agreed to before we shook hands. He and Greg did all the work. I also took up a bunch of leftover shirts, underwear, and socks, a couple of bottles of cava, and a few of the other remaining supplies for the trip.

Greg, Kelly, and I got back into the Winnebago. I took the front seat beside Kelly.

"Congratulations, man!" said Greg, reaching out his hand to shake mine. "This had been a *schlooby* great trip."

∷

Greg went to a cupboard and took out a ring-bound notebook that had the front and back covers ripped off, so it was all just paper, no cardboard.

"Well, I guess it's the last day of the trip. I had a couple of options for the Duchamp of the day, but now I'm gonna go with this one. I think it's a good one for you. You can keep it and use it, to remember this trip."

He opened the notebook all the way, so that the two pages that had been at the beginning and end of the notebook were touching each other inside, and he handed it over to me.

"This one's really tough," he said. "Do you have any idea?"

I looked down at the notebook in my hands.

"Harder than the black ball?" I asked.

"Oh, way harder," he said. "I don't even think *I* would get this one. Do you want me to just tell you?"

I looked up at Kelly, who shrugged to let me know she had no idea herself.

Greg explained that the Duchamp of the day was the obscure *Door, 11 Rue Larrey*. In 1927, Duchamp hired a carpenter to create a door in the corner of a room, so that when it was opened for the entrance in one wall it closed off the entrance in the other, thereby contradicting a French proverb that said that a door had to be either open or shut.

The spiral notebook was the same. When you opened it all the way, it was as if it was closed. What had been the outside was the inside.

Greg gave it to me and told me I should keep it.

⁛

The trip back to Medford passed by so fast that I could hardly believe how long it had taken us to get to Philadelphia. Greg and Kelly wanted to know why I had decided to take an apartment, and I tried my best to explain, but really I had no idea. I just felt glad that I had.

Kelly and I stopped to drop Greg off at his place first.

Greg took the black ball off the rearview mirror rather solemnly, gave it to Kelly, and thanked her for driving us.

We unloaded all his stuff, checking it against the original list. I gave him the rest of the new shirts, socks, and underwear that were in the Winnebago, and a lot of toilet paper. I also let him choose as many ties as he wanted. He took nine.

Kelly came over and hugged him goodbye, without any problem, then went back to the driver's seat.

Greg smiled at me.

"Hey, thanks for having me along," he said. "That was a good time."

"Thank *you*," I said. "There's no way I could have done any of this without you."

We shook hands, and he handed a package to me.

"You're gonna need silverware at the new place."

I unrolled the soft cloth package.

It was his travel spoon collection.

I accepted it with gratitude.

∷

As Kelly drove over to my place, we agreed we'd need to meet the next day to totally empty everything out. She helped me load most of the stuff onto my front porch, but the Winnebago would need one more run-through. She said she would bring it back to my place in the morning and would take a look tonight to make sure we hadn't left anything inside.

We stood facing each other on the sidewalk in front of my house.

"Kelly . . ." I said. "*Thanks.*"

It seemed like not enough, but I didn't know what else to say. I didn't know how to thank her for all she had done for me.

"You're welcome, Ish!" she said. "I really enjoyed the whole weekend! It was a blast. Thanks for inviting me!"

And then, finally, after all that time waiting, I hugged her. We just hugged, the way friends do. She smelled great, of course.

Just before she got back into the Winnebago, Kelly reached into her pocket and took out the stabilizing black ball that Greg had given her, holding it delicately between her fingers as if it were a jewel.

"Seen one Ishta-deva; seen 'em all!" she said, handing it over to me with a smile.

∷

I couldn't go back to Philadelphia for about a week because I had to organize a few things, like changing the mail delivery and getting someone to look after the lawn mowing and the snow removal and all that. I didn't know how long I'd be gone or when I'd be back, but I didn't want to come back just because my lawn needed mowing. I wasn't planning to sell my house. I was a fact millionaire. I was going to keep places in different cities, at least for a while.

I also put my symptoms on a regime and started carrying around the notebook Greg had given me so I could write down how much time I spent on anything obsessive. I went over and took a look at the ivory of Abraham and Isaac, but I only stayed for five minutes, as I had specified in my notebook.

Greg and I met at our old Starbucks to say goodbye. He was the same as always. I told him to come and visit.

"I should come and visit you down in Philadelphia?" he said.

"Yes, Greg," I said. "You should come down and visit me in Philadelphia."

He was silent for a second.

"Do they have a lot of indoor billboards advertising peace, love, and understanding down there?" he said.

"Because it's the City of Brotherly Love, you mean?" I asked, puzzled.

"No. Because 'hippie ad hall' is an anagram for Philadelphia," Greg replied. I laughed.

Several months later, he surprised me by sending a letter saying he would like to take the train down to visit me.

He braved the trip by himself.

We had a *totally fun* time together.

::

I flew to Philadelphia, taking everything I wanted to have with me in two suitcases. I got to my apartment around 3 PM in a taxi. Gary let me in and gave me a key. He let me know what I already knew, that my check was good.

I walked into the apartment, and there was my chocolate grinder, resplendent in color *and* form. I put my suitcases down and stroked it.

My first few weeks in Hippie Ad Hall were mainly devoted to finding a good source of organic chocolate beans because I had forgotten my beans in Medford. Eventually I found a great little chocolate shop that could sell me raw Ghanaian chocolate beans. One Tuesday night, I sprinkled some roasted beans around the grinding table, grabbed the handle on top, and walked around and around my table until the beans had been crushed.

Looking at the mess I had made on the previously pristine surface of my beautiful grinder, I thought of a line from Duchamp's notes to *The Bride Stripped Bare by Her Bachelors, Even*: "Readymade Reciprocal: Use a Rembrandt as an ironing board."

I took a spoonful of the chocolate dust using one of the spoons Greg had given me, then boiled up some milk, added a few spoonfuls of sugar and more chocolate dust, and made myself a thick, slightly chunky hot chocolate, which I drank standing at my front window, looking out at the bustle on the street below.

That was an amazingly good chocolate grinder.

My drink was fantastic.

::

My regime went very well in the coming weeks. I found that once I had established a set of rules about things—how long I could wash for and when; how much time I could spend looking at a thing; how much exposure to contamination I had to take on each day—it started to become a pleasure to follow them. I filled up pages in my spiral notebook with different kinds of organizational tables and charts, observations about what worked and what didn't, and quotes from the books I started reading about behavior therapy and about OCD. I scheduled two hours every morning to go in search of somewhere new to have a cup of coffee, and when I did, I would sit down with my notebook and study and think about it.

One day I admitted on paper that my suits were a symptom. The next day, I forced myself to start dressing more casually in just jeans and a shirt. It felt odd, but it was easy enough to just do it.

After about two months, my methods were working so well that I was finding myself, for the first time in years, with a lot of free time on my hands. I not only was not spending hours staring at art in museums, I wasn't even visiting any museums because I recognized that my former relationship with them had become a symptom. I didn't know what to do with myself. I thought about getting a job, but my only qualifications were fastidiousness, an undergraduate degree in psychology, and an intimate acquaintance with all things Duchampian. These did not seem likely to land me anything that would be interesting or lucrative enough to tempt me. I was, after all, still a fact millionaire, and even though I now had to pay for two places, I still lived pretty cheaply.

I thought about trying to find the Ready Maids, but I felt the day we had spent together was a special time that couldn't be regained, so I never did go back to that Walmart.

After a few days of wondering what to do with myself, I went back to Medford just to make sure everything was OK, and it was. I met Greg at Starbucks, but I didn't get to see Kelly that time.

When I came back to Philadelphia, a few weeks later, I realized that there was only one thing that really interested me: my regime. I hadn't totally cured myself, it was true, but I had by then edited down my symptoms to such a small part of my life that it was as good as a cure. I decided I should share my accumulated wisdom with the masses and write a book about my experience with OCD and what I had done about it. I bought myself a tiny netbook computer for $249 (complete with a three-year warranty!) and set out to become a self-help book writer.

::

One sunny weekday morning I woke up, found my morning coffee, and decided that the best thing for my book would be to do a little research. I hadn't been to an art museum since I had moved from Medford, but I wanted to see what I could make of art. Art, for me, was both a symptom and a cure. It was a symptom because I stopped too long in front of it. It was a cure because I felt peaceful and obsession-free when I was focusing on it. I thought I might be able to write something useful about the relationship between your Ishta-deva and your diagnosis.

I wrote out a schedule for the visit to make sure I wouldn't get stuck on any piece in the museum and set off on the long walk to the Philadelphia Museum of Art. I never took public transit. I liked walking.

When I arrived, I walked around back so I could go in by the same west entrance that we had used when we had the Winnebago. It felt good to go in again.

I walked over to the ticket booth and found the same beautiful black lady there yet again, as if she never left. It seemed like a lifetime ago that I had walked in wearing full makeup, as Rrose Sélavy.

I smiled when I saw her.

"Abeni."

She looked up at me blankly. She was not wearing her nametag. Of course she could not have recognized me without my Ready Maid makeup.

"Abeni. You don't have any idea who I am, do you?"

She looked at me and shook her head.

"I'm sorry," she said. "Do I know you?"

"No," I said. "No. You don't."

I reminded her about my last visit, about my being dressed up and drinking champagne and paying cash for the eight adult tickets. She remembered me then and showed me her great white teeth, her nose crinkling a little when she smiled.

"So that was you! Well, welcome back! No makeup today?"

She stood up to look me over, I guess to see if I was wearing a dress or anything like that.

"No. It was a one-time thing."

"What can I do for you?" she said.

"Abeni," I said. "I don't know why I like saying your name so much. Sorry. But I do. I love your name."

She thanked me and told me it was an African name meaning "we asked for her and we got her." I thought that was extremely cool.

"Abeni," I said. "I was just going to buy a ticket for today. But now I am wondering if I should rather be buying an annual pass. Because I just moved to Philadelphia. And I may end up coming here a lot."

She explained the tiered membership plan to me.

You could buy a membership for just $65, which might be a good deal if you went often enough, considering that it costs $14 to go in once. I noticed that you also got free entrance to the Rodin Museum, which I still hadn't visited and wanted to see. It turns out that you can get in there free anyway.

You could also become a supporter or a sustainer or a sponsor or a patron or, for a big two grand, an associate.

"Abeni, what do you suggest?" I asked, awash in choices.

She smiled.

"Well, obviously we do encourage people to buy one of our supporting memberships, and we would appreciate that support. But it's totally up to you.

"Oh, and the other thing I should tell you is that the supporting memberships are all almost totally tax-deductible."

I had become very fond of tax-deductible expenses. In fact, my accountant had me deducting practically everything by then because I was allowed to deduct costs related to writing my book, and pretty much everything I did was relevant to writing my book.

I was also wondering if I would get my money's worth paying by the visit, since I was on my regime. I couldn't linger in the museum. I had time limits.

I looked over the list.

"We also have a very good reciprocity program, so a membership here will get you into many other museums all around the United States for free."

"Abeni, you've sold me. I've made up my mind. I'm going to become a 'sustainer.' Only because I think it has the coolest-sounding title. I'd probably go for being a sponsor or an associate if it came with a better title. Like 'baron' or 'champion.' You should sell those titles. No one should have to pay two grand just to be an 'associate.' It seems a little unfriendly to call someone an associate. It sounds like you are an organized crime syndicate, not an art gallery.

"The only problem, Abeni, is that I do not have $300 on me."

"Well, you can pay with a credit card."

"I don't have a credit card either. Cash or check."

"Do you have a debit card?"

"Ah, yes. That I do have, Abeni. That's cash."

"Well, we take debit!" said Abeni.

I handed over my card. While she was waiting for it to go through, she said, "So, not drinking champagne with your friends today?"

I shook my head slightly.

"That was a one-time thing too. We were having an odd day. Good, but odd."

"You guys seemed like you were having fun!"

"We were. We had a lot of fun that day. But I don't usually dress up like a woman and drink champagne all day."

She handed the card reader over to me.

"Was it someone's stag party or something?"

I smiled and looked down to punch in my PIN.

"No. We were actually buying a chocolate grinder that day. That's why we were all dressed up and everything. But it only took us a few minutes to pick it up, so then we had the whole day, and we came out here."

"You guys had to dress up in drag *to buy a chocolate grinder?*" She wrinkled her nose again a little when she laughed, showing those perfect teeth.

I had to admit it did sound diagnosable.

"Yeah, well, I know. It sounds pretty weird. It's a long story. I guess you could say that the whole purchase was basically a piece of performance art. The chocolate grinder was based on Marcel Duchamp's *Chocolate Grinder* and is a piece of art itself. But it really does grind chocolate. You know Duchamp's chocolate grinder? You guys have three images of it here."

I handed back the card reader.

"Sure. In the Arensburg gallery. I think there's only two though. *Chocolate Grinder #1* and *Chocolate Grinder #2*, right?"

She handed me my paperwork. Someone was waiting in line, so I had to go, even though I would have rather talked to Abeni.

"The third one is in *The Bride Stripped Bare by Her Bachelors, Even*. No wonder they have you selling tickets. You're not ready to be a museum guide!" I said.

She smiled.

"Oh, OK. I didn't know about that one.

"That's everything you need. Your membership card is on top there. Enjoy the museum."

"Bye, Abeni."

I felt the same feeling talking to her that I had felt when I was first hanging out with Kelly in Boston. I knew what I hadn't known then: what that feeling was called.

Happiness.

::

I did Cy Twombly and Brancusi to warm up. Then I went in to the Duchamp room, where I was hoping to write my bit for the day.

I stood in front of *The Bride Stripped Bare by Her Bachelors, Even* and opened the notebook Greg had given me on our last day. I looked left and down at the malic moulds, toiling away beneath their bride.

No, not *their bride*.

Toiling away beneath their *idea* of a bride.

They looked alone and a little sad. I wanted to help them turn that *schlooby-pie* machine, to get them grinding some chocolate.

I looked right and up at the Bride's Cinematic Blossoming, the most feminine object in the piece. The Bride's halo. The Milky

Way. The empty cartoon thought bubble, a pointer to the idea that the artist could never portray.

An empty space for the viewer to fill in.

I wrote "All art is a delay" in my notebook, dotting the final period extra hard for good measure, as if that would settle the matter once and for all.

I got up and walked across the gallery to the tiny room that held *Given: 1. The Waterfall, 2. The Illuminating Gas.* I stood looking at the old door with two small peepholes in it. That is a great piece of art because of how it forces you to look at it. You only get to catch a glimpse of it through a tiny peephole. You couldn't just stare at it for hours even if you wanted to.

I didn't walk all the way up to the door to catch a glimpse of the piece again. I just stood looking at the door from the back of the gallery, then wrote "Cranston, Connecticut: Constrain, connect, cut." I quickly drew a line in my notebook beneath that and wrote, "Ask and ye shall receive," as if I were working out a syllogism and the last line was the logical consequent of the two lines I had written above it.

I smiled, dotted the sentence, closed the book, left the gallery, and walked through *European Art From 1850 to 1930* and quickly down the stairs to the ticket booth. Abeni was still there, and when she looked at me with recognition, I looked at her, still smiling.

"Leaving so soon?" she said.

"Yeah, I guess so. You know, since I am a member, visits are more or less free now. As long as I come back often enough, Abeni," I said, continuing without pausing. "I'm sure you have a very full life and maybe you don't have any more room in it for new people . . . but I was wondering, if you do, um, have any room in your life for . . . new people, if you would let me buy you dinner one day? Or lunch? Maybe one day this week or next week? Or *the week after*?"

She looked at me without saying anything for a few seconds.

"Coffee'd be good too," I added, to break the silence.

"Why?" she finally asked.

"Well. You know. Like *a date*. Or whatever you want to call it. A *get-together*. *Going out*.

"Just so you and I can talk together and maybe eat or whatever. Because, um, I . . . well, to tell the truth, I just think you're totally beautiful and I'd way rather look at you than *any* thing in any museum, so it would make me really happy to see you sometime for . . . like, maybe an hour or two."

She paused again.

I could tell she liked being told how beautiful she looked. It was just the truth.

"Well, thanks. I dunno. I don't usually go on dates with complete strangers."

"I know. Neither do I, Abeni! Especially with someone like you. Because I have no way to know that you aren't a serial killer. Gorgeous but deadly. Which is why I think we should only meet in a public place where there are lots of people around to . . . um, be sure that nothing bad happens to me. I'm willing to take the risk of eating with you if you can promise me that kind of backup to protect me."

She crinkled her nose, cocked her head a little, then reached for a pen and scribbled a number on the edge of a museum map, which she handed over to me.

"Well . . . Let me think about it," she said. "Call me in a couple of days. What's your name, anyway?"

Call me Ishmael, I thought.

Call me Ish.

"My name's Isaac," I said. "It means *May God smile*."

INSTANTANEOUS STATE OF REST

After I walked out of the museum, my heart was beating fast, and I could feel my face flushing. I was scared and excited. I could hardly believe I had asked the beautiful Abeni out and gotten her phone number. I was still holding the map in my hand, but as soon as I got out onto the steps, I sat down, opened my notebook, and placed it carefully inside so I wouldn't lose it.

The next two days passed slowly. I made no progress on my book. On the third day, I forced myself to wait until exactly 6:38 PM, so it wouldn't look like I had just counted down the minutes until exactly 6:30 PM. Then I dialed the number written on the art museum map.

"May I speak to Abeni?" I asked.

"Sure," said a young woman's voice on the other side. "Just a second."

I heard her calling Abeni's name.

"Hello?" I heard her say.

"Hi, Abeni. This is Isaac. You know. The guy who bought the sustainer pass at the museum. Who asked you out, I guess. Well. I don't guess. I know I did. I don't know why I said that."

"Yeah, sure. Hi, Isaac."

"I was just wondering if you had any time to think about maybe meeting me for dinner or lunch or coffee or anything? We could also do a bubble tea or a shaken green tea lemonade at Starbucks, or just meet for even a glass of water somewhere. Or just go for a walk."

Stop talking! I thought.

"I've been thinking about it," she said.

"Oh."

"I guess I can risk having dinner with you," she said, "in a bright public place with several well-marked exits and a lot of people around."

I imagined her smile.

"Abeni, you know I wouldn't have it any other way myself. You can never play it too safe. *Everyone's* a serial killer these days."

That made her laugh.

I told her I didn't know any good restaurants, so she told me one that she liked, and I said it would be great and I would see her there a week from the coming Friday at 6:30 PM.

Dinner! Dinner.

Yup.

A dinner.

I hung up, washed my hands for exactly 30 seconds because I thought they were sticky, and then called Kelly to tell her I had a date and ask her what I should do.

She said I should just be myself, and that it would go great.

When I called Greg to tell him, he agreed with Kelly, especially since *Abeni* was an anagram for *A Be-In*, which consisted of three abstract words. The original Be-In was a gathering of hippies in San Francisco in the sixties where everyone was supposed to just be cool and loving.

"So," said Greg, "a. That means she's just a really cool person, and b. It means you have to be cool and loving when you're with her."

::

In the following days, I began to study my chocolate grinder with an eye to improving my grinding technique. When I first started using it, I turned it continually in one direction and would go around maybe three or four times without really paying attention to the grinding drums, just walking. But if you turn all in one direction like that, you get some fairly big chunks that break off and find their way into some place where the drums don't bite as hard because of the way they were designed. Some of those chunks never get ground up.

If you want a really fine grind, you have to pay attention to what is happening to the beans. You can't just go in one direction without looking. You have to keep looking at what you're doing, sometimes grinding forward, sometimes backward. You have to get down on your knees and study the grounds. You have to learn that different regions of the drum have different grinding characteristics.

The chocolate grinder doesn't just do it all for you. You have to work with it.

::

Waiting for Abeni, I decided to grind some special chocolate for her. For a present. I called Kelly to see if she thought this was outside of the realm of normality, and she thought it was OK as long as it was just something small. Apparently you can't give anything big to someone on a first date, just in case you're wrong about feeling crazy about her or in case she panics because she thinks you're more serious about her than she is about you. Girls like it if you like them, but you can't like them too much too soon.

I spent the next few days trying different combinations of ingredients, trying to get a hot chocolate mix that was not just the pure bitter thrill I drank down with pleasure every day, but something more delicate: something sweeter, richer, delicious, and inviting.

Not just sugar dissolved with ground beans.

I can't tell you all my ingredients because I still keep the recipe secret so no one else can do it my way. I'll just say there is more than one kind of sugar, more salt than you might expect from the sweet taste, a teensy bit of instant coffee (so it will dissolve), and pinches of at least two common spices.

And a couple of other things I am not even going to hint at here. Sorry.

When I was inventing it, I had the perfect inspiration: Kelly's lemon and sawdust perfume. Of course, I didn't want my hot chocolate to taste like *that*. But I wanted it to have the same effect on people that Kelly's perfume had on me. I wanted people to inhale and smell possibility and beauty, think courageous new thoughts, go inside themselves and find that there is more to them than they have ever imagined.

It wasn't easy, but I did have a lot of time to work on it.

::

The final recipe came together for me on about the third day. I had spent a happy few days trying a bunch of things by then and made notes about them all in my notebook. I knew that I was getting close, but nothing smelled as excellent as Kelly's perfume.

I stood up from my kitchen table and stretched. On the kitchen counter I saw the small black stabilizing ball, the Ishta-deva that Greg had given to Kelly and Kelly had given to me. I picked it up and gave it a trial bounce on the floor. It was very bouncy. I bounced it off the floor again. I walked over and bounced it off the floor, against the wall, and back into my hands. The tenant below me, Carl, was an accountant who only used the place for his business during the day, so I knew it wouldn't bother anyone.

I bounced it off the floor, against the wall, off the chocolate grinder, and into my hand.

Boing boing boing.

Soon after that, I figured out how to bounce it off the floor, against the wall, off the chocolate grinder, back off the wall again, and right onto my waiting hand. *Boing boing boing boing.*

If I missed the right spot on the chocolate grinder, the ball would bounce off in some unexpected angle, and I'd have to chase it all around the room to try again. It took a while to get good.

Soon I had it going with the full four bounces so that my right hand threw it precisely into my left hand, and my left hand threw it precisely into my right hand, which is harder than it sounds. I got that going pretty fast. It was a little like juggling with just one ball.

When I got that move down, the recipe came to me like magic. I hadn't even been thinking about it. Suddenly I understood how it had to be done, just like that. I put the stabilizing ball down and wrote the recipe in my ring-bound notebook.

I didn't even bother testing it until the next morning because I was totally sure I had it right.

::

After what Kelly said, I decided that I was just going to give Abeni enough mix to make one cup of hot chocolate. Kelly thought that enough powder to make just one cup of hot chocolate would be a perfect gift for a first date.

I wanted something nice to put it in.

I thought about this for a while. Finally one afternoon, I walked over and pushed the buzzer at Hawk's place. He was surprised to hear from me, but he listened to my situation over the intercom and told me that he'd be happy to make me a box.

"It can't look too expensive!" I said. "It's just a first date. It has to look like it was cheap."

"OK. Got it. It'll look cheap."

"How much will it actually cost though?"

"For a good customer like you, Ish," he said, "on an important occasion like this, I'll make a small cheap-looking chocolate box for free."

I went over to get it a couple of days later in the rain. It was great to be back inside his place. I leaned against *The Bride Stripped Bare by Her Bachelors, Even* while I took off my wet shoes.

Sitting on the white sofa, Hawk explained that he had tried some metal boxes, but they seemed a little over the top to him. So in the end, he had made this simple little white box out of cardboard, about two inches cubed. The bottom part was just a folded box, taped together with white paper tape. The top was made of folded rice paper. It had a little red silk string on it, and when you pulled it up, the whole top opened up in a circular fashion, like a petal opening out. You were supposed to use the folded-out top like a funnel, to pour the chocolate into your cup.

It was perfect.

I knew Hawk wasn't going to take any money. I asked if he liked chocolate. He said he did, so I gave him a little sandwich bag of the chocolate powder I had brought along for him, just enough for one cup. He poured it into a prototype box that he had kept and told me he would make it soon. I told him I'd make him some more sometime if he wanted it.

He did.

I still make it all the time for him these days.

We shook hands when I left.

::

Later that week, Kelly called me to let me know that she had thanked Greg and me in the acknowledgements of her thesis, "for teaching me about the Bride." Greg and I were both really happy about that.

::

My mother's last few months were a much better time than any period in the year before it had been. She stopped obsessing about the pills and about dying. She started listening to the radio and watching TV again. She and I watched a lot of comedies together. She never doubted my word, and she never asked me about the pills again.

The slow-moving car finally hit Julia. She died in her sleep about two weeks before her birthday, not in her garden but in her bed, at night, without any help from me or, so far as I know, anyone else.

It is true that someone came and took her body away soon after she died and that she really did get cremated very soon after that, so I never saw her again after her body was found.

I never touched it. I am not sure I wish I had. My mom was gone. It would have felt just like any body.

::

On the evening of the actual date, I was completely calm. To me, it was a no-lose situation. At the very least, I would get to spend an hour or two with Abeni. That seemed like a totally wonderful worst-case scenario.

I shaved carefully, laughing about how the Ready Maids had made me shave three times before they would put on my makeup. I put on a familiar pair of jeans and a new blue shirt with a collar, made in China.

The restaurant Abeni had chosen was a modern place, with bright orange, slightly retro seating, expensive martinis, huge pepper grinders wielded by the waiters, and a minimalist menu listing an odd assortment of foods. I got there five minutes early, so I was sitting down in a booth when she showed up five minutes late.

I stood up smiling.

"Hi Abeni!" I said.

She was wearing a simple red cotton blouse and black jeans. She looked so great, it was ridiculous. She looked perfect.

"Hey, Isaac," she said, putting down a large blue handbag on the seat beside her.

"Thanks for coming out. I figure we can break the windows by hurling the pepper grinders at them if either of us turns out to be a violent serial killer," I said, pointing to the enormous grinder in a passing waiter's hands. She smiled at me.

After she sat down, she told me a bit about herself. She had a master's degree in English literature and was thinking of maybe going into law school or advertising, she wasn't really sure which. Meanwhile, she was passing time working at the museum.

I told her about my own degree in psychology and my interest in art history and how I didn't exactly work in the usual sense of the word because I was a private investor now because of my inheritance (Kelly had told me that I shouldn't mention the exact amount on a first date) but that recently I had begun writing a book about my time as an obsessive-compulsive and how I got over it. She wanted to know more about that of course. I told her a little, mainly just about how I had made up the regime and how it pretty much just seemed to work for me. I didn't get into all the exact details because giving people too many details isn't normal and because I didn't want her to think I was crazy. By then I wasn't crazy. I just had habits.

She told me, like everyone does, about how songs sometimes get stuck in her head, and she told me she had gone to see a shrink for about six months when she was an undergraduate, for "general angst." She didn't seem too freaked out by the OCD, and I was staying within the normal bounds of bathroom visits and all that anyway, so she knew I wasn't just some totally crazy freak.

We talked a little about some art we both liked, especially Brancusi because she knew his stuff pretty well and liked it. That was nice for me to hear. She told me what is was like to work in the museum and how she had one coworker with a degree in art history who was really snotty to museum visitors if they came in and didn't seem to know exactly what they were talking about. I told her I thought she seemed really good with customers, especially since she had treated me so nicely when I had come in that one morning drunk and dressed as a woman. I told her that was one reason I wanted to go to dinner with her.

So then of course we talked a little about what I was doing that first day I had seen her. I told her all about how I came to Philadelphia to buy a chocolate grinder, and how Greg and I were doing little Duchamp pieces every day, and how I had met Kelly before that. I didn't get into too much detail about how long I had spent at the museums in those days.

She asked me why I had decided to stay in Philadelphia, but I still didn't know for sure myself, so I pretty much just had to make that part up as I went along.

Talking so much about the trip to get the chocolate grinder reminded me of the chocolate, so I took it out of the plastic bag I had carried with me and pushed it across the table to her. I told her what it was and that I had made it myself, so she pulled up the silk tab and smelled it, which seemed to go over pretty well. You don't get the full effect until you put it in hot milk, though. She liked the box, so I told her that my friend had made it for me, the same guy who had made the chocolate grinder for me.

She told me a few funny stories about her two roommates, and then we were finished with dinner. I wanted to pay for it all myself, but she insisted we should split it, so we did.

"Thanks for coming out to dinner, Abeni," I said, smiling and extending my hand over the table to shake hers. "I really appreciate that you said yes."

"Well, it was fun, Isaac," she said, shaking my hand. Hers felt great. I didn't want to let go, but of course I did.

"Maybe we can do it again sometime."

And then she was gone.

::

When I got home, I threw all the notes for my book into the recycling container. Then I sat down to write this book instead.

::

Kelly told me I shouldn't call Abeni again for at least a week after the first date.

But three days later, my phone rang.

"Hey, Isaac."

"*Abeni*," I said, trying to hide my amazement at hearing from her.

"I was just calling to let you know I made that hot chocolate you gave me the other day."

"I hope it was OK," I said, trying to sound nonchalant.

"I havta tell you, Isaac, that stuff is like the nectar of the gods! It was totally amazing! How did you make that?"

A wave of joy warmed me, spreading up through my chest and across my face.

Smiling broadly, I bounced the stabilizing ball off the floor, onto the wall, against the chocolate grinder, off the wall again, and back into my hand, perfectly.

My mother would be so proud of me. I had decided I would master bouncing that little black ball, and I had *schlooby-pie* well mastered it.

"First of all, you know, I grind my own chocolate," I began.

Printed in the United States
by Baker & Taylor Publisher Services